"W

"This may be news to you, but you aren't the only person alive who's suffered." Now that Jonathan had started, he couldn't seem to stop. "You're all shut away, wasting the most precious gift of all, life itself. You're—"

"How can I get myself to rely on you, to share things with you, when I know I will never come first?"

"And how can I turn my back on the people—the *children*—who need me, for someone who does not?"

"Is that what you think? That I don't need you?"

Jonathan shrugged. "I don't know what to think."

Dear Reader,

February is the month for hearts and flowers, and this month's Superromance selections definitely call for a few hearts to be lost—and found.

In Patricia Chandler's *Mooncaller,* Dr. Whitney Baldridge-Barrows knows she should hate Gabriel Blade. He's planning to turn the Havasuapai village where she works into a tourist resort. Instead, she finds she's losing her heart at the bottom of the Grand Canyon....

Texas journalist Lacy Kilpatrick comes home to a family feud. Though her family calls sexy Austin Fraser "the enemy," and forbids her to see him, Lacy discovers she has other ideas. Lynda Trent weaves lighthearted romantic magic in *If I Must Choose.*

And sparks really fly between Tatum McGillus and Jonathan Wright. In Tara Taylor Quinn's *McGillus V. Wright,* hero and heroine stand on opposite sides of the law. Besides that, the timing is wrong, and the two agree on absolutely nothing. This is one relationship that will need a miracle in order to survive.

Louisiana author Anne Logan sets *Dial "D" for Destiny* in her home state, where Lisa Le Blanc is hot on the trail of her missing sister, Dixie. And the trail leads straight to Gabriel Jordan. But the man denies ever speaking to Dixie. Still, she's sure he knows more than he's telling, and sticking close to him is the only way to discover the truth. Strangely, her heart seems to be in danger, too....

And speaking of hearts and flowers, this year's edition of Harlequin's popular Valentine anthology, *My Valentine,* features short stories by four favorite Superromance authors—Margot Dalton, Karen Young, Marisa Carroll and Muriel Jensen. Be sure to look for it wherever Harlequin books are sold!

Happy Valentine's Day!

Marsha Zinberg,
Senior Editor, Superromance

Tara Taylor Quinn

McGILLUS v. WRIGHT

Harlequin Books

TORONTO • NEW YORK • LONDON
AMSTERDAM • PARIS • SYDNEY • HAMBURG
STOCKHOLM • ATHENS • TOKYO • MILAN
MADRID • WARSAW • BUDAPEST • AUCKLAND

ISBN 0-373-70584-0

McGILLUS V. WRIGHT

ABOUT THE AUTHOR

Like many authors, Tara Taylor Quinn uses real life as a springboard for her imagination. When a man who had committed a crime against someone she knew was released from jail, the authorities informed the victim that he was no longer behind bars. The victim's distress at hearing the news made Tara question the wisdom of the current laws, and—presto—a new story idea was born.

Readers will be delighted to hear that Tara is now hard at work on her next Superromance novel, which is sure to be another page-turning read.

Tara lives in Scottsdale, Arizona, with her husband and young daughter.

Books by Tara Taylor Quinn

HARLEQUIN SUPERROMANCE
567—YESTERDAY'S SECRETS

Don't miss any of our special offers. Write to us at the following address for information on our newest releases.

Harlequin Reader Service
P.O. Box 1397, Buffalo, NY 14240
Canadian address: P.O. Box 603,
Fort Erie, Ont. L2A 5X3

For Chum—the love lives on

CHAPTER ONE

THE TASTE OF FEAR STUCK to Tatum's tongue like cold metal. She tried to take comfort from the iron bars that separated her from the world's undesirables, but they were only an illusion, mocking the freedom that she no longer felt she deserved. It didn't seem to matter that she wasn't actually living side by side with the dangerous criminals she had spent years putting away—she often felt like one of them now.

"How ya doin', Ms. McGillus?" Jim Marsh, model prisoner extraordinaire, greeted her with his toothy smile.

Tatum forced herself to acknowledge the man who always seemed to be mopping the stained tile of the state penitentiary's visitor holding cell. "Getting along, Jim. How about yourself?"

Feeling as stiff as the contours of her tailored blue suit, she stood just inside the cold concrete chamber, waiting to be directed toward one of the fourteen heavy doors in front of her.

What would he look like this week? Would his cheeks have sunk even lower? Would the deep grooves crisscrossing his once-lively face have become even more pronounced? She supposed there could even be bruises, though she had been relieved over the past months to have seen no evidence of physical abuse.

"Waitin' for your daddy?" Jim piped up, obvious in his eagerness to take advantage of the opportunity for a little conversation. Pop had told her that Jim claimed he was in prison for a crime he did not commit.

Tatum nodded, unable to bring forth any further civility. She had ceased responding to Jim Marsh's congeniality many months before. Yet the man continued to interrupt her precious hour with her father each week, even though he had to be aware that Pop only had those sixty minutes of life every week. Tatum almost allowed herself to wish that the easygoing Marsh would do something to forfeit the minimum-security privileges that allowed him the freedom of a custodial position within the prison. But then who would Pop have to talk to? Marsh was the only inmate with clearance to have contact with Pop. Other than Danny, he was Pop's only friend.

"He's been lookin' a little peaked this week, Ms. McGillus. Maybe you ought to talk him into visitin' the infirmary," the friendly man persisted. Tatum felt herself getting irritated by the sound of Jim's tongue sucking against his teeth.

"I'm sure he's fine, Jim, thanks," she replied.

She could not allow the man to see the anxiety that his words had sent coursing through her. She had to remain strong. There was nobody left to pick her up if she fell.

The minutes ticked slowly by, interrupted only by the swishing mop and Marsh's occasional sucking sounds. Pop was almost five minutes late for visiting hour.

Since the night Pop had murdered Cale's killer in cold blood, Tatum had been slowly losing her grip. His being in prison was as much her fault as it was his, and if anything happened to him while he lived behind bars, she knew her life would no longer be worth living.

"McGillus visitor, room nine," a stern male voice crackled impersonally over the aging public-address system.

For his own safety as well as Tatum's, ex-detective Jack McGillus had been given a private visiting schedule, two hours prior to the rest of the inmates.

Smiling warmly to disguise her stress, Tatum pulled open metal door number nine and stepped inside the tiny visiting booth. Her smile faded to straight-lipped tension when she noticed the empty cubicle opposite her own. Something was wrong.

Slumping down into the metal folding chair, Tatum cradled her forearms around the telephone receiver resting on the yellowed Formica counter in front of her and tried to calm her stomach. She stared impotently through the shatterproof window in front of her. Where was Pop?

Tatum's lips stretched into an instant smile as the door in the opposite compartment finally opened, but her effort was lost when a grim-faced guard appeared in the gap—alone.

He picked up the telephone on his side of the glass and motioned for Tatum to do the same.

"Ms. McGillus?"

"Yes?" Tatum spoke into the cold receiver, unconsciously reverting to her court voice in an effort to divorce herself from whatever was coming next.

"Mr. McGillus is in the infirmary, ma'am," the uniformed man explained, looking at her through the glass separating them.

Tatum felt the blood drain from her skin. Someone had gotten him.

"How bad..."

"He's all right. He was having some chest pains this morning, but they were only heartburn. The doctor just wants to keep him hooked up to a monitor a while longer as a general precaution."

"You're sure he's okay?"

"Yes, ma'am. I give you my word, straight from the doctor's mouth."

"When can I see him?" she demanded next, unable to acknowledge the man's compassion for fear of breaking down completely.

"Technically not until visiting time next Sunday, but you can try to pull some strings to get in during the week sometime, since you missed today...."

"TATUM! To what do I owe the pleasure of your pretty face amid these old gray walls?" The prison warden, a long-time friend of the McGilluses, smiled up at her as she poked her head into his office. Danny always pulled the Sunday shift to give his next in command, a family man, the day off.

"It's Pop," Tatum replied, returning the older man's welcoming smile.

Daniel Torunta sprang up from the cracked vinyl chair behind his desk. "Jack?" he asked, alarm spreading across his features. "I haven't heard any trouble today. What's happened?"

"Don't worry, Danny," Tatum reassured hastily. "Your security measures are apparently holding up admirably. Pop's in the infirmary. Word is that he's just had a spot of heartburn, but the doctor wants to be positive before they send him back to his cell."

Obviously relieved, Danny walked to the front of his desk and propped himself against it. He folded his arms across his massive chest, warm understanding replacing the anxiety in his expression. "And you didn't get to see him today, did you?"

Tatum moved forward to place her hand on the man's burly forearm. "I don't want to take advantage of you, Danny, or put you in any more of an awkward position. I just want to know if it's against policy to allow a special visiting hour in a case like this."

Daniel took Tatum's slender fingers into his hand. "First off, young lady, *you* have nothing to do with my position, awkward or otherwise. Jack McGillus was one hell of a police detective—one of the best. He spent a lifetime serving the people of this state, protecting them from the scum of the world. It would be the sickest irony of all to throw him in with all the trash he sent down.''

Tatum couldn't avert her eyes as Daniel's gray gaze pinned her own. She stared up at the wrinkled face in front of her and swallowed hard.

''What I'm saying, sweetie, is that whether or not I know that you cook a mean enchilada casserole has nothing to do with the protection I'm giving your daddy. I'd do the same for any other good cop who wound up in here.''

''But the state would have every right to come after you for the manpower you've spent to protect him. There's no way around his guilty verdict, Danny—he openly confesses to the murder.''

Daniel stood up straight and put his hands on his hips. He faced her with a glare that had cowered many prisoners and guards before her. ''Wait just a minute here, young woman. Do you even hear how you sound? Yeah, it's true that Jack confessed, but are you already so brainwashed by the system that you've lost your ability to see into people's hearts? To consider motives? What about your brother? Have you forgotten Cale? Doesn't his memory matter anymore?''

Tears sprang to Tatum's eyes, blurring her vision, but she would not allow them to fall. ''I see Pop's heart, loud and clear, Danny. I live with it beating inside my breast with every breath I take. *I* don't blame him for shooting Kanish. How can I? It's the thought that counts, right? And in that particular crime the thought was just as much mine as Pop's. He just happened to have a gun handy at the right time."

Daniel stepped forward, grasping Tatum's shoulders in his hair-roughened hands. "Are you out of your mind, girl? You're no murderer. You're a warm and caring young woman. Jack was trained to get the bad guys, and that's just what he did, except that he chose not to follow the rules that last time."

Tatum met the older man's eyes wearily. "You just asked me if I'd forgotten Cale," she said. "I'll never forget him, Danny. I'll never forget the way he died or the rage I felt when I heard that his murderer was being set free. Ever since we received that due-notice letter from the Florida authorities telling us about Kanish's release, I was obsessed with avenging my brother's murder. That's a year and a half of rage. And do you know what? I was *relieved* when Kanish was finally dead. I was actually glad that a human being had lost his life.

"I haven't lost myself in the system, Danny. It's just the opposite. I can't blame Pop for what he did. Not only was I part of the motivation behind his crime, but I condoned what he did. And because of that I'm afraid I can't even do my job anymore."

"What're you talking about? You're one of the best damn lawyers I know. You get the ones that matter the most, and you do it by the book," Daniel said, softening his grip on her shoulders and rubbing them gently with his palms.

Tatum shrugged. "I don't know, Danny. I now understand how a good person—even a law-abiding detective—can sometimes have a valid reason for killing someone. Do you know what I'm afraid of? I'm afraid of standing in front of the witness chair, looking at the person sitting there and seeing that he is a good person who was driven to commit a crime by something beyond his control. I'm going to be looking for it, understanding it and not fighting as hard against him as I should be."

Danny's glance narrowed as he listened to her. "You having more troubles at work?" he asked. Tatum had led him to believe that the harassment she had been subjected to after Pop's arrest had stopped—that the county supervisor had decided that having a felon's daughter on his staff was not going to hurt his political career after all.

Tatum shrugged again. She wished she had not said as much as she had. Her problems with her superior were her own. She peered up at the man who had been a part of her life for as long as she could remember. "Can I see him, Danny? Without jeopardizing your position?"

Daniel nodded slowly. "How about Wednesday, say from four to five?"

Tatum's eyes filled with grateful tears. "Thank you," she whispered, leaning forward to wrap her arms around the big man's middle. For one brief moment, as her head rested against his solid chest, she felt as if she were still a little girl with an adoring father and a big brother to make everything in her world all right.

Daniel buried his gruff features in Tatum's hair. "Please don't be so hard on yourself, honey. Hell, no one wanted that bastard dead more than I. But it doesn't change who you are."

Daniel's words shattered her fragile illusion. She was not a little girl anymore, and there was no one to take care of her but herself. It was time for him to stop babying her.

"Everything changes who you are, Danny. How could it not? How could anyone bury a brother and not be changed? I took an oath to uphold the law, I've been hired by this state to prosecute the bad guys, but I don't believe it was wrong for my father to have killed a man. You don't think that's going to have some effect on me?"

Tatum gave Danny one last squeeze before straightening and heading to the door. Only time would tell just how far-reaching the effects of that due-notice letter were going to be. She had already lost so much. Was she going to lose the career she loved, too, all because some nameless authorities had taken it upon themselves to notify her and Pop that Cale's murderer was being released from jail?

She shivered as she stepped from the stale air-conditioning within the prison walls to the scorching

afternoon heat under Arizona's August sunshine.
Wednesday was still three days away. That would
make it ten days since she'd last seen him. Tatum
could not remember a time when she had gone ten
days without seeing the man who had been both
mother and father to her for practically all her thirty-
two years.

The thought panicked her. In the past months all
the things she had counted on in her life had been
stripped away, leaving her alone and desperate. And
the worst part of it was the fear that she wasn't going
to make it, that she might lose control and be hauled
away by some stranger.

She concentrated on the blue sky above, the sun's
heat caressing her skin. Her car was right in front of
her. If she made it through this year in one piece, she
was never going to put herself in a vulnerable position again, Tatum promised herself as she unlocked
her sand-colored sedan. She was never again going to
risk her heart and soul to the vagaries of life—to
things beyond her control. The price of pain was too
great. She wanted nothing more out of the rest of her
life than work-filled days and quiet nights.

Pointing her Taurus toward Phoenix and the office in which she had practically lived since Pop's arrest, Tatum forced her personal demons aside and
tried to focus on the work that lay ahead of her. She
needed to put in the time on the highly publicized
Rhodes murder trial. Her career had been on shaky
ground ever since her father's conviction, and she

knew that the Rhodes trial could be her last chance to convince her superiors that she was still the right woman for the job. And she hoped the long hours of concentration would allow her to escape into blessed numbness long enough to recover the necessary equilibrium to see her through a few more days.

It was Sunday. The state capitol building would be quiet, peaceful—no ringing telephones, no people. She should be able to accomplish a lot—if only she didn't have those nagging doubts about Bobby Rhodes's guilt....

JONATHAN WRIGHT SPED along the semideserted streets of downtown Phoenix toward the state capitol building, attempting to catch up with his Sunday-afternoon schedule. He had attended church as usual that morning, a practice he'd kept up even before he had been advised that a token religious commitment was necessary to a senator's image. The service had run long, and now he had almost thirty minutes' worth of schedule to squeeze into seven.

Lately, Jonathan had caught himself wondering what it would be like to have a private life, to have more than a fleeting liaison with a member of the opposite sex, to have a real home, but he never seemed to get much further than wondering. He was what he did. His public conscience had been instilled within him in the womb.

Which was one reason why, at two o'clock that afternoon, Jonathan found himself charging up the

steps of a county office building on his way to a
desktop publishing system. He needed his due-notice
bill to pass during next winter's session, because the
children he cared about more than anything else in his
life desperately needed that due notice if they were to
ever have a chance at normal lives. As founder and
director of the Children's Crisis Center, he had seen
too many children who lived in constant fear of repeated abuse. Jonathan was determined to use every
spare moment he had over the next couple of months
to lobby for the bill that would protect them.

The bill was the real reason Jonathan was an Arizona State senator, not the small salary the state paid
its local legislators. His primary allegiance was to his
social work career, and he had no political ambi-
tions. But he was willing to do whatever it took to
protect the kids.

Certain that no one but he and the security guard
would be in the county building on this hot August
Sunday, Jonathan jogged around the corner at the top
of the stairs with a total disregard for his professional persona. Before he could stop himself, Jonathan catapulted into a coffee trolley that was rolling
past the stairs and fell down on his suited backside.

"Oh!"

The startled feminine exclamation surprised him as
much as his fall, and he quickly scurried to his feet
before the faceless female could come around the cart
and witness his humiliation.

As soon as he regained his six-foot-high perspective, he glanced across the cart and was startled to find a cool, collected lady in blue gazing back at him with finely sculptured features.

"I'm sorry, are you okay?" he asked despite the obvious fact that she at least had not suffered from his thoughtless dash. He noticed as he looked away from her curious blue eyes, down past nicely rounded breasts, that even her coffee had remained intact.

"I'm fine. But I'm not sure about you," the raven-haired woman said with a hint of a smile.

"I'm also fine," Jonathan said a little too forcefully. "I mean, just fine," he added more softly. He resisted the urge to brush off the seat of his pants. He didn't care to have any more attention drawn to that particular part of his anatomy.

"What were you doing anyway?" she asked, glancing back to the stairs he had just bolted up.

Jonathan was tempted to try to convince her that he was working out, that he was another Sylvester Stallone in the making, but he wasn't sure how he could explain his suit and tie.

"Hurrying, I guess," he answered with a chuckle. He had no idea who this woman was, but whether she was the cleaning lady or the mayor, she was doing a good job of making him feel aware of her.

"I'd offer you some coffee, but I have hours of work ahead of me and need every drop I've got. There's more down the hall, though. You can help yourself as you pass by." She pushed her cart, loaded with a thermal warming pot, cream and sugar, past him and down the hall.

Jonathan stood watching her voluptuous hips, outlined seductively through a fashionably snug linen skirt, as they swayed beneath her waist-length mane of jet black hair. He felt as though he had just been punched in the solar plexus, and the sudden tingling in his groin had nothing to do with his bruised tailbone. In all of his thirty-six years, Jonathan had never met a woman who had affected him as immediately, as forcefully as the beautiful stranger just had.

Before Jonathan could force his legs to sprint after her, the alluring woman was in the elevator, riding away to an unknown floor. Jonathan's first instinct was to jump on another elevator and search the whole building until he found his mystery lady, but he knew too well that he had other obligations to fulfill, other duties that went above and beyond personal gratification. For the time being he contented himself with a silent promise to ask around about her at the first opportunity.

Jonathan had only served about a third of his two-year state senate term, and since the majority of the time he had been in office had been spent in session, he had not yet become familiar with the people in the local government buildings. But this lady was too distinct to go unnoticed. He would find her again.

In the meantime he had some flyers to design....

CHAPTER TWO

"YOU LOOK TIRED, POP. Are you sleeping okay?" Tatum asked the following Wednesday afternoon. She looked at her father through the window separating her cubicle from his. "Tired" was an understatement, she thought to herself—Pop looked haggard. Tatum felt as if she had the weight of ten children resting upon her back.

"I'm sleeping just fine, girlie. And before you ask, I'm eating just fine, too. The food's really not half-bad here. At least I don't have to fix it or help with the dishes." Pop's voice crackled over the receiver, sounding endearingly familiar but lacking the robustness to which Tatum was accustomed. He grinned at her through the glass.

Swallowing the lump in her throat, Tatum grinned back. "So have you been reading lots of dirty magazines?"

"Naw. They're all beginning to read the same," he told her, but Tatum did not quite trust the twinkle she saw in his sunken eyes. "'Course, the pictures are still halfway decent," he continued, taking obvious delight in his daughter's blush.

"Oh, Pop, how did *you* ever raise two such charming, well-mannered children?" Tatum teased, returning her father's smile. Pop always could make her smile. "Don't you do *anything* constructive around here?" she charged into her receiver.

"I beat the pants off Torunta in chess this week," he countered, resting his elbows on the Formica counter in front of him.

"So how many steak dinners does that make?" Tatum asked. She scrutinized her father through the glass, noticing new wrinkles in his too-pale face.

"Let's just say you better start collecting on them soon, or he'll be ten feet under before he pays up," he said.

Tatum blinked back affectionate tears. Pop had never let her down—ever. She didn't trust herself to speak. Teary words would definitely put a damper on the teasing banter that gave these fleeting minutes a hint of normalcy.

"You find yourself a hunk like your old man yet?" Pop asked after a few moments. He had been trying to marry her off for years, but Tatum had been aware of a new urgency in his attempts since he had been in prison. It made her nervous. It was almost as if Pop wanted to make sure that she would not be alone before he gave up.

"Not yet," she answered her father, quelling a momentary vision of dark brown hair atop dark brown eyes—eyes that were laughing at her over a coffee cart. She had no idea why the stranger's image had insisted on hanging around in her mind for the past three days. Sure he was great looking, but the world was full of great-looking men.

Pop asked several questions about her career, and Tatum answered them as vaguely as she could. There were the ethics of client confidentiality to consider, but she also knew that unless she was very careful, Pop would figure out that things were not entirely rosy.

For once she was grateful for the knock on the door of Pop's cubicle, followed by the appearance of Jim Marsh's toothy grin. She looked at the man's graying hair, his premature wrinkles, and wondered what he had to be so cheerful about.

Jim waved to Tatum from behind Pop's shoulders, leaned down to say something that made Pop smile and then backed out of the cubicle. The door swung shut behind him.

"There's a bit of a ruckus down the hall. We'll have a couple of extra minutes to visit," Pop said. His voice was upbeat. There was no indication that he was aware that as long as the other prisoners were out and about, the walk from the visiting cell to his own would not be safe for him.

Tatum tried not to let her worry show. "I guess today's our lucky day, huh?"

Pop matched her smile with one of his own and spent the next ten minutes telling her the knock-knock jokes he had come up with since her last visit. Eventually they worked their magic. Tatum was laughing so hard her jaws ached by the time the guard's face reappeared on Pop's side of the visiting cell.

"Honey?" Pop stopped Tatum just as she was about to hang up the receiver.

Tatum held the phone to her ear, looking up to meet his suddenly serious eyes.

"Let it go, baby. Be at peace. I am," he said. He hung up then, blew her a kiss and left his cubicle without looking back.

Tatum's hand was still holding the receiver as she sat, frozen, for a moment, staring at the now-empty space across from her and wishing she knew how to grant him his request.

TATUM THOUGHT AGAIN about her father's request as she sat alone in her office Thursday evening. How could she be at peace when she feared that the past year and a half had made her incapable of doing the job she loved? Bobby Rhodes's case was spread on the desk in front of her. The case was so clear-cut that even a law student could fight it and win. The young Mexican had been convicted for killing his brother-in-law. A neighbor had overheard Bobby threaten to kill Roy Ingram just hours before Roy was found shot to death in Bobby's home. There were reports of a heated argument between Bobby and Roy just before Roy's death. There were no suspects other than Bobby, no one who may have had reason to want Roy dead. The case was a classic open-and-close variety, and yet Tatum still did not have even an opening argument.

She looked up as Montgomery, the county superintendent and her immediate superior, stopped by her office on his way out. "You've been here late three days this week. What're you working on that's so all-fired important?" he asked, clearly perplexed.

"Just looking over the Rhodes case," Tatum admitted. He knew she didn't have any other big cases on her schedule at the moment. He had made sure of it. He wanted Tatum's full concentration on this one. If it had been within his power, he probably would have prevented his newest district attorney from trying the Rhodes case altogether.

"I realize the media has gone to town with the kid, but it's an open-and-shut case. You could do it in your sleep. Every piece of evidence fits the puzzle so snugly that you don't need any glue to hold them together," he insisted.

Tatum knew what he was saying. He was telling her that if she blew it, she'd have no excuses. "Yes, sir," she agreed with him. "I'm just memorizing names and dates to reassure the jury that I've done my homework."

"Yeah, you do that," he said, sounding more as though the idea had come from him. "The guy on defense, Duncan, may be a rookie, but he's supposed to be good. And you don't need me to remind you, Tatum, that everything that happens in this office, everything you do, reflects on me. With your father sitting in jail, you're resting on pretty shaky ground here," he added, repeating the thinly veiled threat that she had been hearing, in one guise or another, since Pop's conviction.

Tatum knew better than to reply. She was not up to another battle. Montgomery waited for her stilted nod, waved goodbye and left just as she had known he would. Tatum felt like crying.

Maybe she was trying too hard. Maybe she was inventing problems where there were none. Maybe if she could just relax, the feeling, the certainty that the defendant was guilty, would come over her. Lifting her long black hair away from her neck and shoulders, as if to remove the tension gathering there, she took one last glance at the mass of facts in front of her. It didn't work. The problem was still just as heavy.

Dropping her arms, Tatum gathered up the papers and started to put them back in their file when she saw a strangely familiar figure fly past her doorway. With a spontaneous rush of pleasure, she jumped up to investigate, her heart pounding swiftly beneath her breast. She was only halfway around her desk when the energetic man was back, framed in her office doorway.

"So I finally found you," her handsome comrade of the coffee cart stated as he walked into the room and sat in one of two vinyl chairs in front of her desk. Tatum took in his lithe, trim form. He had the type of body that looked great in a suit. His broad shoulders filled out the jacket, while his slacks tapered easily on lean hips.

Tatum felt her heart lift as she watched him. Returning his grin, she went back to sit behind her desk. The man had made her smile for the second time now—that was reason enough not to excuse herself immediately. She glanced down at his light gray suit, the same one he'd worn when he bumped into her coffee cart. "Your, uh, *you* appear to be completely recovered," she commented.

Jonathan was feeling too smug at having found her again, however accidentally, to feel embarrassed. "Nice of you to notice," he replied. He had a sudden impulse to run his finger along the curve of her lips.

"Don't you—"

"What are you—"

They both started at once and then laughed. Jonathan liked her laughter. It sounded good—sexy, if a little rusty. "So, do you work all the time, or just after hours?" he asked, gesturing to her half-loaded briefcase. He noticed the nameplate pushed to one side of her desk. Tatum McGillus. County Attorney.

"I work when I have work to do," she told him. "I could ask the same of you, you know."

Jonathan conceded her point with a nod. Both times he had seen her, after all, he too had been in the office after hours.

Tatum McGillus. Jonathan recognized the name with surprise. He had heard of her father, of course.

McGillus was that Phoenix police detective who had murdered his son's killer after the killer had already served his time. It was believed that the detective had been keeping tabs on the other man all the way from Phoenix to Florida, following his case in minute detail, just waiting for him to be released from prison so he could follow through on his obsessive plan of murder. Jonathan looked at the obviously successful woman across from him, wishing now that he had followed the case more closely. Tatum McGillus must be one hell of a strong woman.

"So, do you eat?" he asked. He had another batch of flyers to print, a speech to write and bills to pay, but suddenly nothing mattered as much as spending a little time with this woman—doing something nice for her. Each time he had thought of her this past week, he had felt invigorated, revitalized. Now that he was with her again, those feelings only grew stronger.

Tatum smiled. "On occasion."

"Alone?"

Tatum did not take offense at the man's boldness. As come-ons went, his was rather obvious, but refreshingly so. Somehow that made him less threatening. "Sometimes," she conceded. Let him make of that what he would.

He shifted in the seat, anchoring an ankle across his knee and placing his hands on top of the gray sock he had just exposed. "Tonight?" he asked, staring her straight in the eye.

Part of Tatum—the sensible, strong, lawyerly part—could not believe she was allowing this conversation to continue, but even an island needed sustenance of some sort. Tatum couldn't help welcoming his attention for a moment.

"Probably," she finally said, holding his brown-eyed gaze steadily. She knew what was coming. She also knew she was going to refuse him. But she couldn't help wishing she had met him a few years earlier, when she had still had something left inside of her to give away—when she still had the courage to reach out, to risk getting burned.

"So, what do you say we play hooky for a couple of hours and have dinner someplace touristy? We could leave our work behind and just enjoy the evening—kind of like two alcoholics going out for a soft drink."

Tatum's refusal caught in her throat. She suddenly felt like Cinderella being given a chance to go to the ball. He was offering her the chance to step outside of herself, to escape everything, leave the past months behind and live a few hours as she would if she were still the carefree person she had been before Cale died. He was asking nothing more intimate than a game of make-believe. How could he have known that a chance for controlled escape was the one thing she would have a hard time refusing?

"I've never played hooky," she admitted. She sat still, behind her desk, as if any movement of air in the room would whisk the chance away.

"Neither have I, for that matter, but I've heard that the only way to experience real fun is to sneak it."

When he put it like that, Tatum found it even harder to refuse. She obviously had more in common with this man than the memory of a coffee cart. It sounded as if he needed some time away from whatever pressures he was carrying almost as desperately as she did. There was nothing personal about this, she told herself, merely two overworked people taking a brief time-out.

"I don't know your name," she protested. Even to her own ears, her excuse sounded like no more than a pretense of resistance.

"It's Jonathan Wright," he said. "Like yourself, I'm a public administrator, and I need a night off."

Jonathan Wright. The new state senator. She had heard good things about him, about his dedication to his causes. But oddly enough she couldn't remember hearing a single thing about his private life.

She forced herself to ask the necessary question. "Are you married?"

"No."

Tatum leaned across her desk, offering him her hand. "Hello, Jonathan, I'm Tatum." Just for tonight, she was willing to play along. Tonight they were just two people, Jonathan and Tatum, who needed a release from the stresses of their lives.

Tatum simply accepted the feeling of warmth that surrounded her whole body as his fingers closed over hers. She was merely along for the ride—a much-needed, heartily welcomed escape from reality.

"Well, Tatum. Seeing that you didn't share your coffee with me the last time we were together, I say we start there," Jonathan said, finally releasing her slender hand but still holding her smoky blue gaze with his own.

Jonathan suddenly felt more lighthearted than he had since he was a kid. His whole life had been spent with the cares of others on his shoulders, and he had carried the weight willingly. But for the first time in his thirty-six years, those cares seemed to float away of their own accord.

He waited while Tatum finished loading her brief-case and locked her desk, then led her out to the parking lot. They decided to leave Tatum's sedan parked where it was, and took Jonathan's Bronco to Monti's, a legendary hangout near the university where they could escape into anonymity.

Set on the edge of the Arizona State University campus, in the heart of Old Town Tempe, the white stucco building held more than twenty separate dining rooms of various sizes. Mr. Monti served the best cuts of beef, at a fraction of the usual cost, and all of his meals were accompanied by a basket of home-made Roman bread. Tatum found herself munching on the thyme sprinkled crust as she studied her companion.

She already knew what she planned to order, but Jonathan was studying the menu as if he hadn't eaten in a week. She smiled at his intensity. She would bet it had been a while since he had taken the time for a full-course meal. Tatum could not remember the last time she had eaten more than a sandwich on the run, either. She found herself wondering if he had a woman somewhere who would like to have the chance to cook hot meals for him. Most of her hoped he did. And the small part that did not . . .

With great care she studied the Mexican tile mosaic that made up the pool of the fountain beside their table. She was not going to let herself ruin this evening with thoughts of the outside world. She had been offered a rare opportunity, a brief detour from the road her life had taken, and she was going to enjoy herself, she determined firmly as she watched the room's dimmed lighting reflect glints of bronze in Jonathan's dark brown hair. His earnest brown eyes and firm, steady jaw were the perfect foil for lips that were almost too generous. Tatum found herself wondering how close a woman could get to those lips without surrendering completely.

"So what did you decide?" she asked quickly as Jonathan laid his menu aside.

"The filet, I think. How about you?"

Tatum's stomach did a little dance as he smiled across at her. She had no idea what made this man so different from all the others she knew, but just the fact that she was there, sitting across from him, told her that he was.

"The same," she answered. It was what she'd always ordered when she had come here during her law-school years. The memory was a good one. Suddenly she wanted the evening to last a long, long time.

They talked all the way through dinner as if they were old friends who hadn't seen each other in a while but were completely comfortable in each other's company. They discovered that they both were closet sitcom rerun fanatics, that Jonathan liked to hike while Tatum preferred escaping into a steamy book, and they both liked water sports. Her favorite ice-cream flavor was mint chocolate-chip, while he went for the fudge ripple.

"I've always wanted to travel," Tatum told him over after-dinner coffee. "There's so much I haven't seen, so much I don't know."

She was startled when Jonathan looked up at her, almost as if he were feeling sorry for her.

"I'd been everywhere that was nowhere before I was ten years old," he admitted with a half-guilty shrug. "My parents met while they were both members of a mobile army medical unit during the Korean War. After the war was over, they returned to the States, stayed long enough to get married and have me, and then we were off again.

"We lived mostly in underdeveloped countries, working with the natives. I didn't appreciate it as much then, but these days I've come to see the advantages of living in a society with no cars, no sky-scrapers, no telephones ringing off the hook all day."

His gaze met Tatum's and he paused, his eyes holding her captive, as if there were two conversations
going on, one between two people who had just met,
and the other between two souls that were already
melding together. Tatum's heart was pounding when
he finally broke the contact to rearrange the silver-
ware on his empty plate.

"My folks are into educating the underprivi-
leged," he said as if the silence had never been.
"Medical practices constantly need to be updated, of
course, but introducing books and modern farming
technology is equally challenging. As I got older, I
was glad to be a part of their work. I remember one
time when I was about twelve. An infectious virus had
broken out in a village about a day's ride from where
we were stationed. I went along with Dad to deliver
some antibiotics to the people there. When we got
there, there was one baby who had been hit particu-
larly hard—probably because he was so young. With
the help of the antibiotics, they were able to save the
baby. I'll never forget the happy tears that streamed
down that mother's face when they told her that her
child was going to live. I think I knew then that I
wanted to go into some kind of social work."

He seemed to think he was lucky to have had such
a childhood, but Tatum couldn't help feeling a little
sorry for him. Had he ever known a carefree summer
day, a trip to Disneyland, the magic of bright lights
and bundles of presents on Christmas morning? Had
he ever had his own room, shelves full of toys, a best

friend? His folks had thrived on their philanthropic work, but had they taken time to play with their own little boy? Had he missed completely the wonderful years of make-believe that precede the responsibilities of adulthood?

"And to think that my biggest worry was which pair of blue jeans looked the raggiest or had the biggest bell bottoms," Tatum said, feeling a sudden twinge of guilt.

Jonathan smiled at her remark and embarked on a comical dissertation of some of the costumes he'd tried on over the years, ranging from sarongs to loincloths.

"You actually wore a loincloth?" Tatum finally interrupted. Her mind was filled with the dangerous fantasy of seeing his lithe, lean masculinity covered only with a scrap of animal hide. She reached for her glass of wine in an attempt to control her thoughts.

"I only tried it on! Once," Jonathan defended himself with a grin.

Jonathan refused to let Tatum pay her share of the bill. He suggested that they take a walk through the rest of the mosaic of unique shops and eateries that surrounded the university and was known as Old Town Tempe.

Despite the lateness of the hour, Tatum was not ready for the evening to end and accepted his invitation without hesitation. She needed the peace the evening offered more than she needed the restless sleep that had haunted her nights for more months

than she could remember. Her stomach fluttered as
Jonathan took her fingers in the warmth of his grasp
and they set off down the street.

Hand in hand they looked in shop windows,
watched the college students and reminisced about
their own college days. Jonathan seemed as eager as
she was to prolong their fairy tale, and not once did
either of them break their unspoken promise to leave
their present lives somewhere in the future.

But eventually the evening did have to end, and
Tatum swallowed her disappointment when Jonathan finally suggested that they head back to get her
car. The drive back down to the county building was
all too short, and in a matter of minutes, they were
parked beside her car and Tatum was searching
through her purse for her keys.

She jumped when Jonathan pulled the purse from
her hands, but did not protest when he pulled her
across the bench seat into his arms. Tatum was not
inexperienced. She had had her share of boyfriends
who for one reason or another had never led to mar-
riage. She had even had a lover for a year during college, but she had never before experienced the
adolescent thrill of necking in the front seat of a ve-
hicle. But with Jonathan, in this evening out of time,
it just seemed right somehow. She welcomed the
contact as if it could somehow make the last hours
more real, more tangible. She wanted something to
take with her when she returned to reality.

There were no demands as his arms tightened around her, no threats of vulnerability. After all, what could actually *happen* in a public parking lot? Their fairy tale was simply continuing a few moments longer.

Girded by the protection of make-believe, Tatum surrendered to Jonathan's caresses, waiting for his kiss. He made her feel safe in a world gone mad, special in a soiled life. He had taken her out of herself for a few precious hours, provided her with an evening out of time, a chance to rest from the turmoil overshadowing her life. And he had taken the same sustenance for himself.

His lips met hers softly at first, reassuring her. But as she responded, his touch became hungrier. She shivered with unexpected desire as he explored her mouth fully, slowly, as if trying to learn more about her without the words they had denied themselves.

Closing her eyes against reality, Tatum clung to him. Had she been thinking, she would have been alarmed by the suddenness of her response to him. But she was not thinking. She was caught in a sensual haze unlike any she had experienced before. She caressed his back and shoulders with a pressure that held him securely against her while his hands roamed up and down her torso, as if memorizing the feel of her.

There were no thoughts beyond the moment, no awareness other than the rightness of their physical communication. No danger that things could get out of hand with a steering wheel taking up so much of their space.

His fingers stroked along her back and sides, making her shiver, until finally he grazed the side of her breast. His touch was as light as silk, but even as she was leaning more fully against him, Tatum stiffened. Warning sirens were suddenly ringing so loudly in her head they drowned out her moan of pleasure. *Complete loss of control was just around the corner.* She jerked backward, out of his arms.

Her nerves were singing, her body trembling for more, but she knew things could go no further. She leaned back against the seat, her instincts screaming at her with an overwhelming mixture of conflicting needs—security and resistance, desire and safety.

But one thing she knew for sure. She and Jonathan had been dangerously close to crossing the invisible boundary between fantasy and reality. He was a very attractive man, but she had no business getting intimate with him. She had no intentions of getting involved.

And yet, at the same time, it bothered her to think of the impression she had made, responding to his good-night kiss so eagerly, and then pulling back so abruptly. Though it made no sense, his opinion mattered. She wanted to be able to remember this night as something good, special, and to think that maybe Jonathan would do the same. Her hesitant gaze finally met his under the dim light of a street lamp shining through the windshield.

Jonathan let a finger run along her swollen lips. "I'm not sorry I kissed you, but I am sorry it made you uncomfortable," he said in a husky whisper.

Tatum remained silent, unable to tell him she was not uncomfortable. She tried to smile but ended up looking away from him, studying the rows of empty parking places surrounding them.

Jonathan slid a finger under her chin and urged her face back toward him. He kissed her once more, softly, almost platonically on her slightly swollen lips. "Thank you for tonight. It was wonderful," he murmured.

Tatum did smile then, meeting his glance once again. "For me, too," she whispered as if afraid that the sound of her voice would break the fragile wall surrounding them in their fairy-tale world.

He saw her into her car without another word. Just as she was about to drive away, he motioned to her from the front seat of his Bronco. Tatum pushed a button to lower her car window. "I'm going to see you again, lady, in the real world," he warned through his own opened window. His voice resonated in the deserted parking lot. Before Tatum could reply, he was gone.

Tatum smiled, but the grin soon turned wistful and then disappeared completely. She wished she could take him up on that promise, but as she drove away she felt the return of her current circumstances as if they were an actual physical weight cascading down upon her, covering her head, and then her shoulders, and continuing down to pool in her lap. Her grief for Cale, for Pop, her floundering career—all lay heavily in her lap. She had learned the hard way that when all was said and done, she alone was responsible for her welfare. She was traveling the long, slow road of learning to rely only on herself and she could not afford any detours. She wasn't sure she would ever find herself again if she got lost. And there was no one at home to come looking for her anymore.

But in spite of her fears, her troublesome thoughts, she found herself wishing that she could see Jonathan again someday, in the real world just as he had said. For the first time in more than a year, she had felt a kind of peace tonight. And she was pretty sure that she had helped Jonathan to feel it, too. Heaven help her, but she didn't know if she was strong enough to turn her back on that.

FIVE DAYS LATER Tatum was standing at an intersection, waiting for the traffic light to change, when she saw the flyer. It was attached to a nearby pole, and she gave it a quick glance, then tensed up and read more carefully. Someone was trying to get a new law before the Arizona State legislature, and they were going about it in a truly tacky way.

But it was not the lobbyist's novice attempts at campaigning that had Tatum trembling with rage as she ripped down the flyer before marching across the street. It was the law he proposed.

Some ignorant do-gooder had determined that Arizona victims needed to be told when prisoners were released from jail. On the surface Tatum could agree that a victim had the right to know what happened to the person who had victimized him. But she knew first-hand that no good could come of the knowledge. Why should anyone have to live with the bitterness of knowing that the person who had wronged him was now free? Or if the victim had been a casualty of murder, how could his family be expected to cope with the destructive resentment? Not all families could handle that much acid burning away at the fragile structure of their rebuilt lives....

Tatum continued down the block toward her car, but she could not forget the ripped-up propaganda she had left back at the corner in the sidewalk trash bin. As soon as her day's work was done, she was going to find out who was supporting the proposed bill and do whatever it took to ensure its demise. She had as little choice in the matter as Pop had had when he had pulled the trigger on James Kanish.

It briefly crossed her mind that, as county attorney, she could be flirting with a conflict-of-interest charge, but her conscience would not allow her to let the bill pass uncontested. She would just have to fight without her credentials.

She took several deep breaths as she stood unlocking her car in the one-hundred-ten-degree heat and forced her thoughts back toward the witness interview ahead of her. She could not afford to blow this case, and she needed every scrap of evidence she could find to convince herself that Bobby Rhodes had indeed killed his brother-in-law. She had all the facts, but something still did not feel right....

"WHO KILLED your husband, Jenny?"

"I don't know...I don't know...I don't know." The distraught young woman, sitting beside Tatum on the threadbare couch, huddled forward as sobs shook her skinny body.

Having never even had a mate, let alone lost one, Tatum could only imagine the extent of the woman's suffering. But she could empathize with the tragic fear and hopeless sense of loss that pervaded the woman's run-down but spotlessly clean home that Tuesday morning. Jenny Ingram had lost not only her husband, but stood to lose her adored brother, as well.

"Do you think your brother killed Ray?" she pressed a little harder, hating this part of her job even while she recognized that for the good of society it had to be done.

"No." The conviction behind the one word struck a momentary panic in Tatum's chest. Two weeks ago, after days of studying seemingly conclusive evidence, Tatum had finally given in to intolerable pressure from her superiors and indicted Bobby Rhodes for a murder she was not positive he had committed. She did not need more doubts; she was looking for something to make her sure.

"Why not?"

"Bobby would never lower himself to the level of street scum. There've been times when all he had on his back was his dignity, but he always wore it well."

"Even when he was angry?"

"Especially when he was angry." The young Mexican woman was calmer now, apparently comfortable with the straightforward questions Tatum had expected would confuse her.

"But he was arrested six years ago for assault," Tatum continued relentlessly.

"I was jumped on my way home from work. If Bobby hadn't gotten worried when I didn't show up right on time, I'd have been a lot worse than jumped."

"Why didn't he explain that to the arresting officer?"

"Because that's not the way things work around here. Bobby took the rap, was released on probation, and the jerk who attacked me got off clean. But he never bothered us again. If Bobby had ratted on the guy, I'd have been as good as dead."

Tatum was not naive enough to be surprised by the twisted code of honor, but she still believed in the system enough to think that Bobby should have allowed the law to prosecute his sister's violator.

Unless Jenny was lying...

Tatum let the silence stretch for a moment, allowing the young woman to ponder the seriousness of her situation, and took the opportunity to study the home that Jenny had shared with the two men in her life. But though her trained eye took in every detail of the shabby home, down to the spidery cracks in the walls and the near-empty box of tissues on the scarred wooden table in front of her, Tatum saw nothing that could lead to her missing piece; nothing was out of place, nothing too much in place.

Her searching eye settled on a picture on the side table, depicting a much happier Bobby than the one she had met earlier in the month. Tatum couldn't help feeling sorry that life had wiped away the young man's smile. Every time she had interrogated him over the past weeks, Tatum's respect for Bobby had grown. She would almost go so far as to say she liked the Mexican. He had been understandably upset at his detainment, but he had never become belligerent or angrily profane while repeatedly professing his innocence.

Tatum was all too aware that her reactions to the suspected murderer would only confirm her fears that she was no longer capable of doing her job. Maybe she was too understanding, too empathetic with the young man just because he seemed like a decent individual—because he didn't look or act like a hardened criminal. After all, she wasn't the only one who had questioned Bobby—surely the others had good reasons for thinking him guilty.

As she studied Bobby's picture, hoping to find anything that could lead to the clue she was seeking, Tatum was suddenly reminded of Jonathan. Though

Bobby was darker skinned, both men had clean-cut brown hair and dark eyes. But it wasn't the physical similarities that drew Tatum. The men seemed to share something deeper, less tangible than a physical resemblance—an aura of strength, an air of being determined to live decently.

As had been happening on and off since the previous Thursday, Tatum felt her mind begin to wander. She wondered where Jonathan was, what he was doing, who he was doing it with. Abruptly she reminded herself that his actions were none of her business. She could not risk getting involved, could not risk the possibility of being hurt. Her heart was just too battered, and she was just too scared of losing the tenuous control she was managing to keep on her emotions. She was already facing the possibility of a career gone sour and she wasn't sure she was going to be able to handle that. . . .

"So how do you explain your husband's death?" Tatum blurted suddenly into a silence growing tenser by the second. She needed to wrest some kind of gut reaction from the woman, hoping for some sign that would snap things into place.

A fresh wave of tears streamed down Jenny's bony cheeks.

"I can't," she admitted helplessly.

"Do you deny that when you left for work that night, he and Bobby were arguing?"

"No."

"What was the fight about?" Tatum asked almost wearily, expecting the same "I don't know" answer that was all Jenny had offered to date each time she had been questioned about what really happened that night.

"Me. Roy got angry sometimes. He didn't mean any harm. He'd only done it once before, I swear, but Roy slapped me that night. Bobby walked in right as it happened. It was my fault, really. I was nagging at Roy again." The wet tissue in Jenny's hand ripped beneath her troubled fingers before landing forlornly on a pile of similarly mangled tissues in a trash can next to the couch.

"Roy hit you?" Tatum sat up straighter, watching the younger woman with the shrewdness of her barrister's eye. Her sympathy for Jenny Ingram grew. "I thought you didn't know what they were fighting about."

"Bobby told me to stay out of it. He said if I didn't know anything, everyone would just leave me alone. But I'm afraid he's not going to be able to help himself out of this one. Ms. McGillus, my brother did not kill Roy."

"Who did?"

"I don't know," Jenny cried.

At Tatum's look of disbelief, the pretty young woman continued defensively. "I really don't know. Don't you think I'd tell you if I knew, and get Bobby out of that awful place?"

"I don't know what to think, Jenny. You've lied before, you've admitted living by a mixed-up code of honor, you admit Bobby and Roy were arguing, you admit Bobby almost killed a man once before to protect you, and your neighbor heard Bobby threaten Roy just half an hour before your husband was shot to death with a stolen gun—a gun of the same make and model as the one your brother purchased illegally two years ago. You tell me."

"I wish I could, Ms. McGillus, but whoever killed Roy is still out there, free to kill again. If you put Bobby away, you'll be making a big mistake—an innocent man will go to prison. What if he dies in there?"

DIE IN JAIL... die in jail...die in jail... The words were a nightmarish litany raging through Tatum's mind as she drove back to her office. She was already burdened with the guilt of her father's imprisonment. How could she live with the nagging doubt that she was at least partly responsible for the permanent caging of another decent, perhaps innocent human being? Yet if the man was guilty, as all the evidence seemed to indicate, how could she not?

Tatum was a good lawyer. She had never, ever wanted to be anything else. She had been elated when she had been elected county attorney for one of the largest counties in Arizona. She had been certain she had found her place in life—until lately.

Was she doubting Bobby Rhodes's guilt because
the instincts that had led her through years of successful practice told her he was innocent? Or had the
past months of being on the other side of the fence,
emotionally if not physically, taken away her edge?
Was she too empathetic, wanting an acceptable reason for committing an unholy deed, or was she missing something that could prove the man's innocence?

CHAPTER THREE

TATUM HAD A MEETING with one of her assistant prosecutors later that afternoon to review the young lawyer's case against a small-time drug trafficker. She savored the young man's enthusiasm, was impressed by his insights and enjoyed the hours she spent with him. But as five o'clock rolled around and he offered to buy her dinner—friends only—Tatum was not even tempted to accept his invitation. Not only did she have a pile of mail to sift through and the founder of the due-notice bill to search out, but she simply did not wish to spend the meal comparing one dinner date with another, especially since she suspected that the young prosecutor would come up on the short end of the stick. He just wasn't Jonathan.

JONATHAN RAN up the steps of the city building that evening, taking them two at a time. He had barely had time to shower and change into his suit before rushing off to make a speech at a charity benefit dinner being held to update the center's plumbing. He had a due-notice appearance to make in an hour on the other side of town, but he didn't mind the rushing if it meant he might see Tatum again. He had been trying for five days to steal some more time with her and had finally grown desperate. Half an hour would have to do for now.

He adjusted the package he was carrying, checking to see that the cartons resting inside were still upright, and bounded up the last flight of steps.

She was sitting at her desk, just as he had been picturing her for five long days, head slightly bent, long dark hair mingling with the papers on the desk in front of her. She'd hung her suit jacket on the back of her chair and was wearing only a cream silk blouse that seemed to caress her flesh as she moved to write something. Jonathan had never seen her without the added width of shoulder pads before, and he was struck by the fragility of her slim, feminine shoulders. He wanted to cradle them against the solidness of his chest. . . .

"Uh-hmm. Did you want something?"

His glance moved up to meet hers as her teasing words reached him through the doorway. He entered her office, feeling like the boy who had been asked to stay after school to clean the beautiful new teacher's erasers. Except that no little boy had any business feeling the way that Jonathan did right then. And unless he wanted to ruin what could be a satisfying friendship, Jonathan probably shouldn't be having those feelings, either.

"Many things, but I'll settle for twenty minutes and a carton of half-melted ice cream," he replied with a grin.

"Ice cream!" She jumped up from her chair. "Jonathan, surely you didn't bring ice cream all the way up here. In this heat?" She came around the desk, reached for the top of the bag and pulled it down to peer inside. "What flavor is it?"

Jonathan took back his bag and sat in one of the two chairs in front of her desk, motioning for her to take the other. "What do you think?" he asked, enjoying the pleasure she was getting from this impromptu treat. Most women got excited over flowers and diamonds, not ice cream. Jonathan had never been a flower-and-diamond kind of man.

She took the carton he gave her, eagerly pulling at the lid. "It better be mint chocolate-chip," she said. Her smile of satisfaction when she saw that he had remembered her favorite flavor was worth all of the rushing he had had to do to bring it to her.

Jonathan had brought both spoons and straws, not knowing what condition the treat would be in by the time he got it to her, and together they proceeded to alternately scoop and drink the iced confection.

"I can't believe you did this," she said for the third time as she spooned out another chunk of chocolate. "What if I hadn't been here?"

He had hoped to please her, but he hadn't expected her to be quite so surprised by his simple treat. Surely a woman with her looks and intelligence had

people bending over backward to do nice things for
her. He shrugged in answer to her question, slurping
up the last sip of melted fudge ripple.

"It was worth the chance," he said. "I know what
it's like to work every hour in the day, and then some.
I figured you might welcome a little break."

A small bead of ice cream stuck to her bottom lip,
and Jonathan watched, fascinated, as she licked it
clean. He was surprised by the intensity of his desire
to have done it himself. He should never have kissed
her. If he hadn't been living with the constant memory of her taste on his lips, he wouldn't be so tempted.

He wondered how she would react if she knew just
where his thoughts had been wandering. Was she remembering their kiss, as well? Would she welcome
another one—a more private one this time? Had she
pulled away from him because it was too much too
soon, or just because the place had been too public?
Of course, she could have been rejecting Jonathan
himself, but judging from the passionate way she had
responded to his kiss, Jonathan had reason to hope
otherwise.

"You are a very thoughtful man, Jonathan Wright.
Why is it you've never married?" Tatum's words
broke into his thoughts, an ironic reminder of what
could and could not be, though they did nothing to
dispel the desire that was building inside of him with
every moment that he spent with this woman.

"How could I ask a woman to come share my
home with me when I'm only there forty hours a

week, and thirty of them are spent unconscious?" he asked, summing up for both their sakes the reason why this could go no further than friendship, but also, in a roundabout way, why the friendship was becoming so important to him. He had never before found a woman who worked as much as he did, a woman who would understand his own commitment.

"I see your point," Tatum nodded as she sipped from her straw and then let it fall from her mouth.

Jonathan continued to taunt himself with visions of Tatum in different stages of passion as he watched her sensual enjoyment of her creamy dessert, told her about an air-conditioning problem at the center and listened to her praise one of the young attorneys on her staff. Twenty minutes had never passed so swiftly for him.

He didn't try to hide his regret as he rose to leave. He reached for Tatum's hand as she walked with him to the door and returned the brief pressure she applied to his fingers.

"Don't work too hard," he said, knowing the admonishment could be directed to him, as well— knowing, too, that neither one of them was going to take heed of it. For some reason, the thought comforted him.

"I'm glad you came," she replied.

He carried her words with him out into the night.

THE FOLLOWING MORNING, bright and early, she opened her mail.

A letter, halfway through the stack, was marked private and confidential. She recognized the name on the return address at once.

Mandy Schroeder had been a mere fourteen when Tatum had met her three years earlier—fourteen, afraid and severely bruised, both mentally and physically. While filling in for a sick colleague, Jack McGillus had answered a domestic-violence call and had pulled the girl away from the drunken father who was using her for a punching bag. Used to dealing with drug addicts and pushers rather than innocent victims of child abuse, Detective McGillus had called upon Tatum to accompany him as he delivered the devastated child to the Children's Crisis Center.

Mandy had clung to Tatum all the way to the center, sobbing brokenly into her shoulder, and Tatum had had an unbelievably hard time leaving the girl with those who were more qualified to help her. Though Tatum had lived with visions of Mandy's disillusioned, frightened eyes for weeks afterward, and fought for children's rights many times in court since that time, she had never once returned to the center.

Tatum slit open the envelope.

"Ms. McGillus," the note started, an inked rendition of schoolgirl scrawl.

I don't know if you remember me or not, but you and your father changed my life one night three years ago when you got me away from my dad.

Anyway, you were both so great then, and I need some help and I thought maybe you'd know where I could get it.

I don't know whether you've heard or not, but Senator Jonathan Wright's attempting to get a due-notice bill on the docket for the state of Arizona that would require the state to notify victims when someone who committed a crime is being released from jail and *I don't want to know.* I don't even know if you care if the bill passes, but with what happened with your brother and Detective McGillus, I thought you might, and I don't know who else to talk to about it. I'm not old enough to do much by myself. People don't take me seriously enough yet.

Please don't misunderstand. Jonathan's a great guy. Not only is he my boss, he's also about the best friend a girl could have, but this is one crusade he doesn't understand. How could he? His parents are great people, even if they do live halfway across the world. He has no reason to dread hearing from them.

I'm registered to start college after Christmas, Ms. McGillus. Thanks to Detective McGillus and Jonathan Wright, I have a chance to live a halfway normal life. But Jonathan doesn't understand that it won't be normal if I ever find out that Daddy's been released from jail. He really believes all of the children he helps need the protection of his due-notice bill, but I just want to get on with my life. I don't want the past to keep following me wherever I go. If you could help me, or know where I can go to fight Jonathan's bill, please call me. I'm working as a receptionist at the Children's Crisis Center....

Tatum felt the blood drain from her face as she read. It could not be true. Her new friend, the man who had lifted her heart not once but twice in the past week, was the person she must fight against—in a war that she *had* to win. If any good was ever to come out of all the hell her family had suffered, if Cale's murder was not going to be a complete waste, if Pop's imprisonment was ever going to stand for something, then Tatum had to score this one point for those people who still had a chance to build new lives from shattered ones. She owed it to her family, she owed it to all of the innocent people who could still be spared the hell that she and Pop had been through, and she owed it to a seventeen-year-old girl who had just sent out a cry for help that echoed deep inside her own heart. In the space of sixty seconds, Jonathan Wright had become her enemy.

She'd had no idea that he was so personally involved with the crisis center. She had been under the impression that his concern was with the business end of things, that he had trained staff who dealt with the children. She had not even considered that he might know Mandy—one of the thousands of kids the center helped every year. And she'd had no idea that he was the force behind due-notice. . . .

Tatum slowly picked up the phone. She dialed, disconnected and dialed again. Mandy might not even be there.

"Children's Crisis Center, can you hold, please?" Tatum heard the young voice and was tempted to hang up. "Yes," she affirmed, and waited.

Maybe she should not involve Mandy in her battle. The child had come to her for help, but maybe if Tatum did not offer assistance, Mandy would give up, forget her battle, concentrate on boys and the newest fashions. *And maybe brown cows made chocolate milk.* Mandy had already left childhood far behind when Tatum had first seen her three years ago. Due-notice aside, Tatum could not turn her back on the girl's plea. Yet wouldn't nurturing Mandy's fight against Jonathan—an adult who, by the sounds of things, had been a very positive influence in her life—hurt the young woman far more than due-notice? Or would Jonathan's bill come between himself and Mandy regardless?

"Sorry about that, can I help you?" the voice returned.

Tatum sat up straight. "I hope so," she answered. "I'm looking for Mandy Schroeder. Is she working this morning?"

A moment of silence fell on the line. "Who's calling?" the young voice asked, less friendly now.

"I'm sorry. My name is Tatum McGillus. I—"

"Ms. McGillus! How are you? This is Mandy."

The eagerness in the girl's voice sent a flutter of warmth to the icicle that had become Tatum's heart. Maybe she was doing the right thing by calling Mandy. She certainly hoped so.

"I'm doing fine, Mandy. I've thought of you often over the past couple of years. How've you been?"

"Really good," Mandy replied so convincingly that Tatum believed it. "I graduated from high school in May and have been working here full-time ever since. I'm living with Tom and Louise Gainey and their three kids, and they're okay for a foster family, but hopefully, if my grant comes through, I'll be starting at ASU in January and living in a dorm. I'll still keep my job here, though."

Tatum found herself listening to Mandy's words with feelings of relief, surprised that the young woman sounded so natural, so normal. She leaned forward, resting her elbows against the top of her desk.

"What are you planning to study?" she asked, though she suspected she knew the answer.

"Social work," Mandy said, confirming Tatum's suspicion. "I figure it's something I'd be good at, being able to relate to the victims and all," Mandy said.

"I have a feeling you'd be good at whatever you put your mind to," Tatum said. She spent the next couple of minutes getting to know the young woman the battered girl had become.

"So how's Detective McGillus?" Mandy finally asked the question Tatum had been dreading.

Tatum felt her spine stiffen. "That's one of the reasons I'm calling, Mandy," she admitted. "I got your letter. I had already planned to fight the bill, I just didn't know yet who was behind it."

"Jonathan Wright. He runs the center here. He has the idea that people have a need to know when a criminal who wronged them is being set free. He doesn't seem to understand that some of us are a lot happier not knowing."

"I'm with you all the way," Tatum assured the girl. "I'd really like to see you anyway, so how about if I meet you on Saturday and we can talk more. Would that fit your schedule?"

Mandy laughed. "I'm only seventeen, Ms. McGillus. I don't have much of a schedule. Saturday's fine, but my car's in the shop again. If it's not too much trouble, maybe you could come to the center. You won't have to worry about meeting Jonathan or anything, since he's supposed to be out of town all day...."

IN SPITE OF her lightweight shorts and crop top, Tatum was sweating as she walked through the door of the Children's Crisis Center on Saturday morning. Not because she was hot, but because she was not sure what to expect of a teenager who had been abused and left to build a life that went beyond the memories.

"Is Mandy here?" Tatum asked the elderly woman sitting behind a large wooden desk on one side of the reception area.

"She's in the kitchen. I'll tell her you're here, if you'd like."

"Thanks, I'm Tatum McGillus."

As she waited, Tatum continued to fight a battle that had been raging within her for three days. Should she encourage Mandy's fight against Jonathan? Was she wrong to use the child to fight her own battles? Or would she be wrong to turn her back on a sincere cry for help?

"Ms. McGillus! You really came!" The petite, blond-haired teenager, dressed in neon pink shorts and a crop top similar to Tatum's, flung herself into a startled Tatum's arms. Tatum had not expected the seventeen-year-old she had been conversing with over the past week to look so pretty and feminine. Nor had she expected Mandy's childlike openness. Knowing of the years of beatings the girl had endured, Tatum had expected to be approached with bitter wariness by a woman-child who looked twice Mandy's age.

Clutching the girl to her body with a desperation she could not even begin to understand, Tatum was surprised by a rush of the tenderness she had thought she had lost forever after her brother's senseless murder. There was no thought of distancing herself, no fear of being hurt if she reached out, only an understanding of the struggle it took to live with the aftereffects of violence.

"I told you I'd come. Did you expect the daughter of Jack McGillus to lie to you?" Tatum stepped back to smile warmly at Mandy, but she retained a gentle grip on the younger woman's slim shoulders.

"Not really. I just didn't want to get my hopes up," Mandy admitted with an acceptance that saddened Tatum. By some miracle this young woman was still able to express positive emotion despite the harshness of her earlier years, but she had not escaped without scars. Her words suggested that she embraced whatever goodness life offered her but knew better than to hope for its arrival.

"I couldn't stay away, Mandy. Not just because of my father, but because of you. I'm concerned that I could be getting you into trouble with Jonathan Wright. Not only is he your boss, but from what you've said, he's been a big help to you. And looking at you now, I'd have to say he did a fantastic job." Tatum dropped her hands from the other girl's shoulders, but she continued to hold Mandy's gaze with genuine concern.

Mandy led Tatum over to a brightly upholstered couch. "Don't worry, Ms. McGillus. Jonathan knows I don't agree with the law he's attempting to put on the docket. He respects my right to disagree with him, and told me to feel free to exercise that right. I'm just a kid, so I can't do much to fight the law, but at least I'm helping someone who can. Besides, he knows I'm helping you. He said you two know each other."

Mandy's words hung between them, but Tatum was not ready to discuss Jonathan with anyone, least of all this young woman who seemed to think the world of him.

"And he doesn't mind us working together?" Tatum asked. Even knowing Jonathan, she found that hard to believe. Did it also mean that he didn't mind being Tatum's enemy?

"Probably—but that's Jonathan, always mindful of everyone's rights. And speaking of rights, how's Detective McGillus? Have you seen him lately?" Mandy asked, her eyes filled with an empathy that belied her young age.

"Every Sunday. He's tired but otherwise he looks the same," Tatum parried.

She would not lie to Mandy about the man who had saved the teenager's life, but neither could she burden the young woman with the truth. Pop was looking so exhausted, so broken-down that Tatum was finally beginning to believe he would never be fixed again.

"He'll be up for parole in about five years, won't he?" Mandy persisted, obviously well versed on the details of Jack McGillus's case.

"That's what they say."

"And he's only, what, fifty-eight? That'll make him sixty-three then. He'll still have a good twenty years ahead of him."

"That he would," Tatum agreed, knowing that she needed to change the subject. "I was wondering if you'd be interested in coordinating my anti-due-notice schedule," she said more quickly than she would have liked.

The teenager's eyes lit up with enthusiasm.

"Sure. What do you want me to do?"

"Other than keeping me informed, you mean?" Tatum teased.

"That's nothing. Like I said, Jonathan's always mindful of everybody's right to hear both sides of an issue. He said I could show you his schedule. He leaves a copy of it at the receptionist's desk anyway, so we can always find him if there's an emergency."

Tatum didn't want to think of Jonathan's innate sense of fairness or his willingness to be called on in an emergency—the strength and calm with which he would probably handle the emergency.

"What I had in mind was more like campaign manager," she said, pulling her thoughts back to the matter at hand. "You'd be in charge of working as many of Jonathan's appearances into my schedule as you can manage, and then letting me know when to be where, to tell our side of the story. There may be other things to arrange, phone calls to make or errands to run as we go along. I'll compensate you for your time, of course."

Mandy's smile fell flat. "It all sounded great until the compensation part. I don't want to be your paid employee, Ms. McGillus. I'd like to be your friend."

Tatum felt an unwanted rush of respect for the man who was apparently at least partially responsible for helping this previously abused youngster reach out to life's opportunities again and brave the real possibility of rejection. It was one of life's cruel ironies that that same man was also the force behind due-notice.

"Then friends it is. And no more of this Ms. McGillus stuff. You're making me feel old." Tatum held out her hand to the girl and was warmed all the way to her barren heart when Mandy's ice cold fingers clutched hers fervently.

"You're sure Jonathan won't be angry with you?" she asked one more time, wanting to be sure that Mandy was not putting herself in an awkward situation because of a momentary rush of youthful outrage.

"I'm sure. He says I have to stand up for what I believe in, though I'm sure he'll continue to try to influence me where his bill is concerned."

TATUM WAS IN COURT for most of the next week, prosecuting a drug charge. And with her continuing investigation of the Rhodes case, it was well after midnight by the time she got home most nights. She knew she would not be able to keep up the pace for long or continue to avoid Jonathan Wright's calls indefinitely, but she was just not ready to deal with him.

"You look tired, Tatum," Mandy announced after a burrito dinner the following Thursday evening. The two had shared several meals over the past days, planning strategy, narrowing their due-notice objections down to clear, concise facts.

"Bobby Rhodes's trial is due to start three weeks from Monday," Tatum explained, knowing that her young friend was following the extensive media coverage of the case.

"Are you going to prosecute him if you still aren't sure?"

Tatum glanced up, shocked by Mandy's words. Tatum had never told Mandy that she wasn't sure about the case, only that she wasn't sure she was done investigating it. She started to laugh off the young woman's concern, until she saw the worried look in Mandy's eyes. "I have to, Mandy. I indicted him. I can't ask the court to ignore the substantial amount of evidence I've presented, just because of a *feeling* I have."

"But what if he's innocent?"

"What if he isn't?"

Tatum got up to clear the table, leaving Mandy in the dining nook while she carried the shredded cheese, tortillas and other burrito fixings into the adjoining kitchen. She laid them on the tiled breakfast counter and proceeded to put everything into air-tight containers—methodically, calmly, without thought. Or so she wished.

Mandy's intuitiveness was forcing on Tatum decisions that she still was not prepared to make. When was she going to know if she had lost her edge? When an innocent man went to jail? Or when a guilty one was set free?

Instead of clearing her mind, the past two weeks of extensive investigations and long hours of rereading testimonies had done nothing but increase Tatum's confusion. Everything—including a lack of any other possible suspects—pointed to Bobby Rhodes's guilt. Except the man himself. Tatum had met with Bobby several more times, yet not once had she been convinced that he was guilty of murder.

Yet she could hardly tell one of her colleagues that she was not sure about the rightness of prosecuting an open and shut murder case. Since her father's trial, they all held her at a distance, as if wondering if she, too, were going to break the laws she had sworn to uphold. She was not even sure she had enough faith left in herself to take a stand, anyway.

"I got those letters sent out like you asked. Everyone on Jonathan's campaign schedule now knows about us. I only hope we get some calls inviting us to give our side," Mandy said, coming into the kitchen with the dirty dishes.

Tatum lifted a corner of the lid she had just secured, letting the air out of the container. She looked up as Mandy stopped in the middle of the room, dishes in hand.

"Don't look so worried, honey. People love a good fight. They'll call. Just to add a little spice to dull meetings, if nothing else."

Mandy smiled and headed toward the sink, turning on the water to rinse the plates. But as she glanced back over her shoulder at Tatum, her smile faded again.

"Jonathan asked about you again today."

Tatum kept her gaze firmly directed at the refrigerator, rearranging things on shelves that were only half-full.

"Did he?" She really wished he wouldn't involve the teenager in whatever was not going on between them.

Mandy loaded their glasses in the dishwasher.

"Mm-hmm. He just asked if you're all right. He said he's been trying to get a hold of you but keeps missing you."

Tatum heard the question behind Mandy's innocuous statement. She knew that despite the due-notice issue, Mandy thought the world of Jonathan. She only hoped the teenager would understand why Tatum and Jonathan could not be friends. She closed the refrigerator and joined Mandy at the sink, taking the rinsed dishes as Mandy handed them to her and putting them in the opened dishwasher.

"My time's been kind of limited...."

HER TIME FINALLY RAN out on Saturday afternoon. Jonathan was spending two hours outside the public library that afternoon, attempting to fill up a petition with due-notice supporters. And Tatum knew she was going to have to be there.

A crowd had already gathered outside the library by the time Tatum had parked her Taurus in the lot beside the building, but even then she could pick out Jonathan's thick brown hair and sturdy, blue-suited shoulders. She attempted to dam up the flood of emotion that swam within her as she watched him. Why did she feel such an affinity with the man? She had no place in her life for a man—any man, let alone Jonathan Wright. Right now she had to aim all of her concentration at saving her career, and store up her strength in case she did not. She was hanging on to her grasp on life by a moth-eaten thread. She did not have enough faith in her ability to hold on if she were to be faced with any more emotional upheaval right then. And relationships, even the best of them, caused upheaval.

Besides, what did she have to offer anyone? Sundays spent in a prison visitor cell? An unstable career? A heart in cold storage? No, it was much better that she just stick to the course at hand. She knew that.

Jonathan's congenial public image was firmly in place as Tatum approached the table he had covered with petitions and pencils. He acknowledged her presence with a quick glance up and down her pink linen skirt and matching crop jacket, but never paused in the conversation he was having with a middle-aged couple.

Tatum waited until Jonathan had said his piece, watching as he moved on to a young mother with two children. She intercepted the middle-aged couple just as they were about to sign one of Jonathan's petitions, and engaged them in a conversation of her own. By the time she was through with them, they were walking toward their car without having signed.

The two hours passed quickly and almost easily if she discounted the couple of times she had caught Jonathan watching her with a questioning look on his face. Tatum almost wished he would get angry with her for losing him signatures. Maybe then she would be strong enough to resist him.

She was still embroiled in a discussion with an elderly lady when Jonathan began collecting his petitions and pencils. She felt her heart jump as he locked up his briefcase and leaned casually against the wall of the library. He was going to wait for her.

"I'll be giving this some serious consideration before I feel comfortable supporting Senator Wright's bill, missy. Thank you for your time," the old woman finally said before turning to make her way down the walk.

Tatum quickly gathered her purse and keys, intending to follow the woman, but Jonathan grabbed her elbow before she could get away.

"Hold on a minute, lady. I'd like a word with you," he said none too patiently.

"We really have nothing to discuss. I'm well within my rights as a private citizen to be here," Tatum replied without attempting to pull free from his warm grip.

"I'm not questioning your rights, just your motives," Jonathan told her, guiding her out of the way of pedestrian traffic to a bench on the small patch of lawn outside the library. "Arizona is one of the few states that do not currently have a due-notice law to protect its citizens," he told her as if that fact alone made it necessary to create one.

"Protect its citizens?" Tatum laughed harshly. "Come down from your clouds, Jonathan. Would you like to live your entire life knowing that someone who had done you wrong, who had ripped your life apart at the seams, was living and loving as freely as you please?" she charged. If only she could make him see how wrong he was, maybe he would drop this damaging campaign.

"But what about those people who are victimized a second time because they were unaware that their perpetrator had been released from jail?" he countered.

Tatum hugged her purse to her chest. "Parole statistics state that very few criminals actually return to the scene of the crime that put them in jail in the first place," she announced. She was not just waging a passionate, impulsive battle here. She wanted what was best for the greater number of people. And as far as she could see, nine times out of ten, when it came to due-notice it was best to live in blissful ignorance.

"What would your victim actually *do* upon receipt of that information anyway?" she continued. "Would he get a new lock? Change his name? Live on the run? Being victimized in the first place would have prompted him to take whatever precautions he could to provide for his safety. Yet if you tell him that the individual who hurt him is out there, he won't have another moment's peace. He'll always be looking over his shoulder, watching for someone who in reality is probably far away, strapped to a mortgage payment somewhere.''

Jonathan put his things down on the ground beside the bench and stood directly in front of her.

"But what about the domestic crimes?" he demanded. ''The times when a convicted family member does return and sometimes even succeeds in taking a life he left behind the first time? I've seen too many abused children at the center who've barely had a chance to recover once before they're hurt again. Sometimes they don't make it back for a second shot at recovery. And it could all have been avoided.''

Tatum understood what he was saying but she knew that the percentage of children who suffered the fate he described was very small. Most of them became wards of the state and never saw their abusive family member again. Most of them, like Mandy, didn't want due-notice. And she couldn't deny that she had her own, equally desperate reasons for fighting due-notice.

"So you're willing to trade the peace of mind of millions for one or two possibles?" she accused.

"You put more value on peace of mind than on life itself?" he countered.

"No!" Tatum denied his heartless view of her. "Come on, Jonathan. You're in public service. You know that in a society such as ours rules have to be made for the good of the majority, not the few," she said. Her eyes implored him to understand, to see that she cared just as much as he did—maybe more.

Jonathan sat back down on the bench, his arms folded across his chest, seemingly considering what she had said.

Tatum's tension escalated with his silence. Beating due-notice meant the world to her, but she hated fighting with this man. Barely two weeks ago he had been the prince of her fairy tale. "So where do we go from here?" she finally asked, unable to stand the silence any longer.

"I guess we let the people decide," he conceded with a frown and a shrug. "It's their law."

"And you won't try to stop me from fighting you on this?" she asked.

"I won't try to stop you, but I won't stop, either," he conceded. "I believe in the people's right to hear it all. It'll be up to them to determine what's best for them."

It was not the victory she had wanted, but it was better than she had expected when she had come here this afternoon. Jonathan was every bit the man she had first thought him to be. Honest. Fair.

"So why haven't you returned my calls?" he asked her as they continued to sit side by side on the bench, both looking straight ahead.

Tatum's common sense told her to get up, to leave, but whether she wanted to acknowledge it or not, there was more unfinished business between them that had to be settled. She sat beside him, absorbing his heat and his nearness for a moment before looking over at him. "There's no point, Jonathan. We had a nice dinner together once. Why not just leave it at that?"

Jonathan studied her features for several moments, until Tatum was afraid he was going to accept a decision she had not yet fully made.

"Because your mouth tells me one thing, while your eyes say another," he finally replied, reminding her of the soft words they had shared that night in his truck. "I'm in no way desperate for companionship, Tatum, female or otherwise. And I've long since passed the stage of immaturity where the chase means more than the catch. I simply want to spend some time with one woman who intrigues the hell out of me. What's so wrong with that?"

Reasons sprang from everywhere, assaulting Tatum's mind, but she could not voice them. Neither could she lead him on. "My well's pretty dry right now, Jonathan," she said simply.

His brown-eyed gaze bore into her, as if he could read the words she wasn't saying. Tatum glanced away, not sure that he couldn't. "I don't have anything inside to give away," she said, wishing he would just understand and not ask anything more of her, but afraid that he would do just that.

Jonathan turned her face back toward his, reminding her again of that night in the front seat of his

Bronco. Things had been so perfect then, for such a short time. "Who says I'm asking?" he asked.

He was confusing her; her own desire to give in to him was frightening her. "What do you want from me?" The words were torn from the depths of her barricaded heart.

He rubbed his knuckles along her cheek, caressing her as gently as a breeze. "A friend."

Though she knew with every fiber of her being that she was in danger, Tatum could not avert her gaze from the caring she saw in his eyes. "Why?" she whispered. "Why would you want to bother?"

Jonathan sighed. "I don't know why, Tatum. I only know that for some reason it matters. I'm not looking for any kind of commitment. You're right, that would be crazy. Nor am I in any position to give one. I'd just like an opportunity to see, to get to know you better, maybe laugh with you now and then." He reached out to brush her bangs from her eyebrows.

Tatum looked away to the empty table that had been set up earlier for their signature session. "But we're enemies," she said, half in question.

"Then why do I feel more like a friend?" he challenged her. "I'm not saying the bill won't be a problem, but I can tell you this, being my friend doesn't mean you have to share all of my opinions."

Tatum looked up at him again, trying to judge his sincerity. Could they do it? Could they be personal friends and public enemies at the same time? Could she be his friend, period, without risking her peace of mind? And what would happen when she won, when the bill was defeated? Would they still be friends then? Could she handle it if they weren't?

She thought of all the other complications in her life—her self-doubts, her floundering career. She had been honest when she had told him she had nothing to give him. She was still finding out what she could count on for herself. But somehow the words that would banish him from her life just would not come. If he had pushed, she could have walked away more easily. But all he wanted from her was the chance to find another moment or two of the peace they had shared that magical evening out of time. Was that so terrible?

He reached over to cover her hands where they rested in her lap. "I won't try to stop you from fighting the bill, Tatum, as long as you don't treat me like a stranger because of it," he said, issuing what almost sounded like an ultimatum.

Tatum gave in then. She could no longer fight what she knew she really wanted, despite the many very real misgivings she had.

"Just friends, nothing invested but time?" she asked, knowing full well that neither of them had any time to spare.

"Nothing invested but time," Jonathan confirmed.

Neither seemed to care that the words lacked conviction.

CHAPTER FOUR

"HI, TATUM, IT'S Jonathan. Have a meal today. Bye...."

Tatum smiled as she dropped her keys on her desk and sat down to listen to the rest of the messages on her answering machine. He cared whether or not she ate. Who would have thought such a little thing could make a person feel so good inside?

"Tatum? This is Mandy. We got a call from a radio talk show Jonathan's scheduled to do. They got our letter and want you to do the show with him, answering listeners' phone-in questions and things. It's Friday morning at 9:30 at KKVR. You're clear for it. Talk to you later...." There was a click, followed by the familiar beep leading into the next message.

"Montgomery here. Rhodes is still claiming 'not guilty.' Be ready to get him...." Tatum stiffened as the gruff voice of the county superintendent blasted from the speaker. They were due to go to trial in little more than a week. And she still was not ready.

Tatum listened as a couple more messages blared out into the deserted office building, then reached over to shut off the machine. Wednesdays were usually long days in court, and this one had been no exception. She was exhausted. It was almost eight o'clock in the evening, and she had not yet had lunch. She thought of Jonathan's message and smiled again. For someone who barely knew her, he knew her rather well. Tatum sighed as she surveyed the hours of work ahead of her, picked up the phone and called out for dinner.

TATUM HAD TO LEAVE the radio station during the last commercial break of the broadcast on Friday. She knew Jonathan was frustrated about the way things were going, but he didn't say a word to her as she excused herself to the disc jockey. And as much as she would have liked to ease Jonathan's tension, she didn't say anything to him, either. More and more people were questioning the long-term effects of Jonathan's bill. And Tatum was happy about that.

The talk show went so well that the local television station affiliated with the radio station invited Jonathan and Tatum to do a spot on "Arizona Avenues," a talk show that focused solely on Arizona and covered a broad array of topics ranging from where to ski to state tax laws. A date was not set yet, but they both agreed to do the show.

JONATHAN BIT into his second slice of pizza in his office at the center Sunday evening as he waded through the piles of legislative paperwork that had piled up during the week. Each report came in a separate manila envelope. There were three stacks of them sitting in front of him, and the remains of a fourth were already in the garbage can beside his desk. As tired as he was, Jonathan found himself pondering how much of the taxpayers' money went into supporting the manila-envelope business.

Maybe he could put it to Tatum sometime. She would probably have an answer. Jonathan removed his reading glasses for a moment, rubbing his aching eyes as he thought of the woman who could be so much more than a buddy to him if she would let herself. For the time being they had agreed not to discuss the issue of due notice during their private conversations, and it seemed to be working well. Too well, really, Jonathan thought. They never seemed to discuss anything that mattered. And that, more than anything else, bothered the hell out of him.

Tatum stimulated him in a way no other woman had before her. He was attracted to her, yes, there was no doubt about that, but it was more than her china-doll features and sleek feminine curves that drew him to her like metal to a magnet. There was a depth to Tatum that intrigued him. She answered something inside of him that he had not even known was calling out. Yet he sometimes felt as if he did not know her at all.

He had finally met a woman who was no threat to his life's commitments, a woman who was so busy with her own life that she would not expect to tie him down, and he wanted to explore the possibilities between them. If only she were more open with him. If only she gave up on that anti-due-notice crusade. What did she really know about children like Mandy, who *needed* the protection of such a law?

Jonathan drew himself up abruptly, knowing full well that he could spend the entire evening brooding about Tatum, but he also knew that brooding would get him nowhere. Putting his reading glasses back on, he forced himself back to the business at hand. He could not afford to spend an entire evening going nowhere.

He was chewing the last of his pizza and clearing away the end of the third stack of stuffed envelopes when his phone rang.

"Jonathan Wright," he said as he swallowed the last bite of his dinner.

"Detective Charles here, Jonathan," the matter-of-fact tones came over the line. "I've got one here for you, if you have the space."

Jonathan sat forward in his chair, resting his elbows on his jean-clad knees as he prepared himself to hear whatever was to come. You had to have compassion to deal with the children who were victims of the seamier side of life, but you also had to have enough detachment to stomach the facts.

"I'll make room, what've you got?" he asked, his mind already focusing ahead to whatever needs this newest victim might be facing.

"Mostly neglect. Little girl, five-year-old, alone for two, maybe three days this time. Found her in a pop-up trailer up in the mountains. She still had enough water for drinking, but it doesn't look like she's had much to eat. Place didn't have a bathroom. She's not talking.'' Detective Charles reported the facts and only the facts. Jonathan understood that that was Charles's job. He did it well, but he did it with his heart in cold storage. Sometimes that was the only way.

Jonathan's glasses landed on his desk. "I'm on my way," he said. He was already on his feet and around his desk by the time the receiver clicked back into its cradle.

Jonathan did not stop to change out of his jeans, T-shirt and tennis shoes, knowing that anything more formal would probably scare the kid anyway. He did, however, stop by the rec room on his way out.

"Mandy?" he called softly as he poked his head in the door. Ten or so kids were watching a movie, and he did not want to disturb them any more than he had to.

"What's up?" she asked, sprinting toward him. She took one close look at his face and seemed to know. "How bad is it?" she asked before he had a chance to reply to her first question.

"I don't know for sure. She's little, a five-year-old, and she's been alone for a couple of days. Find Cinci and let her know I'm bringing the child back here, will you, please?" he asked, knowing full well that Mandy knew what needed to be done without being told.

Mandy nodded, already turning away toward the kitchen where the house mother was probably popping up a batch of corn. Abruptly she stopped and turned around.

"Jonathan?" she called.

"Yeah, honey?"

"Can I stay?"

"Call the Gaineys and let 'em know," he said, giving her the permission he could not deny. Jonathan had long ago figured out that each time a child came in, Mandy relived her own advent into his life. Each time she was able to help that child settle in, each time she was able to offer comfort or some small measure of security, she was paying back a portion of the debt she felt she owed.

AN HOUR AND A HALF LATER, Jonathan lifted a very dirty, hungry and exhausted little girl out of the front seat of his Bronco and carried her into the bright lights of the Children's Crisis Center. Abby Gressner was a tribute to the endurance of childhood, to the instinct to survive. She still hadn't uttered a word, whether out of fear or for some other reason Jonathan was not yet sure, but according to the doctors who had just examined her, she appeared to be in relatively good health. Thank God they had found her in time.

Both Cinci and Mandy were waiting for him in the foyer.

"Oh, sweet baby, what have we got here?" Cinci murmured softly as she lifted the child from Jonathan's arms to her ample bosom. The forty-three-year-old children's counselor knew all about the ravaging effects of abuse and neglect. She had been half-dead when the authorities had finally taken her from her drunken mother thirty-five years before.

Abby looked at Cinci with huge baby blue eyes, their beauty tempered by the stoic gravity staring out of them. "Cinci, meet Abby," Jonathan introduced softly.

Cinci looked up at Jonathan, a question in her eyes. Jonathan reached out to pull Mandy forward, knowing that the girl was taking in every nuance of feeling in the air. "Doctor says she's going to be fine," he told both women at once. "The rest, we'll just have to wait to see." He could not be more specific than that. In the first place he didn't know much more himself, and secondly he had a feeling little Abby wasn't missing a single cue. He didn't wish to make the child more uncomfortable than she already was by talking about her as if she weren't there.

Jonathan watched as Mandy reached out slowly to brush her hand against Abby's dirty little cheek. Mandy checked the child's reaction carefully, and when Abby did not flinch she continued the caress, drawing Abby's short, unevenly cut brown curls away from her cheeks. "My name's Mandy," she said gently, as if the two of them were the only two people in the room. She waited until Abby's serious blue eyes were trained on her and then continued. "I'd like to take you upstairs and run a nice warm bath for you and then get you into a soft gown. Would that be okay?" she asked, voicing her question in such a way that it gave the child some control.

Abby looked from Mandy up to Cinci, then over to Jonathan and back to Mandy again. For several minutes she just stared, but nobody forced her to come to a decision. No one did anything but wait. Finally, holding Mandy's gaze steadily, Abby nodded. She didn't speak, she didn't smile, but she nodded.

Jonathan saw the joyous relief flash briefly in Mandy's eyes, but the young woman knew better than to approach the confused little girl with big smiles and false gaiety. This was not a situation to be gay about, and Abby was not going to trust anyone who tried to pretend otherwise. He and Cinci waited silently, allowing Mandy to do what she did so well.

"Okay?" Mandy asked again, giving the child a chance to be sure of her decision. Though the detached expression on the little girl's face never changed, Abby's nod was immediate this time.

"Can you walk?" Mandy asked the child gently without talking down to her.

Again Abby nodded mutely.

As slowly as she had done everything else, Mandy took the child's hand in her own and simply held on while Cinci set the little girl on her feet. All three adults stood close in case Abby's legs gave out on her, but as soon as it was obvious that she could stand on her own, Jonathan and Cinci backed off.

Mandy took her eyes from her small charge just long enough to look once from Jonathan to Cinci. "I'll sleep with her tonight."

He and Cinci both nodded. Tomorrow would be soon enough to begin counseling the child.

Jonathan sighed and felt the first stirring of the anguish he knew would keep him awake long into the night ahead as he watched the seventeen-year-old woman-child lead the little girl tenderly down the hall. It was for Mandy and for kids like little Abby that he was determined to win due-notice protection. Somehow he was just going to have to make Tatum understand. Mandy disappeared up the stairs, and Jonathan felt Cinci's plump hand creep into his.

"HEY, LADY, HOW'D YOU like to be kidnapped by a slightly desperate but semihandsome public servant?"

Tatum's head jerked up from the brief she had been studying to see Jonathan framed in her office doorway. A slow smile spread across her face, welcoming him to the room.

"Depends on where he's taking me," she said, laying down her pen.

Jonathan came into her office and propped one lean hip against her desk. "How about a relaxing swim?" he asked.

Tatum felt warm all over as Jonathan's brown-eyed gaze swept over her. Swimming might not be such a good idea, yet short of running away, it sounded better than anything else she could think of. "But you don't have a pool, do you?"

"But I know someone who does," he said, grinning down at her. "Didn't my last phone call catch you right after a late-night swim?"

Tatum laughed at the brazen expression on his face. "Jonathan, you're shameless. If you want to swim so badly, why not just say so? I'll give you my key and directions, too."

Jonathan leaned forward and ran the backs of his fingers along her cheek. The contact was brief and feather light. "I don't want to go alone," he said, all teasing gone from his voice.

"I don't know. . . ." Tatum said, suddenly as serious as he. She knew it was her self-control she was doubting, her ability to keep her growing desire for him at bay.

Jonathan's gaze met hers for a long moment, reassuring her, and then he grinned. "Afraid you can't keep your hands off me, you wanton woman?"

Taking her cue from him, Tatum raised her hands, turning them over and back again, studying them. "How could I be afraid of my very own appendages?" she asked. She knew that she shouldn't accept his invitation, but she also knew that she was going to anyway.

AN HOUR LATER Tatum was no longer sure she'd made the right decision. Jonathan's shoulders and back glistened in the darkness as he swam another couple of lengths in her outdoor pool. She had left the pool lights off to keep the bugs away, but she could still make out the firmness of his buttocks as he thrust his hips up and down, executing a perfect butterfly stroke. She had to fight the images of another, much more intimate activity that his movements provoked. His black swim trunks seemed more seductive to Tatum with their teasing revelations than no suit at all.

Pulling herself up out of the shallow end of the pool, Tatum leaned over to wring the water out of her hair, admonishing herself for breaking the rules she had set to govern this relationship. She absolutely could not risk opening herself up to Jonathan any more than she had already.

As wonderful as Jonathan had been, as peaceful as she felt with him, she knew that if she let him, he would hurt her. She had discovered during their many conversations that he already had a mistress and a wife—his public. And if he ever had to choose between her and it...

Jonathan came up for air at the end of his next lap, stopped himself before kicking off again and glanced up to the concrete sidewalk at the end of the pool. Facing him, right before his eyes was the most exquisite derriere he had ever had the pleasure to study. Like the rest of her wardrobe, Tatum's one-piece swimsuit would probably be considered conservative by the standards of the day, but the sleek violet material cupped her so intimately Jonathan could see her shape almost as distinctly as if she had been wearing nothing at all.

Despite the coolness of the water lapping against his hips, his body hardened in response to the perfectly sculpted woman leaning unselfconsciously before him. She was twisting the long dark tresses of her hair, the only thing about her that she ever allowed to remain free and unfettered, and the act was a seduction in itself. There was something about a woman lowering her hair before a man that sent out that age-old mating cry of unspoken love. For the first time in his life, Jonathan fully understood the fairy tale about the woman who lowered her hair for her man to climb up to her. Jonathan would have given just about anything right then to have the right to run his fingers up Tatum's locks until he reached the body beckoning beyond.

She straightened then and caught him watching her. He had no time to veil his aching desire. She just stood there, staring at him. Yet even from the distance separating them he could see the yearning that flashed in her eyes in response to his own. His silent reply was both a promise and a question. The next move was up to her.

Insidious warmth swarmed within Tatum as she was captivated by the promises in Jonathan's absorbing brown gaze. He would be man to her woman. He would woo her with jasmine and soft music, rather than roses and candlelight. He would raise her to heights she had only read about, and cradle her on her return. He would share everything, catering to her, caring for her, filling the voids left in her life. . . .

Tatum froze as her fantasies were desecrated by the intrusion of reality. She turned away stiffly to pull her towel from the chair where she had left it such a short time before, numbed by the realization that she had almost been ready to make love with Jonathan. And at what cost? If she loved again, she risked losing again, and if she loved Jonathan that loss was almost guaranteed—just as soon as his public called him away. Was she strong enough to give him up when the time came? Was her sanity worth that chance?

Silence, filled with the possibilities Tatum was discarding, stretched for endless seconds while she considered the advisability of hiding out in her bedroom until Jonathan had a chance to get dressed and leave. But she knew he deserved better than that, and so did she.

Wrapped securely in her body-length towel, she turned back to face him. "I'm all done swimming. Can I get you anything to drink?" she asked, nonchalantly, she hoped.

"Have you got any Scotch?" Jonathan asked from the pool. He wanted to wait until she went inside and his body had a chance to cool down before getting out.

"Chivas or Glenlivet?" she asked with an attempt at a grin, obviously relieved that he was willing to ignore what had almost happened between them.

"Mmm. I haven't had that kind of choice in a while. Either one is fine, just leave out the water," he said, sounding as if he had no other desires beyond the enjoyment of a fine glass of whiskey.

Jonathan watched Tatum disappear through the sliding glass door that led into her family room and kitchen. He wasn't quite sure why Tatum was holding herself back from him, but it seemed to involve more than just the issue of due notice or an aversion to commitment. She was still a healthy woman, with normal needs and desires. He had tasted her passion, if only briefly, that night in the Bronco. He had seen the wanting in her eyes tonight. So why was he standing alone in a cold pool of water with her in the house only a few feet away?

By the time Jonathan had dried off and slipped on his sweats, Tatum not only had drinks poured and nachos in the oven, but she had changed into an oversize summer shift that hung clear down to her calves. Jonathan appreciated her consideration, her obvious attempt to take temptation from his grasp; he just wished that someone had told her that a woman's calves were one of her sexiest assets. Why else would his libido be running wild at the sight of them?

"Would you like some?" Tatum asked.

Jonathan's glance shot upward. He was too full of desire to realize that there was no chance that she would be offering him what he hoped she was. She wasn't. Tatum held out a plate of nachos for him. She was already crunching on a cheese-covered chip. Yes, it was definitely time for a talk.

"Thanks, this looks great," he said, forcing out the platitude.

Jonathan reached out to take the plate she held, picking up his drink from the counter at the same time. He took a long swig of straight Scotch before sitting down next to her on one of the bar stools surrounding the island in the middle of her kitchen.

"We need to talk," he said abruptly.

Tatum immediately dropped the chip she had been raising to her mouth. "I don't see why," she said. "We're both adults here, Jonathan, not teenagers who have just discovered that there are opposite sexes. I mean, we can't help being human, but I don't think either one of us is incapable of keeping things as neutral as we agreed they should be," she said.

Jonathan contemplated the chips on his plate. He had forgotten for a moment that he was dealing with a successful lawyer. She was issuing her closing statement, quite well, he might add, before he even concluded his opening one.

He looked up to catch her troubled gaze with what he hoped was a reassuring glance. "We agreed to be friends, Tatum. Nobody said we had to be just friends. All I'm asking for is the natural progression of a caring relationship. I just want us to give this thing a chance—to not give up on it just because neither of us is ready for a huge commitment right now.''

He hoped he hadn't sounded like a rutting male motivated by hormones. He was not looking for quick gratification. He just wanted a normal adult relationship with a woman who fascinated the hell out of him. He refused to feel guilty about that.

Tatum's delicate jaw tightened. ''That is precisely what I'm doing. Why do you even think you're here? Other than Mandy, you are the first person I have brought into this house in more than a year, Jonathan. I'd like to have you here again, but only if you come as a friend—a *platonic* friend. Some things don't change. My life is just as it was that day at the library when you convinced me to give this a chance, and the conditions have to remain the same, as well.''

Jonathan reached out to run his fingers through the long dark hair that was still damp from her swim. ''I'm not trying to tie you down or ask for commitments that neither of us can give, but you can't deny that there are feelings between us. I feel you, Tatum. And I feel you feeling me.''

He had to give her credit. She didn't try to look away. ''I do feel things for you. But that doesn't change the fact that at this point in my life, I have nothing to offer you.''

Jonathan was the first one to finally look away as he stifled his instinctive reply to her words. She had plenty to offer him; she already was giving him more than he had got from anyone in years, but the problem had suddenly, sickeningly become clear to him. Her words had just reiterated the sentiment he heard over and over again at the center whenever a child had been hurt so badly he was afraid to be vulnerable again.

Jonathan felt like a complete fool. He should have seen her need long before now. Hell, she'd even said the words before, that day at the library. Something about her "well" being dry. But she was such a strong woman, so far removed from the needy cases he normally dealt with, he had never even considered that she might be referring to more than a too-tight schedule....

Pushing his plate away, he turned on the stool so that his knees locked with hers. "Tell me about him," he invited softly.

Tatum's startled gaze flew to his face, as if she could read his thoughts through his features. "Who?"

"Your father. I remember some of what was on the news, but I'd like to hear about *him*," he said.

As the silence stretched out, Tatum jumped up from her stool and began clearing up the dishes. It was ironic, Jonathan thought. He had spent his life helping to heal complete strangers, and here was someone he cared about and he hadn't even heard her cry for help. He had admired her for her dedication to her work, not even wondering why such an attractive young woman would choose to live life so completely alone. But now that he knew, he knew he could help her. This was what he was trained for.

"There's not much to tell," she said as she ran water in the sink. "Kanish killed my brother a few years ago down in Florida. They played it off like it was an accident. Said he'd only meant to use the knife to scare Cale into giving up his wallet, but that someone on the street bumped into Cale from behind and pushed him into the blade. There wasn't enough proof to show otherwise. Then, even though he had a previous record, Kanish was released from prison last fall on a technicality. Dad took justice into his own hands," she finished in a monotone, reminding Jonathan of Detective Charles down at the juvenile division. She was scrubbing her cheese grater so hard Jonathan was surprised her sponge was still in one piece.

"None of which takes away who or what you are," he said softly when it was clear to him she was not planning on saying anymore. "You're a beautiful, successful, strong woman, Tatum McGillus."

Tatum turned toward him then, seemingly unaware of her hands dripping soapy water all over her floor. Jonathan's gut wrenched as he caught a brief glimpse of the troubled expression that quickly vanished from her face. He was handling this all wrong. Where was all his training now when he needed it most? Why did it always seem to desert him when he was with this woman?

"Don't, Jonathan," she said in her best prosecutor's voice. "You have no idea, and right now I can't give you one. I only know that everything that I am has changed, and until I can work that out, I can't afford to give up anything that may be left. We can be friends, but nothing more. If that isn't enough, I'm sorry...." She finished less evenly, turning back to her sinkful of suds.

If he had thought it would do either of them any good, Jonathan would have willingly bashed his head against the counter in front of him. What an overbearing ass he had been to presume he could just assure her she was fine and expect it to be so. She was right. He had no idea.

But he knew he wanted to understand. Even from the depths of her own despair, she had touched Jonathan in a way he had never known before. He wanted to do the same for her, to help her to live again. He would wait for her. He had to wait.

Jonathan approached Tatum's bent form as cautiously as Mandy had little Abby the night before. He reached out one hand tentatively and brushed it against the dark, silky strands cascading down her back. He pulled back immediately when Tatum flinched.

"It's okay," he assured her softly. "We'll continue as we have been for as long as you need us to. Forever, if that's what you need," he vowed, wishing with all of his soul that it didn't have to be that way but knowing that he would accept it if he had to. He needed Tatum in his life, one way or another.

Tatum nodded, but she didn't turn around. Jonathan was pretty sure she was holding back sobs. She was not yet ready or maybe able to share her pain with him. Sometimes being a friend meant knowing when to go. With a promise to call the next day, Jonathan left.

CHAPTER FIVE

"BOBBY RHODES HAS AGREED to talk with you again, Ms. McGillus. You can see him anytime," the bored voice of the detention officer came over the telephone line late Wednesday morning. Tatum had been waiting to hear that since noon on Tuesday.

"I'll be there within the hour, thanks," she replied, already gathering up her files. She had just five days until the Rhodes trial began, five days to work a miracle. And unbelievably she may have done just that.

She arrived at the jail forty-five minutes later and had almost no wait at all until she was shown to the door of the interrogation room. Straightening the skirt of her teal blue suit, she went inside. Bobby was there already, sitting up straight on one side of the table, a cigarette burning in the ashtray beside him. His golden brown skin was cleanly shaven, and his hair, though longer than when she had first met him, was neatly combed. Even in his standard gray jail uniform, he didn't look like a thug.

She stood just inside the door. "We've finally identified the gun, Bobby," she said by way of greet-

ing. This young man had already caused her too many
sleepless nights, and if he was the consummate liar she
now suspected he was, she was not going to waste one
more ounce of pity or compassion on him.

Bobby's chin dropped briefly as he took a deep
breath, but other than that there was no sign that he'd
even heard what she'd said.

"Of course, you knew all along whose it was,
didn't you?" she charged, coming farther into the
room.

Bobby met her accusing gaze with a clear brown
stare. "I suspected," he said. His words, as always
came as a surprise. They were well modulated, artic-
ulated, almost highbrow. Bobby Rhodes did not have
the mannerisms of a street punk.

"You suspected," Tatum repeated coldly. She cir-
cled the table at which Bobby sat. "I'll just bet you
suspected. Your brother-in-law was shot to death in
your home shortly after you were heard threatening
him. And the murder weapon belongs to you. Now
isn't this a coincidence. And *you*—" with her uncon-
fined hair forming a shroud around her, Tatum
leaned both hands on the table in front of Bobby,
putting her face so close to his she could see the individual whiskers on his cheeks"—*you*, who've been
the model prisoner, the model defendant, so open, so
cooperative, so *honest*, knew all along that the murder weapon belonged to *you*. Have you been sitting
here so smugly certain that we wouldn't be able to

trace that gun?'' she asked, backing up from the table a few steps.

Bobby held Tatum's glance through her entire attack and continued to do so after she fell silent. ''No,
ma'am, I have not. I knew there were any number of
ways ballistics could have traced that gun to me if it
were mine. I target shoot every Saturday, they could
have gotten a slug from there. The possibilities have
not left my mind since the moment I got here,'' he
admitted, as forthright as always.

Tatum refused to let go of her anger even a little
bit. She *had* to feel sure about this. She just could not
allow the doubts to live any longer. ''Then the not-
guilty plea, the willingness to talk to everybody without protection of counsel, the assurance that you had
nothing to hide was all just a rather twisted but
unique attempt to beat the system,'' she said bitterly.

She didn't know why she was bothering. She had
her answer. Bobby was guilty. So why didn't she just
leave and feel good about the fact that she was still a
good lawyer?

''No ma'am, it was not. I didn't tell you about the
gun for two reasons. First because, as I am sure you
have discovered, where I come from more people have
guns like mine than don't. I bought mine off the
streets a few years back, after Jenny was jumped. We
needed the protection, but I had a police record and
wasn't permitted to purchase a gun in the usual man-
ner. I didn't have an opportunity to determine for sure
that the gun that killed Roy was the same gun. I've

been praying that it wasn't. The second reason I didn't tell you of my suspicion should be pretty obvious. I knew that you or anyone else would react just as you have. It's my gun, so I have to be guilty. As long as no one knew for sure, I had a chance to prove my innocence."

The statements were made simply, sincerely; they rang so true. Tatum felt her anger draining away.

"Did you kill Roy, Bobby? By accident? In self-defense? What?" she asked. Her only hope of pleasing both herself and the law at this point was to get a confession from Bobby and go for a lesser charge.

"I did not kill my brother-in-law, Ms. McGillus," he stated unequivocally. "He was family."

"Then who did kill him? Who are you protecting?" she asked in a last-ditch effort to trap him into revealing something—anything. Time was running out for both of them.

"I would not protect the killer of my sister's husband. I simply don't know who was there while I was gone that night," he answered succinctly.

Tatum watched as Bobby's eyes drifted down to the cigarette that had burned itself out in the ashtray. His lips also turned downward. The man was losing hope. The emotion on Bobby's features was almost unreadable. She doubted that anyone else would even have noticed the barely discernible changes in him, but Tatum was trained to read body language, and she knew. The man was innocent, and if she did her job right, he was going to spend the rest of his life in prison.

If only she could find what she was missing. But she had looked over the testimonies and reports so many times she knew them by heart. There was nothing there to account for her empathy with a suspected killer.

The leftover smoke from Bobby's dead cigarette lingered in the air, and Tatum swallowed distastefully as she ran one last mental check over the evidence against Bobby. Strange how some people were so used to cigarette smoke they didn't even notice it, while other people got sick to their stomachs. Her father had once told her that gunpowder was the same. Gunpowder. Wait a minute. Quelling the sudden ball of hope within her chest, Tatum again reviewed the testimony in her memory. Unusual smell. Gunpowder.

"Bobby, how familiar are you with the smell of burnt gunpowder?" she asked, wondering if she was so desperate for clues she was losing her mind.

Bobby looked up at her with a hint of a grin on his lips. "Come on, ma'am, you've seen where I come from. I learned how to shoot a gun before I learned how to shoot marbles," he said.

Tatum's heart began to thump in her chest. "In your testimony that night you said that the first thing you noticed when you walked back in the door was an unusual smell. It's been assumed all along that that smell was the gunpowder. It's distinctive enough to notice right away, and to most of us, unusual. But not to you,'' she said, coming closer to the table again. But this time, instead of leaning over in an attempt to intimidate, she sat down.

Bobby was watching her intently. "Not to me," he confirmed.

"So what was that smell?" Tatum asked. "Can you remember anything about it? Anything it reminded you of?"

Bobby was silent for several minutes. Tatum could almost feel the memories trying to force their way to the surface of his mind. Finally he shook his head helplessly. "It was just a scent. I had no idea what was going on, and the police who were waiting for me rushed me out of the house so quickly I was left only with vague impressions."

"Do you think you would recognize it if you smelled it again?" she asked. She knew she was really digging deep.

Bobby shrugged. "I don't know, ma'am. It seems like I should, but since I don't really remember what it smelled like, I can't be sure. I remember wondering if my cousin Lily had been there, but then I remembered that she was in the hospital. She'd just had her baby the night before. Jenny'd been with her most of that night."

Being in the hospital and having a baby was a pretty tight alibi, but Tatum knew she was going to check things out just in case. She couldn't afford to overlook anything.

"Was it perfume? Could that be why it reminded you of your cousin?"

Bobby shook his head. "I really can't remember, ma'am. I don't think it was perfume. At least not any kind I've ever smelled before. It was just something I couldn't place. Probably something they brought in when they were taking care of Roy or checking for fingerprints. I don't think it reminded me of Lily, after all. I was just thinking about her because Jenny was supposed to go back to see her after work."

Tatum was disappointed. For a minute there she'd really thought she might have something. "I guess that's it, then, Bobby. If you think of anything else, anything at all, let me know. Otherwise, I guess I'll see you Monday morning in court." Her words reminded them both that they were playing for keeps. She rose from the table.

Bobby stayed in his seat as Tatum knew he had been instructed to do, but she had the feeling that it went against his grain to do so. A gentleman always saw a lady out. "Thanks, ma'am, for trying so hard to be fair," he said as she headed for the door.

Tatum hesitated, but she couldn't turn around again. Somehow she had to get this young man's despondent face out of her mind. She motioned for the guard to come take Bobby back to his cell.

"HI, YOU STILL AWAKE?" Tatum spoke softly into the telephone receiver she clutched in her hand. It was well past midnight.

"Mm-hmm," Jonathan's sleepy voice came back faintly.

"I'm sorry, you *were* sleeping. I'll call you tomorrow," she said quickly, rolling over on her bed toward the nightstand that held her telephone.

"No! Tatum, wait!" Jonathan's urgent tones reached her just as she was about to drop the phone in its cradle.

"Tatum? You still there?"

"I'm here, Jonathan. I really didn't want to wake you. I knew I shouldn't have called. I'm sorry. I'll talk to you tomorrow, okay?"

"No, it's not okay. And you didn't wake me, not really. I was lying here dreaming about you. When I suddenly heard your voice, the dream just kind of continued," he explained.

Tatum felt herself grow warm at his honesty. "Oh," she said, rolling over to lie back against the pillows she had bunched up at least a dozen times in the past hour. Her hair fanned out on either side of her.

"It's okay, really. I'm glad you called. If nothing else, we're friends. You need to talk, you call. I need to talk, I call. That's friends, Tatum," he assured her.

And suddenly Tatum felt better than she had in days. In spite of all the weight she had to carry by herself, she didn't feel quite so alone.

"I've had kind of a bad day," she confessed in a near whisper.

"Tough day in court?"

"No."

"Want to tell me about it?"

"Yes."

"Well?"

"I can't."

"Okay."

Tatum snuggled deeper into her bed, pulling the sheet up to her neck. Her nightshirt rode up almost to her waist. She wished he were with her, so he could massage her stiff shoulders. She tried not to picture him lying in his bed, wearing...probably nothing. "So how was your day?" she asked.

"Not bad. I had a lunch date with one of the governor's aides that lasted until dinnertime, and then spent the evening going through my mail. It sure piles up quickly," he complained good-naturedly.

Tatum wished she could see the tiny duplex he had described to her once, wished she knew where he sat to pay his bills. He was beginning to know her better than anyone had in a long, long time, but she still hadn't seen his home. She knew he didn't spend much time there, but he slept there—every night. And suddenly the fact that she couldn't picture him there bothered her a lot.

"Jonathan?" she asked somewhat hesitantly. After Monday night she wasn't sure she should suggest what she had in mind. And yet, after Monday why not?

"Mm-hmm?" His silky, deep tones sent shivers down to her toes.

"Do you have a free night this week?"

"How do you define night?" he asked.

"Black, long, the office is closed," she said, a smile teasing her lips.

Jonathan chuckled in response. For a second Tatum wished she were with him, in his arms, against his hard, warm chest, feeling those chuckles pass through her—giving life to the hollowness inside of her.

"I'm free Friday after seven," he offered. "What did you have in mind?"

"I'd like to see your house," she said simply. "You've seen mine, but I've never seen yours." She was fully aware of the suggestion implicit in her words, but for the moment she didn't care.

"I don't have a pool," he warned.

"I know."

"I'm not much of a cook."

"It's okay if you'd rather not," Tatum answered in a rush. It had never dawned on her that Jonathan might not want her in his home.

"Oh, I'd rather, honey. I'm just not sure we should. This place is not very big. In fact, it's downright tiny. You. Me. Alone here together. I'm strong, but maybe not that strong," he admitted.

Tatum released the breath she was not even aware she had been holding. For a couple of seconds, she had thought Jonathan was rejecting her. It was disturbing how frightened that thought made her feel.

"How about if I make us a seven-thirty reservation somewhere wonderful and terribly hard to get into. We can stop by your place on the way, but we'll have to leave right away to get where we're going," she suggested.

She could almost see Jonathan shaking his head. "Won't work," he answered. "No place is that wonderful."

"You could drop a key by my office, and I could run over by myself," she said playfully.

"No good. It would drive me crazy knowing you were there, all alone in my territory...." His voice trailed off.

"Jonathan," Tatum protested, drawing out his name on a wail.

"I've got it," Jonathan said with all the drama of a knight in armor coming to the rescue. "We'll invite Mandy over for dinner, and maybe one of the other kids at the center, as well. A chaperone or two. That'll do it."

"Are you going to ask her or should I?" Tatum asked, still grinning at her ceiling.

"You, most definitely. If I ask her, she'll see right through me, and I'd never live it down," he confessed.

Tatum noticed that the tension in her shoulders was gone. This was why Jonathan's friendship was worth the strain. He could make her feel better even after the worst of days.

"And Jonathan? It's the upcoming Rhodes trial. You've probably been reading about it in the papers," she said. She wouldn't talk about her doubts—

she wouldn't let herself need him that much. But she wanted him to know why she was upset.

"From what I've read, it's a cut-and-dried case," he said.

"It's supposed to be," she replied, leaving it at that.

"You're a good lawyer, Tatum. Don't ever doubt that," he said with sudden force.

In truth, Jonathan had no way of knowing what kind of an attorney she was, but his faith in her warmed Tatum's heart. She rolled onto her side and snuggled her face into her pillows.

"Thank you, Jonathan. See you Friday," she said softly.

"G'night, lady," his husky tones came through to her ear.

"G'night," she replied sleepily.

Her eyes were already drooping shut as she hung up the phone.

IT HAD BEEN a long time since Tatum had looked forward to anything, and she savored the feeling as Friday night drew closer. On the day itself, she left her office early enough to shower again, wash her hair and blow it dry. She dressed casually in a pair of pleated khaki shorts and matching crop top, painted her nails, both fingers and toes, and then slipped into a pair of khaki-colored espadrilles. Her makeup, as usual, was just a little blush and eye-liner.

Mandy was ready and waiting on the front steps of the center when Tatum pulled up. Dressed in the inevitable neon shorts and tank top, she looked about three years younger than her seventeen years. As she got up to walk to the car, Tatum caught a glimpse of a striking, curly-haired little girl emerging from behind Mandy's back.

"Hi, Tatum," Mandy greeted enthusiastically as she opened the passenger door of the Taurus and helped the little girl, dressed in shorts and a T-shirt, to climb into the front seat. "This is Abby. Abby, I'd like you to meet a friend of mine, Tatum McGillus. Her daddy helped me out of a tight spot one time and brought me to the center. You can call her Tatum," Mandy continued. While she spoke, she was busily buckling Abby into the middle of the bench seat.

Tatum felt a swell of affection for this young woman, who was so giving in spite of all that had been taken from her. "Hello, Abby," she said to Mandy's young charge. The child simply turned her big blue eyes up to stare at her without uttering a sound. Tatum's startled gaze met Mandy's.

Mandy put her arm along the back of the seat, allowing her fingers to rest lightly against Abby's shoulder. "It's okay," she said to Tatum. "Abby's saving her words for now."

Tatum had no idea what to make of that strange statement, but she knew enough to follow Mandy's lead. For some reason the child must not be able to talk, but Mandy was not going to treat the affliction like anything other than a conscious decision on Abby's part to remain silent. For all Tatum knew, that's what it was.

"So how'd it go at the grocery store yesterday?" Mandy asked as Tatum steered the car toward Jonathan's duplex.

Tatum shrugged. She still hated the idea of fighting against Jonathan on the question of due-notice. Once again she wondered how long it was going to take him to realize that this was one crusade he should not wage. "About the same as the library was," she finally answered. "Jonathan got a few signatures, but he lost more."

Mandy nodded as if satisfied.

"By the way, I listened to the radio show. You sounded great. I bet it helped us out a lot," she said.

Tatum signaled her turn onto Jonathan's street. "It was hard to tell for sure," she replied. "The phones rang for the entire half hour, but a lot of the callers had questions for Jonathan on matters other than due-notice. And I had to leave before him. But the thing to remember here is that Jonathan is the one fighting. He is the one who is trying to get something passed. We only want to keep things as they are. What that means is that Jonathan is going to have to do a lot more convincing than we are."

Mandy's fingers strayed to Abby's hair, pulling gently at one of the child's curls. "Still, we have to convince people he's wrong."

They arrived at the address Jonathan had given Tatum over the phone, and he greeted his three guests as gallantly as a lord of old. With exaggerated pomp he showed them around his small living room, furnished with a serviceable brown couch and matching recliner, ushered them down a hallway that led to a spare room that he had converted into an office and lastly showed them his bedroom.

"Wow! What a humongous bed!" Mandy exclaimed as she saw the king-size four-poster that dominated the room. She walked in to check it out, bouncing on the mattress a couple of times. Abby stood quietly in the doorway, her watchful eyes observing Mandy. Jonathan stole a glance toward Tatum.

Their eyes met in a look that said too much, and Jonathan had to use every ounce of his self-control to keep his body from reacting to the invitation Tatum had not quite been able to suppress. Having chaperones had been a damn good idea—or a damn bad one, depending on how he looked at it.

"So, is it how you pictured it?" he asked Tatum, turning his back on the room.

"Actually it's more," she said. She glanced into the room he had converted into an office. "I didn't realize you did work at home."

"I try to do most of my senatorial work here. That way I can use the place as a tax write-off. State senators may not make enough to live on, but at least there are a few perks," he explained.

Tatum looked toward Abby and wondered if the mute child might be getting hungry. "What's for supper?" she asked Jonathan.

"Pizza," he said, "and it's gonna get cold if we don't eat it in a hurry."

"All right! Pizza!" Mandy exclaimed. "How 'bout some pizza, little one?" she asked Abby, taking the child's hand as they walked back down the hallway.

Abby nodded, and followed the others into the kitchen.

Jonathan pulled two boxes out of the oven and carried them over to the wooden table pushed up against one wall of the kitchen.

"I told you I couldn't cook," he said.

"Aren't those hot?" Tatum asked, surprised that the oven hadn't caught fire with two cardboard boxes so close to the heating elements.

Jonathan collected napkins and cans of pop and piled them up in the middle of the table.

"Naw, the oven wasn't on."

He poured a glass of milk and brought it over to Abby.

Tatum wondered if learning to cook was another thing he had missed out on as a result of his unusual childhood, or if it was simple laziness on his part. She helped Mandy settle Abby into one of the four wooden chairs arranged along three sides of the table, reminding herself that it really was none of her business anyway.

Jonathan ate his share of the pizzas, but he filled up more on the peace surrounding him as he watched the three ladies at his table. From five-year-old Abby, to Tatum with her long dark tresses falling freely around her shoulders, and back to Mandy, his fighter, Jonathan had never seen three such beautiful women. He would probably be willing to come home for dinner every night if he knew that these three would be sitting here waiting for him.

Jonathan shook himself mentally as soon as he realized where his thoughts were taking him. These weren't his women any more than Cinci or the hundreds of other girls who had come through the center were. It was a part of his life he had accepted a long time ago. Just like an ornithologist, Jonathan's purpose was to fix the broken wings so his "birds" could fly away. He handed Abby an extra napkin to wipe up the sauce that was slipping down her chin.

"Cinci said to tell ya the air-conditioning part came in. The guy is coming out tomorrow at ten-thirty," Mandy said as she tackled her third piece of pizza.

"Thank God for that," he replied, eager for the distraction. "I thought Cook was going to pass out from the heat today. I was in the kitchen just before lunch, and her face was as red as the tomato she was slicing. Did the fan help?"

"Yeah," Mandy said. "Cinci found another old fan upstairs and brought it down this afternoon, too. I think they're having cold cuts for dinner, though," she finished with a grateful look at the fourth slice of pizza on the way to her mouth.

Tatum listened silently, more touched by the homey scene than she cared to admit. She remembered a time when she, Pop, Cale and sometimes Danny had shared such conversations at dinner. She had taken it all for granted back then. She wondered if Jonathan had any idea how lucky he was to have his ready-made family whenever he wanted it, or if he ever even stepped away from his public life long enough to miss having a private one.

As more conversation about the center flowed around her, Tatum thought back to those first days of knowing Jonathan. He had been a beacon in her darkness then. He was so much more than that now. He was a man with the courage to make a difference, the kind of man that her father had always hoped she would find one day. Except that he took his obligations to extremes—and she had found him too late.

The ringing of the telephone startled Tatum, but not nearly as much as the strange dread that clutched her as she watched Jonathan leave the room. She heard his voice rumbling in the distance as he spoke to his caller, and though she could not make out any of his words, she could not mistake the solemnity of his tone. Her stomach knotted up like a tangled rubber band. Something, somewhere, was wrong.

Mandy, too, had apparently noticed a tightening, an urgency in Jonathan's voice, and she and Tatum shared a silent, apprehensive look as they waited for his return. Was it the center? Had another child been brought in? Had they found little Abby's parents?

The minute Jonathan walked back into the room, his worried gaze sought Tatum's.

"What is it? What's happened?" she asked at once.

Jonathan continued on to the table, pulled up a vacant chair and sat down beside her. He leaned forward, putting his elbows on his knees and rubbed his fingers along her thigh.

"That was a Danny Torunta, said he was a friend of yours," Jonathan said as if trying to break whatever news he had as gently as he could.

Tatum froze. She tried to speak, to ask whatever she should be asking, but no words formed. No sound came out. Her gaze was glued to Jonathan's.

"Your father's had a heart attack, honey...."

CHAPTER SIX

AS SOON AS HE MENTIONED her father, Jonathan felt Tatum closing herself off from him as surely as if a door had been slammed between them. He longed to hold her, ready to do whatever he could to help make this easier on her, but she held her body away from him, cradling herself. In all of his years of volunteer service, he had never ached for another as he did at that moment.

"Is he...?" she started, but did not finish.

He decided it was probably better to give her the truth all at once. "He's alive, but it doesn't look promising."

Tatum digested his words in silence. "How did he find me here?" she asked after a few moments.

Jonathan watched as Mandy pulled Abby onto her lap, and then he turned back to Tatum. He assumed by "he" she meant Danny. "After he couldn't find you at the office or at home, he called the center. You'd told him you could be reached there through Mandy."

Mandy's straight blond hair blended with Abby's dark curls as the teenager bent her head over the si-

lent child in her arms. "You'd better go quickly,"
Mandy said softly, her cheek rubbing gently against
Abby's hair. "I'll stay here with Abby. Jonathan can
take you to your daddy."

Tatum looked up then, glancing from Mandy to
Jonathan. "I have to go to him," she said as if the
thought had just occurred to her. Her eyes were
glazed, vacant looking. "I have to go now. I have to
see him. Will they let me see him?" she asked.

Jonathan slipped a supportive arm behind her back
as she jumped up from her chair. She didn't lean into
him—didn't even seem to notice him beside her. "It's
all arranged, honey. Danny's waiting for us now."

SURPRISE WAS the first reaction Jonathan felt when
they arrived at the prison's infirmary an hour later.
Not knowing what to expect, he had kept his mind as
blank as possible during the drive. If anything, he had
tried to prepare himself for the sight of a curled-up,
dying, middle-aged man. Jack McGillus looked older
than Jonathan had expected but was propped up in
bed, awake, when Jonathan and Tatum walked into
his room. Awake and waiting.

"Dan tells me you were at this young man's house
having dinner," he said to his daughter, sounding
weak but pleased.

"Oh, Pop," Tatum cried, leaning over the bed to
wrap her arms around the tube-laden man. As Jonathan held back to give her this moment with her father, he caught a glimpse of her taut features and felt

her distress as sharply as if it were his own. What had happened to the detachment that had carried him through a lifetime of other people's traumas?

When several minutes had passed and Tatum showed no signs of loosening her grip on her father, he pulled back and patted her on the shoulder. "Come on, girlie. It's not as bad as all that."

Tatum continued to cling to him for a moment longer before she finally released her grip and stood up. The look on her face, Jonathan noted, was now one of complete composure. This disturbed Jonathan even more, somehow, than the anguish in her face a few moments earlier, or the tension that had lined her face so alarmingly on the long, silent drive to the prison.

"It's just that you feel so good," she told her father with a smile she managed to call up from somewhere. "It's been so long since I touched you...." Her voice faded away on the words.

"So do I get to meet this guy, or do I just gotta let him look at me all trussed up like this without even knowing who he is?" Jack asked, filling in the awkward silence Tatum's last words had left. His gaze was locked on Jonathan.

Jonathan moved forward into the room before Tatum had a chance to introduce him. "I'm Jonathan Wright," he said, holding out his hand to meet Jack's.

Jack's grip was weaker than Jonathan had expected it to be from the man's appearance. The old man was obviously putting on a show of bravado, just like his daughter.

"Same Jonathan Wright that founded the Children's Crisis Center?" Jack wheezed, eyeing Jonathan.

Jonathan nodded.

"Jonathan's a state senator, Pop. He's out to change the world," Tatum said.

Jack looked from Tatum back to Jonathan. "You're not running the center anymore?" Jack asked, his sudden frown accompanied by a grimace of pain.

"Yes, sir. I'm still managing director of the center. Most Arizona senators work full-time jobs while serving their terms."

"Good. Good," Jack said with a slow nod toward Jonathan before pinning Tatum with his muted gaze. "I did some investigating that time I covered for Charles over in juvie and came across the Schroeder girl," he said. "I couldn't leave that poor child there without making sure I wasn't dumping her someplace else where she wasn't wanted." Jack's words were coming more slowly now, more breathlessly. "I checked up on him afterward a time or two, as well. He's a good man." Droplets of sweat were forming on Jack's upper lip.

Tatum smoothed away the gray hair that had fallen across his forehead. "Rest, Pop, please," she implored.

But Jack was not done talking yet. He looked up at Jonathan. "What's your interest in my daughter?"

The question came out as barely more than a whisper, but Jonathan respected the power behind it, and the circumstances that allowed it. He just didn't know what to say in front of the man's daughter.

Jonathan grasped the rail on Jack's bed with both hands. "I . . ."

"We're just friends, Pop," Tatum interrupted before Jonathan had a chance to say anything more.

But Jack obviously saw what he wanted to know as he looked back and forth between the two of them. "Don't let him go, girlie," he wheezed, his gaze coming to rest on Jonathan. Silent messages travelled between the two men. "Don't waste your life. . . ." Jack's voice, which had been coming in spurts between bits of heavy breathing, finally tapered off. His head fell back against the pillows supporting him. His eyes closed.

Tatum glanced over to Jonathan, terror etched across the beautiful face that had been calm just seconds before.

"Jonathan," she cried out, the single word ending in a question.

"Shh," Jonathan said quickly, reaching over to unclench her fingers from her father's limp hand. "He's just sleeping, hon. His heart's being monitored. If there were a problem, believe me, you'd know it. Besides, his color's still good."

He watched while Tatum quickly searched her father's features, looking for any sign that Jonathan might have missed. Finally she looked back up at him, reassured for the moment.

"Let's see if we can scare up some coffee, huh?" he suggested, sliding his arm around her back as he led her out into the hallway from which they had come. The doctor was due back in about an hour, Danny had told them when he had directed them to Jack's room. They still had about half of that time to wait. And Jonathan was going to take Tatum no farther than the coffee machine until she had had a chance to talk with the doctor and find out for herself just what chances Jack McGillus still had.

FIFTY-FIFTY. The doctor's words were still ringing over and over in Tatum's mind an hour later as she rode away from the prison with Jonathan. Pop's life was resting on a fifty-fifty chance, and that was only if he had the will to fight back. Tatum was not sure that he did. She was no longer even sure he should have to. Fight back for what? Another mass of endless days and nights sitting behind bars and sleeping on a bare mattress? And yet, selfishly, she could not even contemplate the alternative.

"Rather than driving all the way back tonight, only to return again first thing in the morning, why don't we get a couple of rooms for the night? We passed a motel on the way in."

Jonathan. Calm strength in the face of emergencies. Tatum had never been more thankful to have his friendship than she was at that moment.

"You don't mind staying over?" she asked.

Jonathan reached across to take her hand, holding it against his thigh. "I want to be here with you."

Tatum nodded, squeezing Jonathan's fingers. The backs of her eyes stung with tears.

Moments later Jonathan pulled the Bronco into a slot in the motel parking lot.

"You want to stay here while I go get us a couple of rooms?" he asked, releasing Tatum's hand as he opened his door.

Tatum grabbed for her door handle. "No!" she said. And then, more calmly, "I'll come with you."

She saw Jonathan look over at her, a concerned expression lining his handsome face. She knew she had overreacted, but she just didn't want to be left with the dark as her only companion, even for a minute.

The heavyset woman behind the desk rose sleepily as Tatum and Jonathan approached.

"You want a room?" she greeted them, pulling a registration form in front of her and picking up a pen.

Jonathan held up two fingers. "T—"

"Yes!" Tatum grabbed his hand. They wanted a room. She wanted a room. One room. For the two of them. She just couldn't bear the thought of being all alone, in a strange room, in an unfamiliar town, during the long, dark hours that were left of the night—

not while Pop lay in a hospital bed with his life slipping away.

The woman pushed the form across the counter.
"Sign here, please," she said, stifling a yawn.

Jonathan slipped his hand from Tatum's to pick up
the pen. But he didn't start writing immediately. He
looked at Tatum, searching her troubled gaze with his
own calm one.

Tatum pleaded with him silently to understand, to
do this for her, to know that she wasn't even sure
what it was she wanted him to do—or not to do.

He started writing.

Five minutes later Tatum was in a clean if utilitar-
ian bathroom, trying to shower the past several hours
away from her body. Jonathan had insisted on paying for the room. But he had put her name on the
register, as well as his, to ensure she could be found
if the prison needed to reach her.

She reached up to adjust the shower head, then
stood still beneath it, letting the hot water cascade
over her scalp to run in rivulets down to her shoulders and around her body. She was wearily contem-
plating the feasibility of standing under that
comforting heat forever, surrounded by nothing more
menacing than the gently soothing water, when she
heard a knock on the bathroom door.

"Tatum, you okay?" Jonathan's voice came muffled through the door.

"I'm fine," she called out. "I'll just be a minute
longer."

Tatum bent over to turn off the faucet and felt the last of the water drip down over her back, sending tingles all over her body. She stepped out onto the white bath mat she had laid out for herself and buried her face in one of the big, fluffy motel towels. She felt a little uncomfortable and, she had to admit, a little excited at the thought of being naked with Jonathan only a few feet away.

Telling herself not to be ridiculous, she quickly dried and wrapped herself in the thick terry robe she had found hanging on the back of the bathroom door. Then, acting as if there were nothing unusual about sharing a motel room with Jonathan, she grabbed up the underthings she had rinsed earlier and swung open the door.

"It's all yours," she said, darting past Jonathan, unable to meet his eyes with her hands full of damp lingerie.

STILL WRAPPED securely in the robe, Tatum was snuggled into the far side of one of the two double beds in their room by the time Jonathan finished his shower. The cool sheet was like a caress against her bare legs, a soothing touch to her flushed cheeks. She listened as Jonathan moved around in the bathroom on the other side of the wall, his clean feet squeaking against the bottom of the tub as he stepped out. She turned her back toward the wall, trying to block out the sensual images flashing through her mind. The water was running again, in the sink this time. He was

probably brushing his teeth with one of the dispos-
able brushes they had purchased from the vending
machine down by the ice machine. Was he preparing
himself for a night of love?

Tatum was not feeling overly fond of herself. What
right did she have to use Jonathan for her own selfish needs? How could she even contemplate losing
herself in his body in an attempt to escape the drudg-
ery of reality for a while? Because if she made love
with Jonathan, that was what it would be—an escape, nothing more.

The bathroom door opened, sending a brief ray of
light out into the darkened bedroom. She watched
Jonathan's shadow as he moved farther into the
room, laying down the clothes he would have to wear
again in the morning neatly across a chair. From what
she could see with her face half-hidden beneath her
covers, he was wearing only a towel wrapped around
the lower half of his body. Were there briefs under
there, too?

Tatum had already seen his naked chest, the night
he had come swimming at her house, and her mind's
eye quickly filled in the shadows left by the dimly lit
room. Flexed pectorals protruded beneath a profu-
sion of springy black curls, which tapered down toward what lay beneath the fluffy white towel. Tatum
felt her nipples pucker beneath the covers.

"You asleep?" His words, spoken softly from the
end of her bed, readied her for his touch.

Tatum rolled over onto her back and looked toward his face in the darkness. There was no point in pretending. Her body wanted him just as badly as her head did not. "Uh-uh."

She watched as Jonathan walked around the end of her bed, close enough for her to catch the fresh, soapy smell of his skin. She tried not to imagine his lean masculine body as she heard the rustle of his towel falling to the floor. She felt the cool air-conditioned air slide across her heated skin as he lifted the covers on the other side of the bed. The mattress dipped beneath her, accepting his greater weight.

Without another thought, Tatum turned to him, moving her face closer for his kiss. She opened her lips to him, hungry for a taste of the passion she had felt with him only briefly before, but she barely registered the firm moistness of his mouth on hers before his lips were gone.

"G'night, lady. If you need me during the night, don't be afraid to wake me," he said.

Stunned, Tatum felt the rush of tears that sprang to her eyes. He no longer wanted her. Just when she was desperate enough to ignore her conscience and give in to the needs their attraction demanded, he was no longer interested. Had she finally frozen him out?

She watched him in the shadows, searching his features for some hint of his thoughts, but he reached out, turning her over to snuggle with her spoon fashion. And as soon as his hard, clothed midsection came to rest against her backside, Tatum understood. It wasn't a question of not wanting. She had known that the time wasn't right, that love between them that night would have been less than it should be, that it would have been for the wrong reasons. She just hadn't realized that Jonathan knew it, too. And while Tatum feared that the right time might never come for them, she was quick to realize that at least this way they would always be friends.

She lifted her arm, allowing him to slide his beneath it. His hand slid over her robe, cupping her ribs, pulling her closer. His heat permeated every pore of her body.

"Jonathan?"

"Yeah?" His breath, stirring the hair on top of her head, sent chills racing down her spine.

"Thanks."

He gave her a quick hug. "Try to get some sleep," he said, pulling the covers up around her shoulders. His voice sounded strained. Tatum settled into her pillow, holding her backside as still as she could, wishing things could have been different for them.

Her fingers ached to touch the hard muscles curved around her, almost as much as a more private part of her ached to satisfy the swollen flesh resting just beneath her bottom. But she knew in her heart that, as things stood, the morning after would not be worth the night before. Grateful for what she had instead, she reveled in the contentment of knowing that he was right there, sharing her air, taking breaths that she could hear, ready to comfort her if she called out his

name. She just had to be sure she didn't call out his
name.

THE JURY BOX WAS FULL. Tatum's practiced eye ran
over the rows of possible jurors, immediately dismissing a couple, seriously considering a few more.
The bitter-looking man with unkempt long hair, a
two-day beard and holes in his shirt was definitely
out. She glanced quickly around the room, taking in
Troy Duncan, Bobby's court-appointed counsel, with
a frown. Though immaculate in appearance with his
perfectly styled black hair, light blue suit and shiny
wing-topped shoes, the man looked bored. Not a
good sign for Bobby.

"Name, please," Judge Keedy's voice boomed out
over the courtroom as he called upon the first of the
hundred or more candidates who had been called for
possible jury duty on the Rhodes murder trial.

"Juanita Marcos," the grandmotherly Mexican
woman replied.

"Have you ever been involved in a court case, Mrs.
Marcos?"

"No, sir."

"Are you employed?"

"Yes, sir. I work at a laundromat."

"Are you married?"

"No, sir."

"Are you aware of any personal prejudices that
might interfere with your service on this case?"

"No, sir."

"Mrs. Marcos, are you acquainted with Robert Rhodes or any members of his family?"

"No, sir."

"Are you familiar with the area of town in which the crime took place?"

"Yes, sir."

"Have you ever resided in that part of town?"

"All my life, sir."

"Counsel?" the judge called, raising his brows in question. Did either of the attorneys present have a problem with the information Mrs. Marcos had relayed? Duncan shook his head immediately. Both men looked at Tatum.

Everyone else in the courtroom turned toward Tatum, as well, waiting to hear if she had a problem with Mrs. Marcos's affinity with the Rhodeses' way of life, but it was the hard stare of the county supervisor, standing in the back of the room, that she felt most acutely. He expected her to use one of her dismissals. There was no reason, according to the constitution, that Mrs. Marcos could not serve on the jury, but Tatum was a lawyer. She knew her way around the system as well as the best of them. She could find some technicality to have the woman dismissed. But in doing so, she would be dismissing her ethics, as well. They were one of the few things she had left.

Tatum's eyes never wavered as she faced the elderly judge and discreetly shook her head. Ninety percent of the prospective jurors were Caucasians. If Bobby were to receive the fair trial that was his right, he should have at least one of his own people hearing his case.

"Mr. Duncan, do you have any questions for Mrs. Marcos?"

"No, sir," Duncan answered. Tatum was not surprised. If he could have an entire jury of people like Mrs. Marcos, his case would be much easier to fight.

"Miss McGillus?"

Tatum's off-white heels clicked across the front of the courtroom as she approached the jury box. Quite deliberately she took a moment to flick her hair back over the shoulder of her tailored beige suit. If Juanita Marcos was easily intimidated, she did not belong on the jury.

"Do you know either of the lawyers on this case, Mrs. Marcos?" she asked when the woman continued to meet her eyes without looking away.

"No, ma'am."

"To your knowledge, are you familiar with anyone who works for or is related to them?"

"No, ma'am."

Tatum returned to her seat behind one of the two tables positioned in front of the judge's bench and witness stand. "No further questions, Your Honor," she stated clearly as she sat down.

Judge Keedy moved on through the list of prospective jurors at a snail's pace. On more than one occasion Tatum had to hold back a yawn. So far, the endless questions had brought forth no other jurors to serve on the case. A lot of the prospective jurors

questioned were only too eager to point out prejudices that would gain them dismissal from jury duty.
Tatum had a suspicion that the high profile of the
case was scaring Phoenix citizens off—probably for
fear of retribution from Bobby's side of town.

During her brief lunch break Tatum found a se-
cluded chair in a corner of the courthouse. She
wanted nothing more than to lay her head back and
go to sleep. She and Jonathan had spent most of Saturday with her father, and she had returned by herself to pass most of Sunday sitting beside Jack's bed,
watching him sleep. He appeared to be holding his
own, for which Tatum was immensely thankful, but
the weekend had still taken its toll. She was exhausted.

"State your name, please." The judge's voice
boomed out for the sixteenth time that day. It was
four-thirty in the afternoon, and everyone, including
Judge Keedy, looked as if they'd rather be elsewhere.

"Lonnie Thomas."

Tatum did not like the sullen expression on the
young man's face.

"Where are you employed, Mr. Thomas?"

"I ain't."

"Have you ever been personally involved in a court
case?"

"Don't even remember, do ya? Ya send a guy's
mama down, and ya don't even remember. That's
rich." The man's face had contorted into an ugly
sneer.

"You may be excused," Judge Keedy repeated for the fifteenth time that day. "This court is adjourned until tomorrow morning."

The gavel sounded, ending the first day of the Rhodes murder trial, and only one of the twelve jurors had been selected to hear the case. Tatum wearily collected her papers and loaded her briefcase. They were in for a long week.

Half an hour later she was seated behind her desk, engrossed in the file spread out before her, when a burly hand suddenly materialized in front of her face. She jerked back, her heartbeat catching in her throat. Her pulse slowed only slightly when she shifted her gaze from the pink message slip in the hand beneath her nose to the stony face of the county supervisor.

"Mind telling me why you were checking up on a Lily Rhodes at St. Joseph's?" he demanded.

Tatum leaned back in her chair, using two fingers and a thumb from each hand to roll her pencil back and forth in front of her. She wasn't going to let him see her sweat.

"Possible suspect," she replied.

"A woman giving birth? You're really digging deep here, young woman." The man's tone of voice alone was intimidating.

"My job is to check out all of the alibis, sir. As you well know, the clue to closing a case is often found in the least expected places," she returned evenly.

Montgomery leaned both hands on Tatum's desk and pinned her with his steely gaze. "Just whose side are you on?'' he sneered. ''I have to admit I'm having severe doubts about *you*, McGillus, and your *ability* to do this job. With your daddy sitting in his cell, this office can't afford any more bad publicity. Have you forgotten what the press coverage on this case will mean to your career—to mine? Representative Stone has promised his constituents that justice will be upheld in this district, and he's using Bobby Rhodes to prove his point. He's got the whole world watching to see him succeed. And you are beginning to be more of a problem than an answer here. First you stall on the indictment, and then today you allow that Marcos woman on the jury. You got some attachment to the Rhodes family I don't know about, Prosecutor?''

Tatum held her calm expression throughout the man's accusations, refusing even to blink beneath his steely stare, but when he turned and left her office without even allowing her the chance to defend herself, her posture crumpled. The pencil broke between her fingers, and her hands began to shake. How much more could she take? She didn't doubt for a second that if she lost this case, Montgomery would petition for her removal from office. He had been looking for an excuse for months. And what would happen to her if he did? The thought terrified her. Was she strong enough to cope all alone?

Yet could she throw conscience and personal ethics to the dogs and possibly send an innocent man to jail? And if she did not, would she be allowing a murderer to walk free?

CHAPTER SEVEN

TATUM SKIPPED a due-notice appearance at one of the local malls that evening to go visit Jack. She found her father no worse, but no better, either. He slept almost the entire time she was there. The doctor was not around, having made his calls much earlier in the day, so there was no more news on Jack's condition. She finally left for home feeling more frustrated and helpless than ever.

And with every mile that brought her closer to her dark, empty house, she felt her tenuous grasp at composure slipping just a bit more. She didn't want to go home, to face all the demons waiting to attack her solitude. Nor did she want to spend the night lost in a strange motel room, with generic motifs mocking the emptiness in her heart. She thought of calling Jonathan. She wanted to call Jonathan—badly— which was precisely why she didn't. She was afraid to lean on him anymore, afraid of how badly she wanted to, afraid that she wouldn't be able to pick up the pieces when he chose his public over her.

Without having made a conscious decision to do so, she pulled into the parking lot of the Mexican restaurant around the corner from her house. She and her father had been there many times, to wind down after a rough day or to celebrate a closed case or a trial won. She would be uncomfortable sitting in the dining room all alone, but they had a small, intimate lounge where she could sit and order dinner without feeling conspicuous. She would be alone but surrounded by people having a good time. Maybe a little bit of their joie de vivre would wear off on her, at least for a little while.

"YOU WOULDN'T HAPPEN to have a light, would ya?" As come-ons went—and Tatum had had more than she cared to contemplate over the burrito special and single margarita she had consumed—this one was lousy. There were matches advertising the establishment in every unused ashtray in the room.

Tatum did not even turn in her seat to see what this particular pickup looked like, although she did like the easy way his voice washed over her. She shook her head, wondering if the margarita was affecting her more than she had thought.

"You want one?" the attractive male voice came again, this time just a little bit closer to her ear.

"No, thanks," Tatum answered, forcing herself not to turn around to see what he offered. All of the other invitations she had had that evening had been easy to turn down. There had been nothing about the men that had even remotely interested her. But she liked this man's voice. It did things to her.

It was obviously time to go home. She must be more worn-out than she thought if she was tempted to allow a total stranger to come on to her. She motioned to Joe, the waiter with whom she had been passing small talk for the past hour. But before she'd had a chance to catch his eye, the disembodied voice behind her started to speak again.

"I'll have a Chivas, straight, and one more of whatever the lady is having, please."

Tatum swiveled her seat around so fast the upholstered arm plowed into the thigh of her handsome suitor. His warm, strong hands reached out to catch her shoulders, holding her still before she could do him any further damage.

"Jonathan!" she exclaimed, hoping he couldn't tell just how desperately glad she was to see him. "You don't smoke, do you? So why did you ask me for a light?"

"'Cause I needed some light in my life," he joked. "So whaddya say, gonna share one of those seats?" He leaned over to murmur his question in her ear, as if he were suggesting a much more intimate liaison than a meal in a roomful of strangers.

Tatum smiled at his nonsense, and at the memory of another dinner they had shared, back when he had been as nonthreatening to her as Prince Charming. He was still holding her shoulders, and the warmth of his skin seeped through her clothes, reminding her of how very real he was. She gestured to the upholstered chair on the other side of her tiny table. "Unfortunately I've already eaten, but please, have a seat."

"Here you go, ma'am, sir," Joe said as he placed their drinks on a couple of little white napkins. "Do you want me to add it to your tab?" he asked, looking at Tatum.

"I've got this one," Jonathan said. Pulling a bill from his pocket, he handed it to the young man.

"Thank you, sir," Tatum said, thankful she was no longer sitting alone at the intimate little table for two.

Joe reached into his apron for the bills to count out Jonathan's change, and placed it on the table. "Can I get you anything to eat, sir?"

"I've had dinner, thanks," Jonathan said, sending the waiter on his way.

Tatum frowned. "You've had dinner?" she asked. If he had already eaten, then why was he in a restaurant? And even if he *had* come in for dinner, it suddenly seemed like way too much of a coincidence that he had chosen the very same restaurant she happened to be at. Though she knew it shouldn't, it made her feel good, really good, to think that maybe he had come looking for her. She was just too tired to fight with herself about it.

"How'd you find me?" she asked Jonathan while they sipped on their drinks. She was watching him in the mirrored wall beside their table. And she had to admit it—she was enjoying what she saw, too.

He shrugged, and his suited shoulders looked just perfect to her. "I drove by your house after the meeting at the mall, waited around long enough to get concerned and was just on my way to make some calls when I noticed your car parked outside here," he admitted.

"Oh." For a minute there, when he'd mentioned the meeting, Tatum's stomach had clenched. She felt a sense of déjà vu, remembering the other time she and Jonathan had shared an escape from duties and obligations, from the sometimes cold and cruel world. He was her friend. This was what they had agreed to that day outside the library—to be friends, occasional companions, laugh mates. It was only because she was so down that his presence tonight seemed to be so much more important than that.

"You look pretty today," Jonathan said as he studied their reflections in the mirror.

Tatum glanced at herself, saw the wrinkles in her red linen suit, a face almost devoid of makeup, hair that showed the signs of having had her restless fingers in it most of the night and figured that it was gentlemanly of him to lie so nicely.

"Thanks." She smiled back at his reflection. "You don't look so bad yourself."

He did look good. Too good. Temptingly good. He must have changed suits and shaved before going to the mall because he showed no signs of a day's worth of wear as she did. His lips were relaxed in a tolerant half grin. His brown eyes were warm and personal as they watched her watching him. And his hair—Tatum was tempted to run her fingers through the wavy mass, to bury them there and never let go. She would never have allowed herself to study him so intimately, but somehow watching his reflection in the mirror took away the threat he imposed and left her aware only of the desire that flared between them.

As if in a trance, she watched as the reflection of her hand moved slowly toward the reflection of Jonathan's head. She saw her fingers sink into the stylishly long strands of his hair, and as she watched, she felt the silky contact not only on her palm and the backs of her fingers, but in the shiver that ran up her arm, as well. She stared, as if caught in a time warp, and concentrated on the sensations she was experiencing between her fingers and down her back.

Finally, with her fingers still sliding slowly through his hair, her glance moved from the reflection of his hair to that of his eyes. He was watching her, and the teasing indulgence he'd been displaying since he had arrived had now turned into a wanting so intense, so necessary that she felt as if she were a part of him already. He didn't speak, didn't ask for or make declarations. And because of his inherent understanding, his willingness not to challenge the walls she had built, she wasn't frightened by the heat in his eyes, only satisfied.

She continued to look into the mirror as they once again communicated without words, falling deeper into the spell she had created, until Jonathan reached up to take hold of her hand. Gently he brought it down and held it in the middle of the round table between them. "I think we'd better go," he said, his voice not quite steady. He motioned for Joe to bring Tatum's tab.

Tatum tore her eyes away from the mirror and shuddered beneath the disappointing intrusion of reality. If only she had met Jonathan earlier. If only she weren't so afraid to take a chance. If only they didn't have the issue of due-notice standing between them. If only Pop hadn't murdered that bastard. If only Cale hadn't died. If only, if only, if only. The world was full of them—too full of them. Every muscle in her body felt tired as she added a generous tip to her bill and signed the credit-card slip.

Jonathan followed Tatum out to her car, a little concerned by her sudden change in mood. Sure, things had gotten a little hotter in there than either of them was comfortable with, but the awareness between them was nothing new. It was certainly no reason for the lines creasing Tatum's forehead or the stiffness in the lips that had been smiling so alluringly only moments before. A stiffness that, as he thought about it, had been present earlier when he had stood undetected in the doorway of the lounge watching her slumped shoulders and unsmiling face.

Jonathan knew she had a lot on her plate at the moment, with her father ill and the Rhodes trial in court, and he was frustrated with his inability to make things any easier for her. Almost as frustrated as he was with her stubbornness, her insistence on keeping him at arm's length.

"I'm glad you came," Tatum said, echoing words of another evening as he held open her car door and waited while she slid beneath the steering wheel.

The sincerity in her voice touched him more than anything else they had shared that evening. "I'm glad, too. Hold on a sec, I'll follow you home."

"That's not..."

He didn't wait to let Tatum finish her sentence, knowing full well she was about to refuse his offer to see her home. He wasn't going to give her that chance. Whether she knew it or not, she needed a friend—and as far he could tell, he was it. He quickly returned to his car and followed her out of the parking lot.

"How about an hour or two in front of the TV?" he suggested as soon as they met again in her driveway. He was ready for her refusal and ready to win her over—whichever came first. "It's time for 'Nick at Nite,'" he said, naming a popular sitcom rerun broadcast that played for several hours each night on a cable channel.

Jonathan knew how to play his cards right. He and Tatum didn't just have a tendency to overwork in common; they were both sitcom rerun fanatics, too. It was something they had discovered that first night at Monti's. There was nothing like a good dose of Donna Reed or Lucille Ball to relax with after a long day. Things in TV land always worked out so the good guys won.

It was a statement of just how tired Tatum really was when she simply nodded and let them both inside.

"Can I get you anything to drink?" she asked, shrugging out of her suit jacket and tossing it on the back of a kitchen chair.

"Just water," Jonathan said, wishing he dared walk over and rub the stiffness from her shoulders. "You feel okay?" he asked.

Tatum shrugged. "I'm just a little headachy. Nothing a good night's sleep won't cure," she said as she took two bottles of water out of the refrigerator, kicked off her shoes and wandered into the living room.

She put the bottles down on coasters on the coffee table, settled into one end of the couch, waited while he sat himself down at the other end and then tossed him the remote control.

"Dick Van Dyke, here we come," she said with an attempt at a grin.

Jonathan wasn't fooled. Either Tatum was not sleeping worth a darn or she was sicker than she was admitting. She looked ready to collapse.

He watched her covertly over the next half hour and was glad to see that by the time Patty Duke was trying to convince everyone that she was her identical cousin Cathy, the lines between Tatum's brows had softened considerably.

He stared at Patty Duke's pert little face, but all he saw was the fire in Tatum's eyes as her gaze had held his in the mirror that evening. Sighing faintly, he thought of the kiss they had shared weeks ago in the front seat of his Bronco. Patty was getting ready for a date with her steady boyfriend, football hero and food-a-holic, Richard. Jonathan was remembering all of the talks he and Tatum had had—the times when just hearing her voice made him feel as if the weight of the world were being lifted from his shoulders. Maybe it was time to see if she was ready to accept what he wanted, more than anything, to give her.

Patty and Richard were back from their date to the malt shop, snuggling on a porch swing, dreaming about their future. Patty slipped her arm through the crook in Richard's elbow, getting closer to him. Jonathan remembered Tatum's fingers running through his hair that evening, her touch as intimate as a lover's. Patty sighed and gazed in Richard's eyes, her innocence an invitation in itself. Jonathan saw again the hunger in Tatum's eyes as their reflection had met his—the honest, open, unconcealed hunger. Richard leaned slowly toward Patty, his intention as clear as his hesitation. Patty was holding her breath, about to receive what she had been wanting more than anything, afraid that Richard would change his mind before she got it.

Jonathan had had enough. He turned to pull Tatum across the couch and into his arms—to convince her that what they had together was much more real than any mirrored image, any television show. Tatum was asleep.

TATUM WOKE UP completely disoriented. For a moment she wasn't quite sure where she was, until her eyes focused on the familiar shadows of her bedroom. But confusion still rankled her. Her last memory was of settling down with Jonathan to watch a little mindless TV. So how had she ended up in bed, half-undressed by the feel of things, with a peculiar warmth against her left side? Afraid to move too quickly, Tatum slowly turned to look at the left side of her bed. She wasn't really surprised when she saw Jonathan lying there, sound asleep.

She knew he had been worried about her. Heck, she had been worried about herself a time or two over the past couple of days. Too many days with too little sleep had finally taken their toll. She was more thankful than Jonathan would ever know that he had been there to help her get through the evening. She had actually slept for several hours straight—a deep, dreamless, strength-giving sleep.

She considered for a moment that something might have happened that she should be aware of, but she quickly dismissed the idea. Jonathan would never take advantage of an unconscious woman, and besides, her body didn't feel at all sated. The familiar aching feeling was stronger than ever.

Tatum tried hard not to be aware of the heat radiating from Jonathan's body beside hers, but she couldn't help but wonder just what he had on under the covers he was sharing with her. Surely he hadn't gone to bed in his suit. Her eyes wandered around her room then, coming to rest on the chair in front of her vanity. Sure enough, his suit was hanging over the chair—the same way he had hung his clothes in the motel room last Friday night. His T-shirt was there, too, but she could not make out any briefs—or did he wear boxer shorts? More to the point, was he wearing them now?

As her thoughts continued to travel along the path of Jonathan's well-developed body, Tatum had a flash of their last moments in the lounge. She and Jonathan had made love with their eyes, and it had felt more right than any physical union she'd ever known before. He hadn't asked her to give up a part of herself, only to take the satisfaction he was offering. She would not have to love him—only to share a beautiful experience with him. Whether either of them had room for commitment in their lives or not, they were still adults with adult needs. Was she being a fool to deny them both the release they so obviously needed? What could possibly be wrong about one friend satisfying another?

But making a rational, logical decision to embark on a physical adventure with Jonathan was a different thing from actually doing something about it. Tatum lay stiff and silent in her bed, afraid to move for fear of disturbing the man lying so dangerously close to her.

Eventually her stillness paid off, and her body relaxed enough to allow her to drift back to sleep....

The next time she awoke, dusky light was bathing the room with predawn intimacy. Tatum didn't have to turn to see if Jonathan was still there. His hands were roaming lightly over her, speaking to her body in a continuation of the silent conversation she had started in the mirror the night before.

His strokes were gentle yet sure as he slowly explored her body. Tatum pictured again the way he had looked at her the previous evening. Jonathan obviously saw something in her that she hadn't even known she possessed, and she wondered, if she could just ride out the storm with him, if someday he would help her to see it, too. She wanted to believe in that possibility.

He touched her hip through the silk of her slip and rested his palm there for a long moment, warming her, allowing his heat to infiltrate her. Tatum could no longer hold back the needy moan that had been caught in her throat since she had first awakened.

She looked up at him then, thrilled by the broad shoulders she saw looming over her, the lips that were slightly parted, the eyes that were looking at her as if at that particular moment, she was the only thing necessary to his living.

"Touch me," he demanded hoarsely. And then again he said, "Touch me, Tatum. Touch me like you did last night, like you can't help yourself. Like you want this as badly as I do."

Tatum glanced back down to his body, to the chest covered in taunting black curls. She could not have fought her desire for him then even if she'd wanted to. It was as if some primal instinct had taken over and she could do nothing but blindly follow its dictates.

She was drowning in desire, but still she hesitated. Not because she wanted to deny him anything, but because she was afraid of the power she would unleash if she touched him. She had wanted him for so long and fought it so hard that she now had the feeling the heavens had opened up before her and the flood of her wanting was crashing forward to consume her. What if she was getting in deeper than she realized?

"There are many forms of loving, honey," Jonathan murmured as she lay still beside him. "Committing yourself heart and soul to one individual is one of them, but not the only one—not even the only right one. Due to circumstances beyond our control, you and I share another kind of closeness, but that doesn't make it any less special," he continued.

His hand lay still on her hip. He didn't pull back, but he didn't force her forward, either. Even now the choice was up to her. The waves of longing were crashing relentlessly toward the shore, and Tatum was afraid there was simply no turning back. They had waited too long, come too far.

"Is it so bad to seek comfort in whatever way you can find it?" Jonathan's words brought her gaze back up to his. And as their glances came together once again, the gates opened completely, sweeping aside any doubts that remained.

Slowly, of their own will, Tatum's hands moved up from the bed toward Jonathan's body. She buried her fingers in his hair, as she had done the night before, but this time she was ready to follow through on her promise. "I want you," she whispered plainly. "I want you so much it hurts."

Jonathan studied her for another, very brief second, and then, apparently satisfied with what he saw, what he heard, he moved his mouth down to cover hers. His first kiss was restrained, as if he, too, respected the power of their coming together. The instant their lips made contact, they both knew the choice was no longer theirs to make. They were both too hungry.

She opened her lips to his, seeking a deeper, more intimate contact, and then met his demanding tongue with an urgency too long denied. She strained against him, needing to be a part of him so desperately that the kiss was almost painful, and still she couldn't get enough.

"You're so beautiful... so fine," Jonathan whispered in between kisses. His hunger made her feel cherished. He devoured her lips and then left them to place worshipful kisses across her eyes, down her face and over her neck. His tongue trailed across her throat, leaving tingles of need in its wake, and then he moved up to her ear. "You are the stuff of my dreams, lady."

There were no words of love spoken, no false promises made, just honest declarations that could be given and received without fear.

"I do want you, Jonathan," Tatum whispered. And from that moment on the fate of the next several hours was sealed.

Whereas moments before Tatum had been unable to move, to touch Jonathan, now she couldn't keep her hands still. She explored his face, his shoulders, thrilling in the masculine strength she felt in him. She curled her fingers in the springy black hair matted across his chest and smoothed the skin of his back beneath her palms. Her lips left kisses all along his neck as she tasted his skin for the first time. She inhaled his musky scent and knew that she had found her anchor in the storm.

Her body quivered under his masterful hands as he took his turn exploring. He caressed her arms, her back, her shoulders, paying tribute to each part of her. He slid his hands down her sides, leaving a path of desire behind him as he found each rib and followed it to its source. Tatum felt completely feminine and wholly cherished as she lay beneath him.

He placed his hand over her heart and held it there, as if protecting her most tender of organs, and then slowly, so slowly she was afraid she was going to go crazy with anticipation, he cupped her breast beneath her slip. Tatum's wandering hands stilled as she became consumed by the pleasure he was giving her. First one nipple and then the other clamored under his skillful fingers, until the two hardened tips were aching for his kiss.

Jonathan slid his hands farther down her body, finding the bottom of her slip and pulling it slowly upward. He viewed each part of Tatum's body as it was revealed to him, his ardor so naked that she felt shy with him for the first time. First her thighs and then her hips were exposed to him, and she saw him studying the triangle of lace and cotton that covered the dark curls of her womanhood. A sharp pool of desire surged within her under his gaze, and she wriggled beneath him, urging him on.

She felt a rush of cool air against her belly and sucked in a quick breath as her breasts were bared to the early-morning light. Jonathan's palm was already caressing one of them even before she'd slid free of her undergarment. As soon as she was able, Tatum looked down her body with eyes adjusted to the semidarkness and watched as Jonathan's strong, masculine fingers explored its contours. Her nipples responded to his gentle pulling, hardening for him again beneath his watchful stare. Jonathan glanced up and caught her watching her own response to him, and she could see his face tense up with increasing desire.

"Do you like watching me touch you?" he whispered, pinning her with his passionate stare.

Tatum looked down her body once again, burning even hotter at the sight of his hands on her. She nodded.

"Do you want to see more?" he asked huskily. His throat sounded as dry as hers felt. She nodded a second time, her gaze locked firmly with his.

Jonathan pushed the covers off the bed, revealing not only Tatum's near-naked body, but his own, as well. Tatum fixed her gaze on his hairy thighs for several tense seconds before raising her eyes enough to see the bulge of his masculinity beneath his briefs. Jonathan hooked his thumbs on either side of his underpants and, lifting his hips off the bed, pulled them down. She watched him, marveling at the firmness of his buttocks, the denseness of the dark hair matted between his legs, and finally, the swollen evidence of his desire for her.

Dropping his briefs on the floor, Jonathan reached for her hand, brought it down to surround him and squeezed once, as though to embed her touch there forever. She felt him quiver beneath her touch, but he didn't demand any further gratification just then. Instead, he slowly removed the one piece of clothing still left between them.

The scent of their mutual desire was stronger now, mingling between them, telling a story all its own. Completely naked, completely oblivious of anything but Jonathan, Tatum lay with him, trusting him completely.

At Jonathan's intimate but gentle touch, Tatum writhed with impatience. They had waited so long; so much had happened before that Tatum no longer had the patience for slow explorations. She needed Jonathan to complete them now, and in her womanly way, she let him know.

She saw him reach for his wallet where he had left it on her nightstand, and waited for him to protect them both, thankful that she had not needed to ask.

She was as ready as he was when he lowered himself between her legs, tested himself against her and then plunged inside her with one heavy thrust. He attempted to hold himself still once her womanhood cradled him completely, but once again Tatum urged him on. She did not need consideration nearly as much as she needed fulfillment. She wanted Jonathan's loving completely.

He set a quick pace for their communion, taking her body to the very edges of consciousness, and Tatum rode along eagerly, surging forward to the release they needed so desperately to give each other. And when it came, she cried out his name over and over again, wanting him to know that it was he and only he who could take her to such a glorious place. She felt him empty himself within her and rode a renewed series of spasms with his until they both lay spent, still joined together, in each other's arms.

A few blissful minutes later, Jonathan took his weight off Tatum and rolled over to his side. Before long they were both asleep. No words were needed to add to what they had just shared. It had all been said, most exquisitely, without words.

CHAPTER EIGHT

TATUM HAD TO MISS another due-notice meeting to be in court on Wednesday. She knew Jonathan was setting up shop outside a grocery store on the west side of town, but she had the selection of a jury to oversee. Seven jurors had already been chosen. Relieved that progress was being made at last, she couldn't help but be aware that the sooner the jury was found, the sooner she would have to prosecute Bobby Rhodes.

"State your name," Judge Keedy ordered once again. Tatum wondered if the man said the words in his sleep, as well. That could get him into trouble with his wife, she thought wryly.

"Travis Sutherland."

"What is your occupation, Mr. Sutherland?"

"I am independently wealthy," the young man stated arrogantly.

Tatum glanced over toward Bobby in time to see the disgusted look that flashed across his face. Bobby came across as the type of man who would put in an honest day's work even if he were a billionaire. He commanded more respect in his clean but obviously old street clothes than Sutherland did with his hand-tailored wardrobe. *And what good are those thoughts going to do you, Prosecutor?*

"Are you married?" the judge continued.

"I've managed to evade that respectable state to date," Sutherland said with a practiced grin.

"Have you ever been personally involved in a court case?"

"Of course not."

"Are you aware of any personal prejudices that may impede you from turning in a fair verdict on this case?"

"I pride myself on being open-minded," Sutherland stated, tilting his head upward as he issued a rote statement he had obviously delivered many times before. Not once did he even deign to glance Bobby's way.

The man was as snobbish as they came, Tatum thought, and she would bet her life that he looked down with pitiful scorn at people less fortunate than he, people like Bobby Rhodes, who had not had his chances in life. Bobby would not have a fair trial with a man like that choosing his fate. People like Travis Sutherland automatically assumed that if a man came from a certain part of town, he was guilty.

Tatum waited for Counselor Duncan, Bobby's attorney, to have Sutherland dismissed. And then she remembered that the other lawyer had already used all of the dismissals allotted to him. She deliberated for one short second before rising from her chair. She had one dismissal left. "You may be excused," she addressed the prospective juror.

She heard an impatient snort behind her and turned just in time to catch the tail end of Montgomery's angry glare. She held her chin up, refusing to cower beneath him. She was doing nothing wrong. She was not so desperate to win this trial that she would compromise her ethics and play sleazy lawyer games in order to do so. If she was going to get Bobby Rhodes, she was going to do so by the books, or she might as well turn in her license to practice law and start looking for a waitressing job some place. She had sworn to uphold the constitution when she had passed the bar exam, and one of its major dictates was that everyone in the United States was entitled to a fair trial. If she couldn't win this one fairly, then she didn't deserve to win at all.

Montgomery turned in disgust and stalked out of the courtroom.

TATUM'S PHONE WAS ringing when she returned to her office later that afternoon. She dropped her things in a heap on the desk and hurried to answer it.

"Tatum? It's Mandy," the teenager said in response to her breathless greeting.

Tatum slid one hip onto the edge of her desk. "Hi, hon, what's up?" she asked, glad to hear the teenager's voice.

"Couple of things," Mandy admitted with little of her usual cheer.

Tatum frowned. "Something wrong?"

"Not really. I really just called to invite you to dinner tonight."

"What time?"

"Cook's taking the night off, so some of the kids and I are going to be making chili. Jonathan said to plan dinner for around seven. Is that okay with you?"

Tatum did some quick calculating. She still had time to get to the prison by five, have an hour with Pop and just about make it back in time.

"Sure, hon, sounds good. Now, what else is on your mind?" Tatum asked. Mandy just wasn't her usual optimistic self.

"'Due notice.'" The answer surprised Tatum.

"And?" she prompted.

"Jonathan's collecting a lot of signatures all of a sudden, and I'm getting worried. He spoke at some big business gathering last night, but he didn't say anything about it until it was all said and done, almost like he didn't want me to know—so you couldn't be there or something. And those are the kind of people with influence."

Tension gripped Tatum. Was she letting her guard down? With the trial and Pop's heart attack, and yes, becoming Jonathan's lover, she had given little thought to the due-notice question over the past few days. She had seen Jonathan again the previous night—the whole night—and he had said nothing at all about the meeting. Was that because they had agreed not to discuss the issue during their private time? Or had he finally realized the damage she could do to his campaign and deliberately avoided telling her? Despite their relationship, he was going to do what he had to do to win his fight. Tatum knew that. His public came first.

"Don't worry, Mandy. He's a long way from home yet, and we'll just have to step up our end of things. I'm not going to let you down or Pop, either," she vowed, meaning every word she said. It was time to do a little propagandizing of her own. "Think you could do some typing for me?" she asked.

"Sure. What do you need?" Mandy asked, sounding better already.

"I'll rough out a letter, explaining our stand, and get together a list of addresses of some of the prominent people in this town. Think you could prepare the letters and send them out?"

"Sure!" Mandy's exuberant tones made Tatum smile.

The telephone was ringing when Tatum flew through her front door a few minutes later, but she ignored it, rushing into her office to collect the supplies she needed to take to Mandy. She listened while her answering machine clicked on and played her brief message. She was on her way back out again when Jonathan's voice came into the room.

"Hi, honey. Just thought I'd try to catch you on the way to see Jack. Mandy says you're coming here afterward, and I wondered if you wanted some company on the drive. Sorry to have missed you. I do miss you. See you in a couple of hours. B—"

Tatum grabbed up the phone. "Jonathan?" she asked, out of breath, hoping she was in time.

"You're there!"

"Mm-hmm." Tatum smiled at the genuine pleasure in his voice. Jonathan would not do anything deliberately to hurt her. Maybe last night's meeting had been a last-minute thing. He could have mentioned it afterward, of course, but surely his failure to do so was just because he was honoring their agreement not to bring due-notice into their private lives.

"You just get home?" His husky baritone sent chills of remembered sensual pleasure over her shoulders and down her back.

"Just leaving," Tatum admitted, "but I could swing by to get you. Are you at the center?"

"I'm at home and I'll be waiting," he promised, reminding her to drive safely before he rang off.

IT HAD BEEN less than a week since Jonathan had seen Jack McGillus, but the older man seemed to have aged ten years and lost most of his bravado. Tatum had not even mentioned the change. Jonathan wondered whether it was because she had been seeing her father every day and so she hadn't noticed or because she was even now, refusing to lean on him even a little bit.

There was another man with Jack—another prisoner, judging by the way he was dressed. Jack lay back, seeming to struggle for each breath as the other man read aloud to him from a newspaper.

"Jonathan, good to see you," Jack wheezed when Jonathan walked hand in hand with Tatum toward the bed. Alarmed to find the older man's grip nonexistent, Jonathan pumped the limp hand anyway and then gently placed it back against the covers.

"It's good to see you, too, sir," Jonathan admitted, wishing he could have known Tatum's father before circumstances and fate had taken his vitality away.

"This's Jim Marsh," Jack said, motioning toward the other prisoner with a barely perceptible nod. Jonathan turned to shake hands with the other man, curious about the man's presence in Jack's room. He had been under the impression that security measures had been taken to protect the ex-detective from the prison's other inmates.

"Jim's been cleared to visit with Pop," Tatum explained, smiling at the older man. "Besides Danny and the doctors, he's the only other person Pop ever sees. Jim, this is Senator Jonathan Wright."

Jim returned Jonathan's handshake. "Never met a real live senator before," he said with a smile, showing the gap between his two front teeth. "I guess I'll be going now that you're here, Ms. McGillus. Nice to meet you, Senator." With his tongue sucking against his teeth, Jim left the three of them alone.

"How's your day been, girlie?" Jack asked Tatum slowly, his breath labored. His eyes were still sharp, though, as they settled on his raven-haired daughter.

"Pretty good, Pop," Tatum reported. "We've just about picked the jury." She told her father, revealing what little was ethically allowed about her day in court.

Jack was silent then, glancing from Tatum to Jonathan and back again. His gaze settled on their interlocked hands just before his tired eyes drifted shut.

Tatum thought Pop had fallen asleep until he startled her by speaking suddenly—disjointed, breathless words that were difficult to catch. "Got anything personal to tell me, girlie?" His eyes remained closed, but Tatum smiled anyway.

"Nope," she said mischievously, figuring that joined hands told Jack anything he needed to know.

Jack nodded, seemingly content with the answer, and turned his head away. Tatum pulled away from Jonathan and, settling herself in one of the two armchairs in the room, pulled a yellow pad out of the bag she had carried in with her.

"What ya' workin' on?" Jack asked sleepily from the bed.

Jonathan was surprised to see that the man's eyes were open again so soon. He pulled the remaining chair up closer to the bed, in case Jack wanted to talk.

"Just some overdue correspondence," Tatum answered vaguely. She continued to write.

Jonathan glanced over to see her head bent over the pad in her lap. Her beautifully free long hair formed a veil around her, falling down to the paper on which she was scribbling furiously. It reminded him of the night before, when the sexy dark strands had fallen down to his chest in much the same way. Tatum had not been bending over him, though—she had been lying on top of him. He pulled himself up abruptly when he realized where his thoughts were leading.

"She's a good girl, despite the mess her pop made of his life," Jack breathed out slowly, his voice barely audible, as he caught Jonathan watching Tatum.

Jonathan leaned in closer to the bed. "I don't doubt that, sir," he stated without hesitation. "I have an idea her pop's a good man himself," he added just as sincerely.

"I did wrong," Jack said distinctly.

Jonathan had been sitting beside sickbeds all over the world since he was old enough to sit still, and he recognized Jack's need to confess, to be heard, to be rid of the guilt. He pulled his chair closer so that Jack wouldn't need to struggle so hard to be heard.

"It was so hard...my son...murdered...gone. Tatum...it took so long to see her smile...again. But slowly...she started to.... And then the letter came.... He was free.... My...son's...murderer...was...free, and they...had to...tell us.... No reason...just tell us."

Jack started to tremble as his watery hazel eyes took on a distant stare. "The bitterness...like bile...for

Tatum, too... I watched it eat away...at her.... You can't expect a man...to live with that.... His family's been wronged...it's his job to right wrongs.... I kept seeing his hands...young, healthy...capable hands...driving a car...holding a woman...when Cale couldn't.... They didn't let us...live in peace... I had to make...my own peace...." The words trailed off as Jack's eyes drifted shut. His wrinkled face relaxed in a semblance of the peace he claimed to have found as he drifted off to sleep.

Jonathan dropped his chin to his chest as Jack's words thundered inside his head. *The letter came... the letter came....* Had Jack received a due-notice letter? Had that letter been the prompt that had sent the older man to prison, rather than a premeditated act of revenge that Jonathan and the press had always assumed was responsible? Jonathan felt his stomach grow queasy as the realization washed over him. If circumstances had been different, this old man could have been his father-in-law, yet he was lying in a prison infirmary because of due-notice.

How many more people like Jack were out there? How many people, unable to fix the problem as Jack had done, were slowly dying from bitterness? And yet how many others would die without the protection by due-notice?

Jonathan glanced toward Tatum's silent figure in the corner of the room, wondering if she had heard her father's broken words. And then it hit him. This was why she was fighting his bill—and why she was going to fight it to the death. She had to. *Why hadn't she told him?*

And what would he have done about it if she had? What could he do about it now? Should he drop the bill? Should he let her and her pop, and others like them, rest in peace?

Jonathan wanted to make her happy, to take some of the suffering from her shoulders, but he had others to consider, as well. He had Mandy and little Abby and dozens of others just like them. Their lives could very well depend on the passage of his bill. Slowly he shook his head, watching sadly while Tatum's pen flew silently across the yellow legal pad.

THE DRIVE BACK to Phoenix was a tense one. Tatum answered quite congenially whenever Jonathan spoke to her, and even initiated a couple of mundane conversations herself, but as usual, when it came to something that mattered deeply to her, she was not communicating. He knew she had to be concerned about her father. He also had a pretty good suspicion that she had heard her father's words. She knew he now understood what the defeat of his bill meant to her.

He cursed silently when he glanced over at her impassive expression and had no clue as to what she was thinking. Was she ever going to share anything other than her body with him? And if she did, could he make her happy?

The proposed due-notice legislation should not have to come between them. He had meant it when he said that the law was for the people, and it was up to them to decide its outcome one way or another. But now he was forced to admit that it was a personal issue, as well. Tatum had deep personal reasons for fighting the impending law, and Jonathan had just as deep a need to see it pass. As hard as he tried, he couldn't find a way for them both to win.

Jonathan knew that the evening was not going to get any better as soon as he ushered Tatum inside the front door of the center. Mandy was sitting at the reception desk, and her terse expression warned him right away that something was not to her liking. She was wearing the stiff upper lip and jutted chin with which she warded off pain. It was a look Jonathan had come to dread.

"Detective Charles called," she said flatly as he and Tatum approached. "They've found Abby's mother. She's agreed to give up custody. A social worker will be coming by to take Abby to a foster home."

Jonathan's gut wrenched as he realized what the future was probably going to hold for little Abby—a series of families who might or might not want her, none of them to call her own. And her inability to speak was only going to make things that much rougher on her. He knew how upset Mandy must be at the news, but he also knew the teenager was going to keep her distress to herself. No matter how Jonathan tried, he had not yet been able to help Mandy to share her pain. Sometimes he wondered if he was doing the right thing by allowing her to work at the center, being a part of all that went on.

"Where is she?" he asked, wondering how Abby was taking the news.

"In the rec room. She doesn't know yet. I was waiting for you two."

"I'll go get her," Tatum said, speaking for the first time since they had come in the door. She hurried off down the hall.

Jonathan approached the reception desk, dropped his keys and reached out to run one hand along Mandy's blond hair. "You okay?" he asked, watching for any sign of emotion on the girl's pretty face.

She looked down at another message she had taken, signed her name and the time in the appropriate blanks and dropped it in Cinci's slot. "Sure," she said with a shrug.

"Mandy..."

But before Jonathan could do more than form the girl's name, she was out of her seat, heading across the room. "I'll go collect her things," she announced on her way down the hall. "She should at least have a familiar nightgown with her to sleep in."

With his hands resting helplessly in his pockets, Jonathan let her go. Sometimes he wondered why he thought he could help these kids.

Tatum came walking down the hall a moment later with Abby clutching her hand. The little girl was dressed in the inevitable denim shorts and T-shirt that seemed to be the standard donations to the center. Jonathan moved forward and bent down in front of the little girl.

"You're going to have a new home, Abby," he explained, not jovially but with a show of optimism. "Some nice people want you to live with them so they can try to make you happy. Will you let them try?" he asked, not even considering what he would do if she said no. He just knew that the easiest way for anybody to handle changes in life was to feel as though the decision came from within.

Agreeable as always, Abby nodded. Jonathan wanted to explain to her that things would be better for her from now on—that she would never again have to live in a place like the abandoned trailer where she had been found—but he honestly didn't know what her future held and he wasn't going lie to her. If she ever needed him or the center again in the future, he wanted her to trust him enough to come back, or at least not to resist if she ever had to be brought back.

The front door opened behind him, and he heard Sylvia Reynolds' cheery "Hello" with a mixture of resignation and feeble hope. His eyes met Tatum's once, briefly, before he acknowledged Sylvia, but the one look was enough. Tatum understood. He turned to face the social worker.

"Sylvia, come in," Jonathan welcomed just as Mandy returned carrying a brown paper bag.

"Jonathan, Mandy," Sylvia greeted with a smile, looking curiously from Tatum to Abby.

"Hi, Sylvia. This is Tatum McGillus, a friend of ours, and this is Abby," Mandy said.

Sylvia stood with them for a couple of minutes, making small talk, while allowing Abby to get used to her a little bit, and then bent to the child.

"Ready to go?" she asked, holding out her hand.

Abby put her little hand in Sylvia's, but her chin quivered just a tiny bit. It was the first emotion any of them had seen from the little girl since her advent into their lives. Jonathan felt his throat tighten up.

Mandy stepped forward. "Here're her things. Just a gown and some underwear," she said, handing Sylvia the bag.

"Thanks." Sylvia took the bag and looked down at Abby with a friendly smile. "Say goodbye, Abby, and tell these nice people thank-you for taking such good care of you," she said.

Mandy leaned forward to give the girl a hug, but Jonathan noticed that she held her body apart as much as she could. When she straightened, her gaze rested somewhere over Abby's shoulder, as if she was just waiting for it all to be over with. Abby looked from Mandy to Tatum and Jonathan, then back to Mandy again. Tears pooled in her big blue eyes and began to stream silently down her cheeks.

"Bye-bye, Mandy," she said suddenly in the tiniest voice Jonathan had ever heard.

He saw Mandy jerk when she heard the little tinkle of Abby's farewell, but her expression remained impassive. "Bye, Abby," she replied, her gaze directed toward the bag containing Abby's belongings.

Mandy had to be elated at the milestone that had just taken place. Abby's speech was a godsend for the little girl. Her chances of being placed in a permanent home, of becoming part of a supportive family, had just improved tremendously. And yet Mandy, who loved the child probably more than anyone on earth at the moment, had not even cracked a smile. She kept her joy all bottled up with her pain, as if she couldn't release one without feeling the other. Jonathan grew more concerned.

Tatum leaned forward to give Abby a quick hug, and then it was Jonathan's turn. Just as quickly as she had arrived, Sylvia left, taking a small part of their hearts with her in the little girl by her side. Mandy turned to leave the room as soon as the front door clicked back into place. At a loss for how to reach her, Jonathan didn't try to stop her.

"Mandy." Tatum's voice sounded with authority from just behind him.

Jonathan swung around in time to see her frown as she gazed at the teenager's departing back.

Even more surprising was the instantaneous response she elicited from Mandy. The girl turned, apparently saw something in Tatum's eyes that spoke to her in a way Jonathan's words had never been able to do and ran to her as if all the demons she had ever carried were at her back. Tatum's arms opened and caught Mandy as the teenager threw herself against Tatum's body, and the two women held each other firmly while sobs shook Mandy's body.

Jonathan had the feeling he was out of place, that a communion was taking place in which he could not be a part, but as he turned quietly and left the room, he felt the beginnings of a smile tug at his lips. For someone who thought she didn't have anything left to give, Tatum sure did a good job of it....

CHAPTER NINE

"LOCK UP, will you, Jonathan? I need a hot bath," Tatum said as she pushed open the front door. She stepped wearily into the house, through her living room and down the hall toward her bedroom without as much as a glance back in his direction.

Jonathan had half a mind to be irritated that they had only been lovers for three days and already she was taking him for granted, but in truth he was pleased—too pleased to stifle the smile that spread across his face. If this was domesticity, he had sacrificed more than he thought by choosing his unusual path in life.

He took his time locking up, enjoying the contentment of knowing that he was settling them in for the night. Pulling his tie loose, he turned off the living-room light Tatum had left burning and was about to follow her down the hall when he decided to make a small detour to the kitchen. If he wasn't mistaken, there was still something left of the wine they had shared the previous night.

He arrived in the bedroom a few moments later, carrying two fluted wineglasses filled to the halfway mark with White Zinfandel. Hearing the tub filling in the adjoining bathroom, Jonathan set the glasses down on one of the nightstands and sat down on Tatum's queen-size bed to slip off his shoes. He placed his socks inside them and then stood up to unfasten the buttons at his waistband. The sound of running water stopped, and the silence was followed by a delicate splash as Tatum sat down in the tub. Jonathan pulled his shirt over his head, undid the buttons of his slacks and eased himself out of them.

The water in the next room splashed lightly, and Jonathan pictured the liquid cascading over Tatum's glorious breasts, the tightening of her nipples. Wearing only his briefs, he picked up the wineglasses and padded into the next room.

The sight that greeted him was even more exciting than what he had been imagining. Tatum lay immersed in the brimming tubful of water, completely covered by a pool of sparkling white bubbles. Her eyes were closed, and the look on her face was almost serene. Jonathan had never been so aroused in his life.

Setting the glasses down on the counter by the sink, he moved quietly toward the tub. Her eyes remained closed as he crouched by the side of the bath. Jonathan's first thought was to plunge right into the water with her and, with a few fierce thrusts, relieve the burning that she had lit within him. But he didn't.

Instead, he trailed his finger through the bubbles, searching for and finding the sensitive softness of her nipple. With her eyes still closed, Tatum strained toward him, slowly pushing herself more fully within his reach. Her nipple teased his palm. Jonathan's erection strained painfully against his briefs, and he inhaled a long, deep breath in a vain attempt to calm his ardor.

The steamy scent of roses that filled the room went straight to his head, making him feel more intoxicated than if he had polished off the entire bottle of wine he had left back in the kitchen. He raised his other hand to her unattended breast. The bubbles tickled his palm as he gently squeezed them, and still Tatum did not open her eyes. He had barely touched the water, yet he felt wet all over, sweating from the exertion it took him to keep from hauling her up out of the bathtub.

"I've never seen anything so gorgeous," he whispered hoarsely as he watched the darkness of his skin, surrounded by the brightness of the bubbles, move against her in stark relief. Tatum moaned deliciously, dropping her head back as she lifted herself up to him, placing herself more firmly within his reach, trusting him implicitly, giving herself to him unconditionally, if only for the moment. The water jostled gently against her as Jonathan leaned down to kiss first one distended nipple and then the other, sucking at her until she was squirming beneath him. The taste of her skin, diluted by the water lapping around her was to Jonathan the sweetest nectar.

He trailed his fingers farther into the water, grazing across her ribs to the flat softness of her belly. He laid his palm across the sleek skin there for a moment, as if he could somehow discover the secrets that lay within her, then moved on to the dark, triangular shadow that was barely visible through the bubbles. His absorption was complete. There was nothing but the tinkling of water, the sweet smell of bubble bath pervading the room and Tatum.

She spread her legs to him without prompting and lay back with her eyes still shut. He gazed at her with renewed ardor, the liquid heat pulsing through him almost more than he could bear. He slid one hand beneath the water and fondled her curls, running his fingers through them before exploring what they concealed.

Tatum writhed beneath his ministrations, expelling little sighs of satisfaction as he slipped inside her, withdrew and slipped back in again. He could feel her tightening around his fingers, the water splashing over the sides of the tub as she moved her hips in time with his thrusts.

He held still within her during the seemingly endless waves of her release. And finally, as her last convulsion subsided, Tatum opened her eyes. She looked up at him even while his fingers were still inside her tight cocoon, her smokey blue eyes filled with an emotion he did not dare put a name to. Slowly he left her.

"You're a special man, Jonathan Wright," she whispered.

"Not nearly as special as the woman I'm looking at," he countered, his raspy voice betraying the need he'd been holding in check.

Tatum stood up. Leaving the water with two delicate splashes, she lay down beside him on the carpeted floor and pulled him toward her. Needing no further encouragement, he stepped out of his briefs, sidled up to her wet body and covered her lips with his own. She tasted faintly of mint, as if she had brushed her teeth before getting in the bath, and Jonathan would have been content to sup at her that way for the rest of his life.

Tatum had other ideas, though. She reached between them and guided him home. After his long wait, Jonathan's pleasure was over almost as soon as it began, his explosion was accompanied by her cries of pleasure.

They climbed into the tub together afterward, leisurely soaping each other's tired bodies. A few blissful minutes later they got out of the tub, dried each other off with fluffy yellow towels and fell into bed. They were asleep in minutes.

The fluted glasses remained untouched on the sink where Jonathan had left them. Due-notice, Bobby Rhodes and Abby Gressner were all cares of a different world, far, far away.

OVER THE NEXT TWO WEEKS, Tatum alternated between gaining sustenance from her memories of that night in the bath with Jonathan and trying to dispel them. Pop was still hanging on, and though he wasn't showing any noticeable improvement, the doctor continued to assure Tatum that the longer Jack held on, the better were his chances for recovery. It was during the long hours she spent in the infirmary, watching her father sleep, that Tatum took comfort from the feelings that Jonathan had awakened within her.

She had seen him pop in and out of the courthouse several times during those two weeks, and in spite of her doubts about him—about them—Tatum found herself wanting his moral support. She still couldn't bring herself to confide in him about her doubts of her ability to convict Bobby Rhodes, but she could no longer deny that his presence was the brightest spot in her life.

The complete jury for the Rhodes' case had finally been chosen, and Tatum spent several days calling witnesses to the stand to present the background facts of the case to the court, establishing the time and cause of death and the deceased's relationship with the defendant. Troy Duncan turned out to be a better lawyer than he had first seemed, and his uncanny cross-examination left shadows of doubt lingering in the air. Montgomery was beginning to growl like a caged tiger. Tatum had to do something—fast.

She arrived in the courtroom fifteen minutes early on Friday of that second week, with only a couple more cards to play. She could only hope that the jury would find one of the cards an ace. Jonathan had said he would try to be there, and she watched anxiously for his lean figure to appear in the doorway.

"All rise."

Tatum stood as the bailiff called the courtroom to order and introduced Judge Keedy just as he had been doing twice a day since they had begun impaneling the jury eighteen days earlier.

"Be seated."

Tatum smoothed the back of her summer gray suit as she slid back into her seat. Montgomery sat next to her, his stiff countenance a constant warning to her to come through or else. The back door squeaked as someone came in late, and Tatum couldn't resist a quick peek over her shoulder in hopes that Jonathan had been able to keep his word. Her stomach settled a little when she saw him slip into a back seat.

Squaring her shoulders, she collected some papers in her hands and rose to call her first witness to the stand. She was as ready as she was going to get.

"Raise your right hand. Do you swear to tell the truth, the whole truth and nothing but the truth, so help you, God?" The bailiff droned, swearing in the first juror, pizza-parlor owner Miguel Sanchez.

"I do." The Hispanic nodded once before stepping up to take his seat in the witness box.

With her long hair swinging behind her, Tatum approached the stand. "Are you familiar with the defendant, Robert Rhodes?" she asked, keeping her voice calm and unthreatening.

"I am." Sanchez sat easily in the stand, meeting her gaze head-on.

"Would you identify him for me now?"

Sanchez pointed to the table of the defense. "That's him."

Tatum took a step backward. "And how long have you known Mr. Rhodes?"

"Bobby an' me go way back," Miguel said, his slight accent becoming more apparent with the longer sentence.

"Would you consider him a friend?"

"Objection!" Duncan rose from his seat next to Bobby. "Counsel is leading the witness," he claimed.

Judge Keedy looked at Tatum over his wire-rimmed glasses. "Is this going someplace, Counselor?" he asked.

"Yes, sir, it is," Tatum assured him calmly while keeping her gaze locked on Sanchez. "Mr. Sanchez's relationship to the defendant needs to be established," she explained.

"Overruled. Answer the question," the judge ordered Sanchez.

Tatum moved in closer to the stand, the click of her light gray heels echoing in the large room. Sanchez remained silent, looking down as he picked at his fingernails.

"Mr. Sanchez?" she prompted.

"Yeah, we been friends, but I don't lie for no-body, friend or no, if it's gonna get my butt in hot water," he blurted out.

Tatum's heart gave a glad little leap, while Duncan snorted in disgust. She herself would not have been allowed to mention the fact that friends are apt to lie for one another, especially ones who live by the un-written codes of the street, but Sanchez had just placed that doubt in the minds of jurors all by him-self.

She stepped back a few more paces and turned to face the courtroom for a moment, catching Jona-than's smile. As she had hoped, Sanchez was looking a little more relaxed when she turned back.

"Do you own a bar called Miguel's Place, located on West Valley?"

Miguel beamed. "Yep. It's all mine."

"And do you remember seeing Mr. Rhodes at your establishment, Miguel's Place, on the evening of June 18?" she asked.

Tatum was doing something a little unusual by es-tablishing the defense's alibi, but she was hoping her strategy would pay off. She had a feeling the infor-mation she had would have more effect on the jury if they heard it up front, rather than in the defensive mode of cross-examination.

Sanchez sat up straighter. "I do," he answered without hesitation. "Bobby came in right at five-thirty an' ordered up a beer."

"You're sure about that time?"

"Yes, ma'am, I'm sure."

Tatum leaned back against the front of the prosecution table and nodded. "Did Mr. Rhodes seem upset to you?"

"Objection! Your Honor, Counselor McGillus is leading the witness!"

"Objection sustained. The witness is not required to answer that question."

Tatum tried to look contrite. She had been well aware that the question would be disallowed, but by reminding Miguel of Bobby's probable mood that night, she had a much better chance of having him offer the information she was seeking.

"How would you describe Mr. Rhodes on that evening?"

Miguel fidgeted with his mustache before answering. "He was mad, but not enough to kill anybody."

Bingo! The old familiar adrenaline was pumping through Tatum's veins. She had her witness in the palm of her hand.

"How long did Mr. Rhodes stay at Miguel's Place?"

"Till after the fights on TV." Tatum had questioned several other people who'd been at Miguel's place that night, and had heard the same thing from everyone except one woman, Bonita Juarez.

"What time did the fights end?"

"Eight o'clock." Two hours after the time of death.

Tatum had already established, earlier in the week, that the time of Roy Ingram's death was believed to have been somewhere between six and six-thirty. She had also shown that Bobby was arrested in the home he shared with Jenny and Roy shortly after eight o'clock on the night of June 18.

She heard Montgomery breathing harshly behind her and took a few steps closer to the stand. "A roomful of men watching a boxing match. Was everyone rooting for the same winner?"

Duncan jumped up from his seat. "Objection, Your Honor! Counsel's question is clearly irrelevant to the case at hand."

Judge Keedy looked over at Tatum. "Counsel?" he said.

"If I will be allowed to continue, Your Honor, the court will realize the importance of setting the scene," Tatum said. The court was going to realize a lot more than that one way or another, but Tatum was trying to keep suspense on her side as long as she could—the evidence would make more of an impact on the jury that way.

"The witness may answer the question, but get to the point, please," the Judge told Tatum. She breathed a silent sigh of gratitude.

"Mr. Sanchez?" Tatum said, looking back toward her witness, "were your patrons all cheering for the same boxer to win?"

"'Course everybody didn't want the same guy. What's the fun in that? We get proper rip-roarin' at

Miguel's when we watch the fights. We do it up right. It's all good-natured fun, though," the Mexican added as an afterthought.

Judge Keedy grunted. Tatum knew it was time to move in.

"And did Bobby join in the revelry? Did he seem to be having fun?"

Fear passed quickly across the man's face. He remained silent.

"Answer the question," Judge Keedy ordered.

"No," Sanchez finally admitted, his chin resting on his chest.

Tatum moved in closer to the stand. "Why not?"

"That broad, Bonita, she'd been hangin' all over Bobby disgusting-like, and he wasn't in the mood to play her games. I told him to go in the back, to my apartment, to watch the fights."

Though she told herself not to, that there was no purpose, Tatum turned around to see Bobby's reaction to his friend's words. She knew she should not have done so. The respectfully though inexpensively dressed young man looked sick.

She turned back to face her witness. "What time was that?"

"Six o'clock," the man replied, looking nervously toward Bobby.

Tatum moved in then, leaning her forearm against the witness box. "And what time did you see him again?"

"Eight o'clock."

There was a slight rumble as the effect of Miguel Sanchez's story pervaded the courtroom.

"No further questions, Your Honor," Tatum stated quietly, and returned to her seat, never once looking across at the defense. She had already made that mistake. Bobby's sickened expression was imprinted indelibly on her mind.

"Counselor, do you wish to cross-examine this witness?" Judge Keedy's voice boomed out over the hushed courtroom.

Troy Duncan only had one question to ask Sanchez.

"Can you tell the court for sure that Bobby Rhodes was *not* in your apartment during the entire time the fights were on?"

Miguel didn't hesitate. "No."

Jonathan stayed until the lunch recess and then offered to buy Tatum a hot dog at a stand outside the courthouse. October in Phoenix was a beautiful, balmy month, and Tatum was quick to accept Jonathan's invitation. She could use a few minutes outside in the sunshine.

"You really got him there on that alibi," Jonathan praised her as they settled themselves down outside the courthouse. "How on earth did you find out that Bobby had left the front of the bar? Sanchez seemed surprised that you knew."

Tatum finished her bite of hot dog before replying. "I just talked to Bonita. Lucky for me, she was so humiliated by Bobby's public rejection that she was willing to risk breaking the unwritten laws by which they live down there. No one lied to me—they aren't dumb—but no one volunteered all of the truth, either, until Bonita." Tatum shrugged, as if denying any credit due to her questioning tactics or the gut feelings that had sent her to Bonita in the first place.

"And I don't really have him," she admitted, smiling faintly at the surprise reflected on Jonathan's face.

"Sure you do," he declared. "The whole place was so thick with tension it was incredible." He took a swig from the can of cola they were sharing.

"I surprised everyone, all right. And I admit, it doesn't look as good for Bobby as a solid alibi would have done, but it still doesn't prove anything. Bobby could very well have been in Miguel's apartment the entire evening just like he says he was. So you see, this really *proves* nothing," she finished. She looked at her hot dog, wondering if she really wanted it after all.

"Eat it," Jonathan ordered, reaching across to raise the bun to her lips. And because his big brown eyes looked so concerned, Tatum took a bite.

"Still, things don't look that good for the defense," he said again, as if wanting to inject her with a dose of optimism.

Tatum took a swallow from the can still wet from Jonathan's mouth. "You're right," she conceded with a hint of a smile.

"I've missed you," Jonathan said suddenly. He caught her gaze with his own and held it. "Who would've thought two weeks could seem like ten years?" he asked softly. He was making love to her with his eyes again.

Tatum didn't look away. "When is Cinci due back?" she asked, the words sticking in her throat. The house mother had left the week before to stay with an old friend who had fallen ill, leaving Jonathan to spend his nights at the center in her absence.

"Sometime this weekend..." Jonathan replied, suggestion nearly dripping from his words.

Tatum looked away from the longing in his brown-eyed gaze, telling herself to be strong. The problems between her and Jonathan were escalating, with his continuing due-notice appearances that she only heard about after the fact. And with the end of the Rhodes trial looming so close, she was feeling more and more internal pressure to pull back, to pull inside herself where she was safe, where she knew she could retreat from the consequences if she lost the trial. What if she really had lost her edge? What if her self-doubts were founded, instead of simply the exaggerated worries of a woman who had been living on the edge? What if Montgomery's threats become more than just threats? And what if, when Jonathan was forced to choose between his public and herself, he chose his public?

Was she strong enough to handle a shattered career and a broken heart, too? She was too unsure of herself to risk finding out. She just knew that if she lost her job, she was going to need every ounce of energy she had to hold herself together, to find some kind of life for herself. She could not afford to waste any strength hurting over a man who placed her second on his list of priorities.

At least Jonathan knew nothing about the very real possibility that she could be out of a job. She could not bear the thought of him watching her fall apart.

She glanced over at Jonathan once more. She felt more alive when she was with Jonathan than she had since Cale was killed. She did not want it to end. "Will you come to me?" she heard herself ask. She and Jonathan might be running out of time, but the clock hadn't stopped yet. Somehow she would prepare herself to lose him when she had to—but not one second before.

His smile lit the kindling deep within her. "You can count on it...."

Jonathan had to leave right after lunch, and Tatum tried to ignore the void she felt when court resumed for the afternoon and she knew she would be fighting without him there behind her. She called Walter Miller, a representative from the ballistics section, to the stand.

As soon as the older man was seated, sworn in and his position identified, she picked up a labeled plastic bag and carried it over for him to inspect. She kept it in clear view of the jury at all times, giving them a picture they were sure to remember. It was imperative to impress upon them the seriousness of the decision they faced.

"Can you identify this?" she asked the gentleman seated before her.

The man's wire-rimmed spectacles slipped down his nose as he nodded his balding head. "It's the gun that was brought to me by the arresting officer on the case of the state versus Robert Rhodes—the gun that was found beside the dead man's body," he said. His words were enunciated with such precision, they reminded Tatum of the law professors she had had in college. Those men of letters had instilled respect; the information they imparted had instilled complete conviction. She hoped Mr. Miller would have the same effect on the jury.

"How can you be so sure? Aren't there hundreds of guns just like this one?"

"There is a pie-shaped chip of paint missing from the left front side of the sight, and the screw holding the casing together was inserted on a slight angle, so it doesn't flesh completely with the casing."

Tatum approached the jury box, holding out the gun with its left side exposed, and carried it along the length of the jury box. She made the return trip with the crooked screw in view. A couple of jurors sat back, as if wanting to keep their distance from the dangerous weapon, but Tatum was satisfied. The jurors had been greatly affected by this piece of evidence. Things were going just as Tatum had planned.

Still holding the gun out, allowing the entire courtroom to get another look at the piece of metal and hard plastic that had been used to kill a man, Tatum walked back to Walter Miller.

"Will you please tell the court your other findings?"

"The bullet taken from the body of the deceased was launched from the weapon in question. The weapon was then matched to ammunition recovered from Sand's Gun and Rifle Range."

"Thank you, Mr. Miller. I have no further questions, Your Honor," Tatum said, returning to her seat next to Montgomery.

Several jurors fidgeted in their chairs, repositioning themselves, sitting back, sitting up straighter, crossing a leg, uncrossing one. A couple of them cleared their throats. One coughed.

"Does the defense have any questions for this witness?" Judge Keedy asked.

Troy Duncan rose from his seat slowly, approaching Mr. Miller with practiced contemplation.

"Tell me, Mr. Miller, just out of curiosity, were you able to find any fingerprints on the gun? Anything to tell us who actually held it the night Roy Ingram was murdered? Who actually pulled the trigger that sent the deceased to his grave?"

Tatum groaned inwardly. The man was too melodramatic, too practiced, too everything. But most of all, he was too good at what he did. She knew the ballistics expert's answer before he uttered it—knew it and dreaded hearing it.

"No, I did not."

Duncan smiled, as if greatly relieved, as if he had not already known what the other man was going to say. "No further questions, Your Honor," he said, returning to his seat with the air of one who had just received an unexpected windfall.

Tatum waited only until Walter Miller had cleared the front of the courtroom before she called her next witness, Detective William Shattles, back to the stand. Detective Shattles had been her first witness, his testimony a basis for the framework for her case, but she had saved a portion of her interrogation for the part of the trial where it would make the most impact.

After a brief reminder of his oath, Tatum was able to get straight to the point. "Mr. Miller has just told the court that he was able to trace the murder weapon to ammunition recovered from Sand's Gun and Rifle Range. Can you verify the accuracy of his statement?" she asked, returning the focus to where it had been before Duncan's little show.

"I can. I brought it in myself. The gun was used for target shooting every Saturday."

Tatum remained completely still in front of the witness stand. "And were you then able to trace the owner of the gun? The individual who spent *every Saturday* shooting at targets, perfecting his aim?"

"I was." Again Detective Shattles's answer was short, succinct—nothing to deter the jury's attention from the information being imparted.

"Will you please identify this individual for the court?"

"The gun belongs to that man." The detective pointed straight at Bobby Rhodes. Every eye in the jury box turned to stare at the defendant. Tatum continued to face the witness stand. "Mr. Robert Rhodes," Detective Shattles said.

It sounded to Tatum as if all the air in the courtroom was let out in one swoosh, as if everybody present had been holding their breaths for the past several minutes. Still she did not turn around.

"Thank you, I have no more questions at this time." She returned to her table with her eyes trained on the scarred brown wood, reminding herself that she could not let herself get caught up in Bobby Rhodes's ordeal. No matter how hard it was, she had to fight with herself to stay neutral. She had to win this case.

Duncan asked a couple of seemingly innocuous questions, trying to cast some doubt on Detective Shattles's testimony, but for once his well-rehearsed histrionics fell short of their mark. Tatum was gaining ground.

Her next witness was the neighbor who had alerted the police to the gunshot sound she heard coming from the Rhodes and Ingram home on the night of the murder. Tatum tread very carefully, remembering the codes of the street that many of Bobby's people chose to live by. She stood directly in front of the witness stand, establishing a one-on-one rapport with the woman seated before her. "Did you hear anything else, anything *before* the gunshot that rang out that night?" she asked.

"Yes, ma'am, I heard 'em arguing again. Seemed like they was always arguing."

"Who exactly is the 'they' you're referring to?" Tatum asked.

"Bobby Rhodes and that loser of a brother-in-law of his."

"Can you remember what the fight was about?"

"Bobby was tellin' that nasty Roy Ingram to leave Jenny be."

Tatum needed more than that. She knew the woman had heard more than that. She just wasn't sure she could get her to speak.

"I'm going to ask you one more question, and I want you to be very sure to remember that you are under oath—that failure to answer as honestly and accurately as you can could result in a jail term. Did you hear anything more that night? Anything Bobby might have said to Roy? Anything that would lead the court to believe that Bobby would kill his brother-in-law?"

The woman was silent for several seconds. She looked briefly at Bobby and then turned away, tears pooling in her eyes. She turned toward the judge.

"Bobby's a good man, Your Honor," she said.

Judge Keedy nodded. "Please answer the question," he ordered gently.

"Bobby gave Roy an hour to git out, to clear all his stuff out of the house and never come back." The woman paused. "He said he'd kill Roy if he ever found 'im in his house again."

One of the jurors gasped. Montgomery smiled. Tatum didn't look at the defendant's side of the courtroom. Her career could very well be at an end if she lost this case, and her heart was shredding a little bit with every step that brought her closer to winning it.

In his cross-examination, Duncan tore the neighbor's confession to shreds, making her look like an ignorant, over emotional, unstable busybody.

Tatum then called Jenny Rhodes Ingram to the stand.

"Raise your right hand..."

Tatum studied her notes while the modestly dressed young woman was sworn in and took the stand—not because she needed any reminders of what was on those papers, but because she was trying to distance herself as much as possible from the work that lay ahead of her. Her stomach was twisted into a painful knot as she took a step back from the witness stand.

"Describe, in your own words, the scene that was taking place in your home when you left for work on the evening of June 18," she instructed the pretty Mexican woman.

"Bobby and Roy were arguing," Jenny answered reticently.

"About what?"

"Me," Jenny stated softly.

"Can you be more specific, please?" Tatum asked, feeling like a dentist pulling teeth from a child without using anesthetic.

With trembling lips, Jenny repeated what she had told Tatum in her home a few weeks before. All through the telling, the girl's brown eyes rested on her brother.

Tatum knew where Jenny was looking, but she did not follow her gaze. "Have you ever known Bobby to be violent, Jenny?" Tatum asked next, moving closer to the prosecutor's table.

Tears welled in Jenny's eyes then, but the accusation in them as she stared at Tatum was plain to see. She shifted her gaze from the judge to her brother, then back to the judge. "Once." Her answer, when it came, was barely audible.

"Did he kill his victim in that instance?"

"No."

Tatum steeled herself to do her job. "Did you do something that may have prevented him from doing so?"

"I pulled on his arm and begged him to let the man go."

Just a few more questions and this would be over. "What did the man do then?"

"Nothing." Jenny sounded more frightened than she had since the trial had begun.

"Why not?"

"He was unconscious."

Tatum paused, hating herself for purposely allowing time for the combined expulsion of air from the courtroom audience to settle upon the jury.

"Please tell the court what happened just before your brother engaged in those violent actions," Tatum said, her stomach cramping so severely she had to lean back against the table.

"I was attacked on the way home from work that night. Bobby was protecting me, that's all," Jenny cried defensively, tears streaming down her cheeks. Tatum felt a wave of empathy for the Rhodes siblings. She would have defended Cale just as staunchly, had the occasion ever arisen.

"He was protecting you," she repeated Jenny's words.

Jenny nodded. "Yes, ma'am, he was."

"So when your brother came home on the night of June 18 and found your husband raising his hand to you, he stepped in to protect you again. He sent you away, and then he had it out with Roy, threatening him, giving him an hour to pack up and get out or he'd kill him. And then he went to Miguel's to wait out the hour. And while he sat alone, in the back of Miguel's bar, drinking a beer, his rage grew.

"By the time the hour was up, he was ready for anything. He arrived home to find Roy still there, not one stitch of clothing packed. Bobby was at his wits' end. He had already tried to reason with Roy, he had already given him chances to get help, but Roy had proven that he wasn't going to do that. As long as he was around, Roy was a threat to you. The man was refusing to leave your home, possibly taunting Bobby with your love for Roy and Bobby's inability to do anything about Roy's presence in your life.

"As enraged as he must have been, Bobby knew of one way to prevent your husband from ever beating you up again. He went for Roy. A skirmish followed. At some point Bobby grabbed his gun. It may even have been meant as just a threat—but it ended in murder." Tatum delivered her closing line just as she had planned, but she had not planned on the bile that rose to her throat at Jenny's stricken look.

"The prosecution rests," she announced without satisfaction as she took her seat. She had to physically restrain herself from pushing Montgomery's hand off her shoulder when he gave her a congratulatory pat. Aside from the fact that she couldn't tolerate his touch, his good cheer was a bit premature. Some of her evidence was strong—the gun, the neighbor's testimony—but much of it was circumstantial, as well. No one saw Bobby return to his home or leave it again. There was nothing solid that proved that his finger had been the one to pull the trigger. Depending on how good Troy Duncan really was, the jury's verdict could actually rest on Bobby's character references, on whether or not the jury believed beyond the shadow of a doubt that Bobby Rhodes could and would commit murder. Tatum had not been able to find one person who would paint Bobby's character as so completely evil.

CHAPTER TEN

JUDGE KEEDY CALLED a recess for the weekend as soon as Tatum announced that the prosecution had finished presenting its case. There was a mass beeline for the door, as if everyone present couldn't wait to be someplace else. Tatum sympathized with them. She would prefer to be just about anyplace else, as well. She badly needed the break the weekend offered, even if the break only brought other concerns to the surface.

Tatum spent Saturday morning visiting with Pop, or rather, watching him sleep. He woke up briefly a time or two, just long enough to be comforted by her presence, but he drifted off again almost immediately. Though the doctor continued to be optimistic, Tatum was not. She knew what was happening. Pop was not fighting his way back. He was ready to die.

About halfway through the morning, Jim Marsh appeared in the doorway, mop in hand.

"Come on in, Jim," she called. The oppressive silence was getting to her. She needed someone to talk to, and Jim had always been more than willing to talk.

Jim mopped his way in, stopping on the side of Pop's bed opposite to where Tatum sat. With gentle, practiced movements, he untangled one of the wires leading to Pop's heart from around the bars on the side of the bed.

"Your pop's a good and lucky man," he said softly, looking down at the sleeping man.

Tatum's shocked gaze met Jim's. "How can you say such a thing?" she asked, looking at the frail, broken image of the man she had adored all her life.

Jim smiled. "Because he is," he said. "He's had it all—a career he loved, children he doted on who actually loved him back and a chance to get even when the world got tough. But most of all, he's found that one thing we all spend our lives looking for—peace. This man's soul is truly content."

Tears filled Tatum's eyes as she listened to the truth in Jim's words. Her tears gave way to a smile as she looked at Pop. When he put it like that, Tatum had to admit he was right. Pop was a lucky man.

"You always seem so content, too, Jim, but you're not, are you?" Tatum asked a few minutes later when the prisoner was mopping the other side of the room. She didn't even know why she asked, except that she had just been given a glimpse into the man with whom Pop had found friendship over these past months, and found that she liked what she saw.

Jim shrugged and kept on mopping. "I do okay," he finally said, sucking his tongue against his teeth. "Most days I just try not to think about much except that I'm glad I'm not cooped up in my cell all day like most of these guys are. But it's kinda hard to be content when you're living in here and know you belong out there."

"What're you in for?" Tatum asked.

Jim was making his way back toward the door. Tatum knew he had a job to do, that he had to stick to it if he wasn't going to lose his minimum-security privileges, but she wished he could stay longer.

"Robbery."

"Did you do it?" she asked, leaning back in the armchair she had pulled up beside Pop's bed.

"Nope. See ya later, Ms. McGillus," he said, and was gone.

TATUM'S HEAD WAS ACHING by the time she got back to Phoenix. She had a load of work awaiting her at home, and even the thought of it made her feel ready to explode. She didn't even want to think about the Rhodes murder trial. Deciding she needed a pick-me-up more than she needed her job at that moment, she stopped by the center to see Mandy. She and Mandy had found a new closeness since the night that Abby left, and Tatum was eager to nurture the relationship. Though Mandy was still a teenager, just a girl in some ways, she had a wisdom far beyond her years. In spite of the difference in their ages, Tatum felt more like a friend than a role model to Mandy.

"Tatum! Am I glad to see you," Mandy greeted her with a hug when Tatum walked in the front door of the center.

Tatum wrapped her arms around Mandy's thin shoulders, taking sustenance from the brief contact. She looked over Mandy's head to the vacant receptionist's desk. "You working?"

"Just off," Mandy replied. "My replacement's getting a pop."

"How about going to lunch?" Tatum invited.

"Sure! Wait a sec' while I get my purse," Mandy said, and bounded off down the hall.

Half an hour later they were sitting on the outdoor patio of one of Scottsdale's casual eateries, waiting for their lunches to be served. Mandy had been talking almost nonstop, jumping from a couple of humorous anecdotes about some children at the center to her optimistic assessment of Tatum's chances of winning the much-publicized Rhodes murder trial. The combination of fresh air and Mandy was doing wonders for Tatum's headache.

"Any word from Cinci yet?" Tatum asked, taking a sip of iced water with lemon. Was Jonathan going to be free to come to her that evening? And if he was, did she want him to?

"Her friend's seeing the doctor this morning. If all goes well, Cinci will be home sometime tonight." Mandy emptied the container of sugar packets and began to reload them, taking great care to place one evenly on top of the next. Her gaze, when she glanced up briefly, was suddenly troubled. "Jonathan's really moving on his due-notice petition. Lots of people are calling," she said cautiously.

Tatum was not ready to hear that. "How many more appearances has he made this week that were not on his schedule?" she asked, the words like congealed glue in her throat. She had known from the start that when it came to the due-notice question, she and Jonathan were enemies. So why did his duplicity upset her so much?

"Two that I know of, a PTA and a businesswomen's group, but I suspect there's probably more."

Lunch was delivered, and in spite of her discouragement, Mandy attacked her burger with the gusto of a typical teenager. Tatum approached her salad with less enthusiasm.

"We've got that Rotary meeting coming up next Friday. We'll be up against more influential power there than you'd find in ten PTAs." Tatum forced herself to appear as if nothing was wrong. This was not supposed to hurt. She had steeled herself for this from the very beginning. "Did you get all the letters out?"

Mandy nodded.

"Good." Tatum took a couple more bites of her salad and then put down her fork. "The most important thing we have to do here is educate," she continued. "Jonathan's going to get enough signatures, that much is obvious. With as many people as there are in this city, and as hard as he's working, it would be pretty impossible not to. But all those signatures do is allow him to file the bill in November. It still has to be looked at by the other senators and representatives during session, and then, assuming they all vote for it, it has to go before the people during the next public election."

Mandy finished off her burger and started on her fries. "So we've still got time," she summed up with a grin.

"Yes, we still have time." Tatum watched Mandy smear her french fry in a pile of catsup and was reminded of just why this fight meant so much to Mandy.

"Do you have any idea when your father is due for parole?" she asked, wishing her young friend could be as blissfully unaware of due-notice as were most seventeen-year-olds.

Mandy shrugged, the grin gone from her face. "He was given fifteen years, but who knows? If he's been good enough..." She left her unfinished sentence hanging between them.

Tatum understood. Mandy didn't know when her father would be released from jail, and furthermore, she never wanted to know. She just wanted him to stay out of her life. Tatum was more determined than ever to see that Mandy got her wish. The girl had suffered enough. No one had the right to force further heartache upon her in the form of knowledge that she did not want. Due-notice *had* to fail.

Tatum vacillated for the rest of the day. She needed Jonathan to come to her so badly she was going crazy with waiting, and yet she also hoped he wasn't going to make it. She could no longer deny to herself that she cared for him, but neither could she let herself give in to that caring. Her life could very well be on the verge of falling apart, and she knew that she couldn't rely on Jonathan to pick up the pieces.

IN SPITE OF all her mental lectures, Tatum didn't send Jonathan away when he knocked on her door at ten o'clock that evening. He was dressed casually in black cotton slacks and a white polo shirt, and Tatum wanted to bury herself against the solidity of his chest and stay there forever.

"Can I come in, or are you just going to ogle me out here for the rest of the night?" he asked with a lazy grin. She hoped, as she watched his gaze sweep over her, that he approved of the silk lounging pajamas she was wearing. She'd bought them on impulse, and the saleslady had told her that they were nonreturnable.

"I guess you better come in," Tatum invited, turning around to walk down the hall toward the living room. If her time with Jonathan was running out, she was going to use every minute she had to create a few more memories.

A long wolf whistle followed her across the ceramic tile, and she turned back, eyebrows raised.

"You sure are a sight for sore eyes, lady," Jonathan said softly as he came toward her. The heated look in his eyes gave away just what he had in mind to appease that soreness.

"You're not so bad yourself, Senator," Tatum replied, turning her bottom to him once more.

She teased him deliberately, swaying her silk-clad backside with playful seductiveness. She wanted him to need her as badly as she needed him; she wanted him to lose control, to see her as the single most important thing in his life—if only for this one night.

"Can I get you something to drink?" she asked as she crossed over to the stereo to turn on some soft jazz.

"Nothing," he answered, following close behind her.

Her heart began a heavy hammering as he slid his hands around her from behind and pulled her back against his body. Tatum snuggled against him, fitting her bottom to his hips, and inhaled the musky masculine scent of him that she loved so much. How was she ever going to live without him?

"You okay?" Jonathan asked from behind her, loosening his grip on her but not letting go.

Tatum leaned back against him. "Fine," she assured him, trying to convince herself it was so. She and Jonathan had the whole night ahead of them, his arms felt wonderful around her, and she was determined to be satisfied with what she had for as long as she had it.

He ground himself against the roundness of her bottom again and, slipping his hands around to cover her belly, began to kiss the column of her neck. His whiskers rasped against her sensitive flesh, sending chills through her spine, alighting nerve endings all the way down her body.

"Did I interrupt anything?" he asked, nipping at her ear.

"Nothing that can't wait another day," she said softly.

She was ready to melt, to give in to the forgetfulness only he could bring, until she sensed the change in him—the briefest hesitation. Though she didn't know what was causing it, she felt his struggle like a physical current. His hold loosened almost imperceptibly.

"I've been hearing about you in the oddest places this past week," he said from his position behind her, sounding as if the words had been forced from him.

Tatum turned around and looked at him, noticing his tense jaw, his unsmiling lips.

"You have?" She wanted to continue what they had started, not face what was to come. His desire was still obvious in his face as he held her against him, but his doubts were even more so. He let her go.

"Mm-hmm. Seems everybody I come across has received a wonderfully convincing letter, urging them not to support a due-notice bill that's due to be presented during the next session of the legislature. It has your signature on it." The fire in Jonathan's eyes had not burned out, but it was dimmer. Obviously she was not the only one who was having doubts about their future together, counting down the hours.

The due-notice issue had finally reached them at home. Deep inside, Tatum had known it was only a matter of time. She met Jonathan's troubled gaze head-on, neither cowering nor gloating. This thing was bigger than both of them, and she had a feeling they were both going to be hurt by it.

"And I suppose you know the guy who's been hitting up the ladies' groups this week, gaining their signatures during meetings I would have attended, as well, had I only known they were taking place?" she asked as gently as she could.

Jonathan shrugged, not denying her charge. Like her, he showed no signs of backing down, of apologizing, of giving in. She could not stop the crushing disappointment she felt as she was finally forced to face what she had already known from the start. Jonathan's public battle was more important to him than she was.

In a sudden flash of awareness, Tatum realized that it wasn't the proposed law coming between them so much as the fact that she had a personal demon for which she needed Jonathan's support, and was unable to get it. Even after learning about Pop, even after realizing the debilitating effects due-notice could have on hundreds of other people just like him, Jonathan could not let go.

Jonathan watched the thoughts chase each other across Tatum's face and kicked himself for bringing the controversy into her living room, especially now, tonight. It had been a long, tiring two weeks. He needed the night of sustenance he had hoped to find in her arms. He reached for her with a desperation born from the sudden conviction that the question of due-notice was going to come between him and the woman he loved more than life itself—because his love for her was strictly personal, and he had been raised to put public conscience before personal gratification.

He had never expected Tatum to do more than attend a few meetings, lose him a few signatures. He certainly had not expected her to write a stunningly articulate letter and mail it out to every important person in the city. If that letter did nothing else, it convinced Jonathan that she was going to fight to the finish, that she was going to use whatever means she had at her disposal, that she just might come out the victor. And he was afraid that the first time one of his kids suffered because of the absence of a due-notice law, he would resent Tatum for her part in the bill's failure.

With those thoughts occupying his mind, he knew he couldn't make love to Tatum that night. It would make a mockery of all he felt for her, tarnish the moments they had already shared, if he were to take her body to bed while he was angry with her person. He would be reducing their love act to no more than an animalistic coupling. He couldn't do that.

"I guess we're both a little tired tonight," he said, knowing his excuse was lame but unable to conjure up anything more honest. He might not be ready to sleep with her, but he wasn't ready to have it out with her, either. Part of him kept hoping he wouldn't have to. That, if given more time, the problems between them would somehow be resolved—or just melt away.

"Yeah, it would probably be best to call it a night," she said with a sigh.

"I'll call you," he said, needing there to still be some stated connection between them.

"Okay," she told him but Jonathan had a feeling she wasn't going to hold her breath waiting for him to do so.

"JONATHAN, I'D LIKE to have a word with you about that bill you're trying to push through. I got a very disturbing letter in the mail this past week, and I'm not sure that following through on this thing is a good political investment...."

"Senator Wright, I signed that petition you had for your new bill, but then I heard that radio show you did a while back with Ms. McGillus, and the more I think about it, the more sure I am that I should withdraw my signature...."

"Senator, my twenty-four-year-old daughter was killed by a young man so high on acid he couldn't remember which side of the road to drive on. She bled to death in the road while he worried about losing his license. I almost lost my wife, too. Not because she was in the car—she wasn't—but because of the anger, the uncontrollable grief. Can you imagine how much bitterness something like that leaves behind? To imagine your baby, your own flesh and blood, suffering, dying without you there, while some punk looks at her and sees only the inconvenience of losing his driving privileges? But things started getting better when the kid was convicted and sent to prison. It didn't bring our Jan back, but it did ease some of the bitterness to know that some kind of justice prevailed, that the kid is not still out there, living freely, laughing, loving, giving the hugs that we will never again have from Jan, maybe even killing again.

"But vehicular homicide is not usually punishable by life imprisonment. That kid could be free again someday. And if your bill passes, my wife is going to be forced to know about it the minute it happens. I'll lose her, Senator. I'll lose her for sure if she no longer has the hope that he's still shut away. And for what? What possible *good* will the knowledge of his freedom do either of us? Can't you just leave us with what peace we have left?...."

Jonathan drove home from church, remembering not the words of wisdom the priest had imparted, but the words of his fellow parishioners before and after the hour-long service. They had not all come to him about the bill, and among those who had, some had been supporters. But it was the words of those who were opposed to due-notice that were haunting him. He couldn't deny that those words had some truth in them. But there were two sides to the issue, damn it, and Tatum, with her lawyering skills, was beating him at every turn.

He pulled into the driveway of his apartment complex, slammed the car door and strode up the walk to his front door, cursing the woman he had left so abruptly the night before.

But when he walked into his kitchen and saw the half-empty pizza box left on his table from last night's midnight snack, he had a vision of Tatum's face the night she had sat in this very room, in the chair at the end of the table, the one now stacked with old newspapers. He remembered how content he had been that night, how right it had seemed to have not only his house full, but his heart, as well.

He loved the woman. He knew he did. He just didn't see how he could live with that love and fulfill his life's obligations, as well.

His frustration was near the boiling point when the phone rang later that afternoon. *Not another one,* he thought as he swiveled around in his desk chair to answer it. He just wasn't up to another view of the seamier side of life right now.

"That you, Jonathan?" he heard when he picked up the telephone receiver.

"Yeah, who's this?" If this was another anti-due-notice crusader, he was going to throw the phone.

"It's Danny Torunta. We've met a couple of times at the prison," Danny's gruff tones came over the line.

"Sure, Danny. Sorry about that, it's been a long day."

"Tell me about it," Danny said. "Listen, Jonathan, I got kind of an odd request here. I just left Jack McGillus. He's been pretty unsettled ever since Tatum left this morning, and I don't need to tell you how important it is that he stay calm. He's been insisting on speaking to you, and I finally promised him I'd call just to settle him down."

"Tatum's pop asked specifically to see me?" Jonathan asked. "Did he say what for?"

"He wasn't saying much of anything, just kept cursing the fact that he was unable to come see you." Danny sounded as baffled as Jonathan felt.

Jonathan didn't know whether Jack would have come with a shotgun or a smile, had he been able, but he knew he had to find out. "Tell him I'll be there in an hour," he said before hanging up the phone and grabbing his keys.

IT HAD BEEN more than two weeks since Jonathan had seen Jack McGillus, and time had not been kind to the older man. Jack's skin was sallow and clung to his bones like wet semolina. But with the aid of the oxygen tube strapped to his face, he was breathing more easily than he had been the last time Jonathan had seen him.

"Thank you for coming," Jack said slowly as Jonathan settled himself beside the sick man's bed.

Jack's voice was reedy with weakness, but his eyes still glowed with intelligence.

"No problem," Jonathan said, unable to tell just yet whether he was there as friend or foe.

"I'm worried about Tatum," Jack said, each word an effort. "She was always such an intense child, took everything to heart, but lately she's so shut up inside herself, I don't think even she knows for sure what she's feeling. She just might stay there forever if she's not forced out."

Jonathan wasn't sure he had any answers for the man. He had been looking for them for himself, as well. "Maybe she's happy where she's at," he said, telling Jack what he had pretty well already decided.

Jack shook his head. "Tatum can never be happy alone. She's got too much love inside her." Jonathan had to be patient as the man formed his words. "She's a strong woman—she just doesn't know it yet—and I think that frightens her."

Jonathan wanted to believe Jack. He wanted to hope that Tatum was capable of loving him wholly, maybe even committing to him, but he was not sure he should. After all the hours they had spent together, the lovemaking, the shared sorrows of her father's heart attack, of Abby's departure, never once had Tatum spoken to him of love or even of deep caring. She spoke only of friendship—the kind she shared with Mandy, the kind she could probably get from a loyal puppy dog. There was nothing to give him hope that when he didn't back down on the due-notice issue, she would still be willing to be his friend, let alone anything more.

"What do you want from me?" Jonathan asked, not sure he was in a position to give whatever Jack was after.

"Not to give up on her," Jack wheezed. "She wore that forced smile all morning. She's fighting, and I don't want her to lose by default."

"How can you be so sure it's me she wants?" Jonathan asked.

"Her eyes. The sparkle came back," Jack said. His own eyes shut while he took in several quick breaths, catching up on the air he was losing while talking.

Jonathan told himself he was a fool for wanting to have it all, for wanting to believe that there was a way he could continue helping those in need and have Tatum for himself, as well. The due-notice issue was a symbol of what life with Tatum would be like. His conscience pulling him one way, his love for her another.

But he couldn't tell any of that to a dying man. Neither could he lie to Jack. "I love your daughter, sir. It's been out of my hands since the first time I saw her," he said, the words ringing out starkly in the sanitized room.

Relief flared in Jack's eyes at the same time that hopelessness flared inside Jonathan's heart.

THE RHODES MURDER TRIAL resumed the following week, with the defense pleading its case. Tatum was not surprised by the character references, but she was surprised that they did not all come from the Rhodeses' side of town. It seemed that everybody who knew Bobby—regardless of where they lived—liked and respected him. He had spent a summer building pools, and families remembered him. He had worked in construction and done landscaping for a couple of years as a member of a yard crew. Owners and contractors rallied to his defense, emphasizing how confident they'd been with him on the grounds.

Tatum could almost feel the steam building up inside Montgomery as the day progressed. His earlier friendliness was less and less in evidence.

When Defense Attorney Troy Duncan called Jenny Ingram back to take the stand, he barely waited for the bailiff to remind her that she was still under oath before starting to question her. His tone with Jenny was so sugary it almost made Tatum sick—not because she wanted the girl to be treated poorly, but rather because it was so obviously insincere. Troy Duncan was the kind of lawyer who gave lawyering a bad name. Tatum would rather quit practicing law altogether than resort to those tactics, no matter how hotly Montgomery breathed down her neck.

"Mrs. Ingram, before the night that Roy died, did he and Bobby ever argue?" Duncan asked.

"Yes," the girl answered, her eyes downcast. Tatum's heart went out to the young woman. She was trying to defend her brother, but she was surely still grieving for the husband she had lost, possibly by Bobby's hand.

Duncan moved forward to lean one arm against the witness stand in a practiced gesture of sympathy. "Often?" he asked. Tatum saw the calculated look in his eyes as he turned toward the courtroom, as if judging the feelings in the air.

"Sometimes," Jenny replied.

"And what were most of those arguments about?"

"Me. Roy pushed me around sometimes. Nothing serious, he almost never hurt me, but Bobby wouldn't stand for it."

"Had he ever actually hit you before the night he died?"

"Yes. Once." The young woman's words were barely audible, even through the court microphone in front of her.

Duncan turned to walk slowly toward the jurors' box, his gaze fixed on the floor as if he were pondering his questions for the first time. "Was Bobby aware of it?"

"Yes."

"And yet it hadn't been enough provocation to murder him," he murmured as if to himself.

"Objection!" Tatum called out, rising from her seat. "Your Honor, he's leading the jury," she accused.

"Sustained. Erase Mr. Duncan's last comments from the record," Judge Keedy ordered.

But the damage had already been done. Tatum knew it, and she knew Duncan knew it, too. He had planted another doubt in their minds, and leaving doubts was all he had to do.

"Jenny, how did most arguments between Bobby and Roy usually end?" Duncan asked, assuming a relaxed pose in the middle of the room.

The young woman continued to stare straight ahead, as if in a trance. "Roy promised to get help, and for my sake, Bobby always let it go. Roy was a good man. He just had some things to work through. I loved him. Bobby knew that and accepted that ultimately the decision was mine, so he always just left the house for a while to cool down."

"Where would he go?"

Jenny shrugged. "Out for a beer someplace, usually. Miguel's, maybe, or the bowling alley."

Tatum studied the jury, watching as the girl's words sank in. Duncan was painting a believable scenario of Bobby Rhodes's possible actions that night. His evidence was highly circumstantial, but much of Tatum's was, as well. And Duncan had just spent days showing the jury what a wonderful man Bobby Rhodes was. Tatum could hardly blame them for having doubts that such a man would cold-bloodedly kill the man his baby sister loved. She had doubts herself.

"No further questions, Your Honor," One way or another, Bobby's fate was now sealed.

Tatum suddenly felt dizzy, short of breath, as she was hit with the realization that she might have missed the real motive, that something else had happened between Bobby and Roy that night to make their argument different from the others. Maybe she had allowed her empathy for the young man to blind her thinking. Maybe she had not tried hard enough to show him as a man capable of murder. Maybe she was allowing a murderer to walk free. Montgomery's stiffness beside her told her that the same things were going through his mind.

As far as she could tell, she had done her best with the trial, and her best had always been good enough in the past. If Bobby was acquitted, then maybe he was not guilty. Her insides were trembling as Judge Keedy called for her to make her closing statement, and she rose to approach the jury.

CHAPTER ELEVEN

TATUM FACED the jurors' box, unsure of herself for the first time in her career. Wanting to appear relaxed, she had left the jacket of her mauve and white suit along the back of her chair. But as she stood before the twelve attentive people, her white silk blouse shimmering against her skin, she felt herself shiver—not a good start.

"Ladies and gentlemen of the jury, I would like to begin by reminding you that a crime committed out of love for another is still a crime, and is still punishable to the fullest extent of the law." Her voice, at least, was strong, reflecting her years of courtroom training. "You must be aware that the defense has tried to build up your sympathies for the defendant, painting him as a likable, well-respected young man. We are not disputing that fact. But it is not Bobby Rhodes's personality traits that are on trial here. Please keep in mind that not all criminals are hardened and mean. You would be setting a very dangerous precedent, ladies and gentlemen, were you to base a man's innocence on his likability. Most child molesters can be extremely friendly which is why children are tricked into trusting them. There have been several religious men who contributed greatly to society and were respected by millions, and who were also guilty of unpardonable crimes. And there have been innumerable family members who killed in defense of another family member. A son kills the father who is abusing his mother, a father kills the man who murdered his son, or a brother will kill the brother-in-law who is a threat to his sister." Tatum delivered her words with a calm confidence that belied the knots of anxiety in her shoulders, the churning in her stomach.

"You have here a young man who was arrested, charged with and found guilty of beating a man severely once before," she continued, motioning toward Bobby while keeping her eyes glued to the jury. "The motive? Removing a threat to his sister's well-being, possibly her life. The record shows that Bobby Rhodes had many arguments with Roy Ingram over Roy's treatment of Mr. Rhodes's sister, arguments which ended with Roy's promises to seek help. So how must Bobby have felt—how would *you* have felt—coming home on the night of June 18, possibly tired from a long day at work, to find his brother-in-law hitting Jenny, *again*. Roy's promises to get help had apparently been empty ones. We have it on record that Mr. Rhodes was angry—very angry. Angry enough to threaten murder.

"As you leave here to deliberate on this case, I implore you to remember the facts. The defendant had a fight with the deceased, went to a bar, drank some beer, had time to deliberate over the deceased's continuous failure to keep his word. Remember, too, the effects of alcohol on the human brain. The defendant has no alibi during the time of the murder. He had plenty of opportunity to leave Miguel's during the fight, to ensure that Roy had done as ordered and removed himself from Jenny's home before Jenny returned from work, only to find that Roy had not even begun to pack and had no intentions to do so. There was plenty of time for simmering rage to become white-hot, for battle lines to be drawn in a war that could only end in death, in a household where there were one too many men at the helm. And there was plenty of time for Bobby, the victor of that sordid battle, to make it back to Miguel's bar by the time Miguel came looking for him. Remember, please, that Robert Rhodes was heard threatening to kill Roy an hour before the murder, giving that hour as Roy's last chance to escape. It has been proven beyond the shadow of a doubt that the murder weapon belongs to the defendant, that his alibi is flimsy, and that his motive is plain.''

Without another word, Tatum turned around and walked back to her seat. The click of her heels on the tile floor echoed like gunshots through the silent courtroom. She suddenly wished Jonathan were there.

Troy Duncan remained seated several seconds after he had been called to make his closing remarks, letting the suspense build. Tatum had to admit the man was good at what he did. She didn't like him. She didn't think he either knew or, worse, cared whether Bobby was guilty or innocent. But she had to admit his control of the courtroom was right on target.

The silence stretched out to the point of discomfort, and then Duncan rose. He approached the jurors' box, made eye contact with each of the jurors and then leaned both forearms along the outside wall of the box. He looked casual, relaxed, almost like a friend involved in a conspiratorial chat.

"Well folks, here we are," he began dramatically, the gravity of his tone conveying the seriousness of the decision ahead of them. Tatum could just imagine the worry lines on his forehead. He was going to have the jurors eating right out of his hand.

"It is up to you twelve people to uphold justice, to make the system upon which we all depend work, to determine the fate of a respected and caring young man." Duncan lowered his head, fixing his gaze on his clasped hands.

"The laws that govern and protect every one of us state that a man is innocent until proven guilty, *beyond the shadow of a doubt.*" Duncan looked up, glancing around the room before settling his sights on the jurors once again. Tatum caught just a glimpse of the steely, pinpoint glare he was aiming at the twelve private citizens before him. "I don't know about you folks, but *I* have doubts. Isn't it possible that Roy Ingram was in some kind of trouble, that someone else visited his home between six and six-twenty that night and had an altercation with him? Isn't it also possible that Roy went to the drawer for Bobby's gun, but whoever was there got it from him, shot Roy and ran away? I think it is."

Duncan hesitated again. "Isn't it *doubtful* that a dependable family man like Bobby Rhodes would *kill* a man, the man his sister loved, when there were other options? Folks, I don't know what happened that night in June, but I do know that we have not yet heard the real story. Please remember that there were no fingerprints on the gun—anyone could have fired that fatal shot. Doesn't that fact alone leave room for doubt in your minds?

"Ladies and gentlemen, Bobby Rhodes did not kill Roy Ingram. He came home ready to make peace, only to find two policemen waiting to take him to jail for a crime he did not commit. He found out that his brother-in-law was dead in the morgue of the downtown police station. And I can tell you he was as horrified as you were when you first heard the facts."

With a single slap of his hand against the jurors' box, Duncan concluded his arguments. He returned to his chair, steepled his fingers under his chin and studied the white brick wall directly in front of him. He was the perfect picture of a troubled man, waiting to hear if he would get a fair shake. Tatum groaned silently. No matter what kind of man he might be, the defendant definitely had an edge with

Troy Duncan fighting for him. Tatum could not bring herself to look at Bobby, not even once.

JUDGE KEEDY REQUESTED the jurors' verdict, took the folded piece of paper that held that decision from the bailiff's outstretched hand, read it and passed it back. The bailiff looked down at the paper in his hand, glanced from Bobby to the jurors to the on-lookers in the courtroom. Bobby Rhodes was told to rise.

"The defendant is found to be not guilty." The bailiff's words resounded through the courtroom.

The pandemonium that broke out after a split second of total silence found its echo within Tatum as she felt her insides cave in. As much as she had been afraid this would happen, she still couldn't believe that it had. The air felt cold against her heated, clammy skin. She had lost—not just her first major case, not just a case that had been raised up publicly to prove a political point, not even just an open-and-shut, win-it-in-your-sleep murder trial. She had lost what little faith she had left in herself.

She was aware of Jenny rushing forward, throwing herself in Bobby's arms, sobbing out months of relieved anguish, and of Bobby, holding his sister securely, his eyes closed in grateful relief. She saw the flash of light bulbs, the rush of reporters trying to get the first scoop, the smiles on the faces of the court employees. She saw the large gathering a few rows back—Bobby's people, his supporters, waiting to pat his back or shake his hand. She even noticed Montgomery pushing his way through the crowd, leaving her standing, frozen with shock, all alone on her side of the courtroom. And when she saw a couple of reporters heading her way, she ran. She had to find Jonathan.

JONATHAN CAUGHT a replay of her hasty departure less than half an hour later on the five-o'clock news. Until that moment he had thought that the trial was not yet over. He watched only enough of the broadcast to determine that somehow Tatum had lost the trial before grabbing his keys. After Saturday night, he didn't know if she would welcome him, but he had to try to see her. He knew she would be hurting—hurting badly, if there had been any truth in what Jack McGillus had told him two days earlier.

He was already outside, locking his door behind him, when he heard the phone ringing. Tatum. She was calling him. By the third ring he was back at his desk, grabbing up the receiver.

"Tatum?" He could feel his heart thudding all the way up to his throat.

"It's Charles, man. This one's not pretty."

Jonathan felt his heart stop for the split second it took him to recognize the detective's sterile tones.

"How old?" he asked, moving through the routine for what seemed like the millionth time and still unable to control the instant of rage that shivered through him as he listened to ugly facts about bruises and a broken bone, stated in flat, emotionless tones. He had a bed left in one of the boys' rooms. Cinci could have it made up and turned down long before Jonathan returned from the hospital with nine-year-old Sammy Lawrence.

He ached for Tatum as he finished his calls and sped away from his apartment, but he forced himself to face some hard facts. Charles had called. Tatum had not yet done so. The world was full of people like Sammy who were not yet able to stand on their two feet, who truly needed him—to whom he had already committed his life. Tatum was not one of his needy children. She was one of the world's survivors. And like it or not, he had obligations to fulfill....

TATUM SPED AWAY from the courthouse with tires screeching, bent only on escaping the hordes of media personnel eager to sink their teeth into her. She drove through the city and headed north, knowing that if she could reach the desert lands beyond Carefree she would be relatively free of their clutches.

Her heart was pumping furiously, but her hands were chilly as she clutched the steering wheel, and her feet were like ice. She had the heater blowing, in spite of the balmy October weather, but she was still shivering. She recognized the symptoms of shock as if she were a passenger looking over at herself, but she continued to drive, concentrating on traffic and road signs, her brain on automatic pilot.

She turned left on Carefree Highway and drove as far as the first one-pump gas station she came to, pulled into the graveled lot and searched frantically for a pay phone.

There was no answer at Jonathan's apartment, but Tatum had not really expected him to be there. Too impatient to wait for the message on his machine to finish playing, she hung up and fumbled through the buttons that would connect her with the center. The voice that answered the phone at the Children's Crisis Center was not familiar to Tatum. Had she dialed the wrong number?

"Who's this?" she asked, trying to instill a cheerful note in her voice. She didn't want to alarm the child.

"I'm Andrea. I'm not really supposed to answer the phone, but it was ringing and Mandy's upstairs helping Cinci get ready for the new boy and she told Laura to get the phone, but Laura's in the bathroom. Who's this?"

"Is Jonathan there?" Tatum asked quickly.

"Nope. He's at the police station, getting the new boy—you know, the one Mandy and Cinci are upstairs getting ready for."

Tatum's heart sank as she heard the news. It could be hours before Jonathan was back.

"Do you know when to expect him back?" she asked, hoping the child was privy to the information. She knew she couldn't hold on much longer. She could feel the acid sting of suppressed tears in her throat and behind her eyes.

"Weeelll, I don't think so. He just left to go to the police station and he told Mandy and Cinci right before he left that Tatum had lost her trial and that if she called they were 'sposed to tell her that he would call just as soon as he gets back, even if it was late. So he pro'bly won't be here for a while. Tatum's his friend, you know. Mandy said so. Hey!" the child paused as if something had just occurred to her. "*You* aren't his friend, Tatum, are you?"

Tatum nodded her head, only half-aware that the child couldn't see her reply. No, she thought, Jonathan wasn't her friend, not the kind she needed anyway. He had known about the trial, had even left a message for her, yet he had still chosen to serve his needy strangers first. Couldn't someone else have gone just this once? Did it always have to be Jonathan who personally picked up the kids who stayed at the center? Tears began to stream slowly down Tatum's cheeks. She had her answer. Jonathan had made his choice—one she could not live with.

"Hey, lady, you still there? You wanna leave a message?" The child's perplexed voice drifted off into the distance as Tatum hung up the phone. There was no point in scaring the child with a choked-up voice. She had no message except goodbye, and that one she had to relay herself.

THE NEXT MORNING, after a night spent driving numbly, aimlessly over miles and miles of desert, Tatum arrived at her office to find Montgomery waiting for her. He was sitting in *her* chair behind *her* desk. One look at the paper in his hand, and she was flooded with the dread that had been creeping up on her since the jury's verdict had been read the previous afternoon. Her removal from office was being petitioned.

"I believe you will find this in concise, ordinary language," was all Montgomery said as he stood, handed her the folded paper and brushed by her to stride out of her office.

Holding the paper carefully in trembling fingers, Tatum sank slowly into her chair. She lifted her hair away from her shoulders, as if even that much weight was too much for her crumpled frame to bear. And then she read the formal notice. The numbness that had been her only companion over the past twelve hours dissipated like air being released from a punctured tire.

She had twenty-one days before she was required to appear before the superior court to answer the accusation. This time it was *she* who would be tried by jury—a jury of her peers. Sitting lifeless in her chair, staring down sightlessly, Tatum felt curiously relieved. The worst had happened and she was still in one piece, healthy and functioning. She had just made it through the worst night of her life and, although it had not been her choice, she had done it alone. She would get through whatever lay ahead, as well. She knew that now.

Tatum left her office, drove home, unplugged her phone, locked her doors and went to bed. She needed to catch up on a night's sleep and then she had work to do. It was too late for her and Pop, but she was going to defeat that due-notice bill and save other victims from the tragic chain of events that bitter despair left behind. Someone had to benefit from all that she had lost.

As soon as she was rested, she had something else to do, as well. During the long hours of the night, she had finally faced the fact that whether she was ready or not, it was time to tell Jonathan goodbye. She just couldn't continue pretending that coming second did not hurt. The longer she pretended, the more painful it was going to be.

JONATHAN SLAMMED down the receiver with a resounding bang. Where in the hell was that woman? He had been trying to reach Tatum since he had finished settling in Sammy Lawrence late the night before, but she had not come home. He knew—he'd spent a good part of the night in his blazer outside her house, waiting—and wondered where he had gone wrong, where *they* had gone so wrong, that Tatum had not even bothered to call him after the trial. And when he finally accepted the fact that she was not coming home, he had driven off feeling lost and confused.

He had continued trying to contact Tatum throughout the day. He'd left innumerable messages at her office and called her private number so many times that the sequence of tones corresponding to her number kept playing back through his head like an irritating tune. Mandy had not heard from her, and she had not been to the prison. No one seemed to know what had become of Tatum McGillus.

Jonathan picked up his keys and stalked out of his office. She may not want to see him—judging by his silent phone, she most certainly did not want to see him. But he had to find her anyway. In spite of the pain her silence was inflicting, he still had to know she was all right.

"Mandy, I'm driving by Tatum's again, and then on to her office," he said as he strode by the receptionist's desk. "I'll call later."

"Tell her I love her," Mandy called to his back as he headed out the door.

Jonathan drove with the demons of hell on his tail, as if he could stop time from catching him if only he could move quickly enough. But even as he searched the city for her, he knew his relationship with Tatum was ending. He was a Wright; his life was public service, and Tatum was getting in the way of that. Sammy Lawrence would need him soon, and Jonathan would be further damaging an already injured boy if he could not go to him with one hundred percent concentration.

And there were Tatum's needs to consider, too. Even though she had not called, even though she had not turned to him during her difficult hours, Jonathan had been achingly aware over the past twenty-four hours that if Tatum had called him after the trial, if she *had* needed him, he would not have been able to be there for her. He had been with Sammy.

Jonathan's gloom suddenly lifted as he pulled into Tatum's driveway and saw her car parked beneath the carport. His relief was staggering. He pulled up behind her Taurus and barely had his key out of the Bronco's ignition before he was bounding for her front door. Bypassing the bell, he pounded on the door and tried the knob. Locked. He pounded a second time, impatient to see her, to reassure himself that she was all right, to reassure her. He would just see her through this time, and then he would find a way to walk out of her life.

Jonathan's impatience turned to concern when his third knock went unanswered. Was Tatum in there? Was she all right? He ran around her house, looking in windows, trying to get a glimpse of anything that would tell him if the house was occupied. But the blinds were all drawn, and he was left staring at his own tousled reflection. Alarm spread through him.

Back at the front door, Jonathan pressed on the bell, wondering which window offered the best access for breaking and entering. He would never forgive himself if something had happened to Tatum.

The dead bolt clicked back. Jonathan straightened, his heart pounding heavily in his chest, not sure what he would see when the door finally opened—not even sure of his welcome. Whatever he had been expecting, it had not been the half-asleep, half-dressed beautiful woman who fell into his arms. Jonathan held on to her with everything he had.

"Jonathan," she mumbled against his shoulder, "you shouldn't be here.... It'll only make it harder.... I shouldn't want you here . . . but please, just hold me for a while before you go. Please?" Her voice was thin and husky with sleep, reaching into Jonathan's heart, to the place that ached because he'd let her down.

He led her back into her house, shut and locked the door with one arm still around her, then picked her up to carry her back to her bed, letting go of her just long enough to slip out of his shoes. His body quickened as he lay down next to her and she nestled her silky bottom into his groin, but his heart and mind willed his body to be still. He wrapped both arms around her fine-boned body, settling her head in the crook of his shoulder, smoothed her hair down between them and kissed her neck gently just once. Then he lay as still as stone, willing her back to sleep. This was not a time for lovemaking, but rather a time for loving.

TATUM'S BODY WELCOMED the long-denied rest as much as her mind soaked up the chance to escape into oblivion. Jonathan spent the night with her, waking

her once to coax her to eat some soup and toast
sometime after dark. But when she woke up in the
morning, he was gone. Still too tired to analyze either his coming or his going, she made a sleepy trip to
the bathroom and fell back into a bed still warm from
his presence.

She awoke later that morning feeling surprisingly
refreshed. Her life didn't look any rosier, but she felt
more ready to handle the weeks ahead. She had work
to do—the hearing before her peers to prepare for, a
due-notice bill to defeat. The long-awaited Rotary
meeting was scheduled for the following day, and
Tatum planned to spend the next twenty-four hours
loading her guns in preparation for what could be her
most important battle.

She plugged in her telephone and started to call
Jonathan, wanting to hear his voice, to thank him for
feeding her the night before, to ask when she was going to see him again. But she drew back her hand before it ever reached the receiver. As much as she
wished things could have been different, in her heart
she knew it was time to stop kidding herself. Their
time was up.

CHAPTER TWELVE

TATUM WAS FIGHTING with everything she had as she
stood at the podium in a private meeting room at the
Paradise Wyndham Resort Friday afternoon. The two
hundred Rotarians she faced were a captive audience. She could feel the hard stare of the well-dressed
man seated behind her reaching the fragile, lonely
part of herself she was trying to bury forever. She
straightened her shoulders beneath the shoulder pads
of her plum-colored tweed jacket.

"And so, gentlemen, I ask you to place yourselves
for the moment in the lives of those innocent victims, or families of victims, who are striving to hold
on to a fragile new beginning after enduring more
than their share of the world's repulsiveness. What
purpose would a letter, a brutal reminder of past vi-
olations, serve, other than to provide the root for a
destructive bitterness to grow?"

With years of courtroom practice her voice was
controlled, unemotional. "Could they right what to
them would appear to be a great injustice? Could they
maybe petition to have their violator sent back to
prison? Or could they be at peace with the fact that
the individual had served his lawful term of penance

and deserved the freedom granted him, while the scars they carried, the memories, were with them forever? Do you have that much forgiveness in your heart?''

She looked out over the sea of masculine faces. "If your wife was assaulted, would you be able to live with the fact that the person responsible for changing her life forever was living freely, enjoying life's many rewards?''

Tatum's voice fell silent for a moment, allowing the attentive and influential business owners to absorb her words. No one moved or spoke. No sounds could be heard at all, other than the whirring of the central air-conditioning, until Jonathan sighed heavily from the seat behind her. She wished she could pull her hair down from its professional knot on top of her head. Maybe that would relieve her headache.

"Senator Wright's support for this bill is based on the assumption that a victim can protect himself from further abuse if he's notified that a prisoner is due to be released from prison. In theory, I embrace his view, but I am a realist, gentlemen. What is a victim going to do upon receiving this information? Wouldn't he have taken measures to ensure his safety after he'd been violated the first time? Wouldn't you have?'' Again she made eye contact with as many of the individual members of her audience as she could.

"Very few victims have anything to fear, but by forcing the knowledge of a prisoner's release upon them, we would be instilling in them, probably for life, an awareness that their violator could be just around the corner. Are we to have a society consisting of paranoiacs and witness-protection pawns? Aren't we in essence freeing the prisoner, but by announcing the fact, taking away the freedom of his victim?''

Tatum paused, surrounded by the thick silence that rang with her words. She could almost feel the tension emanating from Jonathan as he sat behind her, but she remained stiffly in position, her speech the center of attention in a roomful of sober-faced individuals. No one knew that at that very moment her heart was breaking. *You told me this wouldn't happen,* her heart cried out to the man behind her. *You told me we could separate the public from the personal. But public is all that you are. And the failure of due-notice is far too personal for me to be able to let go.* She had to break the chain of failures that had befallen her and Pop since the day they had read the letter from the Florida authorities. For the sake of all the victims to follow, she had to succeed in this battle.

"I thank you for your time, gentlemen, and would be more than happy to answer any questions you may have," she concluded with a softening of her features, but without smiling.

"Ms. McGillus, as district attorney, isn't your office personally responsible for supplying much of the information that leads to a prisoner's parole?"

Tatum cringed inwardly at the public mention of her title, a title that only she knew was tenuous at best, but she faced her questioner with outward calm.

"Yes, sir, it is."

"And do you feel confident enough in your staff, and in the American justice system, to take responsibility for the well-being of the victims of this state were they to remain ignorant of an offender's release from jail?"

"I do," Tatum swore without conceit. She was not upholding her faith in her ability to do her job, but rather in the checks-and-balances system she had dedicated her life to representing. After Cale's death, Kanish no longer had the power to hurt her and Pop—it was only the knowledge of Kanish's release from jail that had done that.

The questions continued to flow, and Jonathan joined Tatum at the podium, but as the afternoon wore down, it was he more than she who was having to defend his cause. His peers were questioning the validity of his due-notice proposal.

Tatum felt his heat as he stood beside her, acting as though he had never seen her before in his life. Their suited shoulders brushed, and brushed again. She inhaled the familiar scent of his soap until she almost choked on it. And while she cried inside for what she was losing, she continued to face the roomful of men before her with as much detachment and poise as she could muster. She tried to tell herself that she could not lose what she had never had, that Jonathan had never been hers to begin with. But the thought did nothing to ease the ache in her heart.

After the meeting was over, Tatum pulled up her Taurus beside Jonathan's Bronco and waited. She and Jonathan had some business to finish. It was time to cut off the loose ends between them.

JONATHAN WAS more tired than he could ever remember being as he left the coolness of the Rotary meeting room behind him and headed for his Bronco. He could feel his support for due-notice falling, and the thought scared him. He was going to have to fight harder, which translated in his mind as dirtier, and when he did that he was going to lose Tatum forever.

He was not really surprised to find her waiting for him as he approached his car, but he wasn't happy to see her, either. He felt as if his back was up against the wall and he just didn't see a way for him and Tatum to win—not together. But neither was he ready to let her go.

She looked so beautiful as he approached her, but so distant, as well. He wondered why he was not more relieved that she obviously knew it was time to call it quits, as well. That should make it easier to do what he had to do, shouldn't it?

"Mind if I follow you home?" he asked as he reached her, too weary to bother with platitudes.

"My home?" she asked. She clearly did not think that was such a good idea.

"I won't stay long."

And he wouldn't. Nothing could come of prolonging this except more pain for each of them. But neither could he just walk away from her in a public parking lot. He loved her, for God's sake.

Tatum studied him for a long moment, and Jonathan could only imagine what thoughts were running behind her inscrutable, but unexpressive gaze. She gave him no clues. Finally she just nodded.

JONATHAN FOLLOWED Tatum through to her kitchen, accepted a glass of iced tea that he didn't want and perched on a stool at the breakfast bar. He searched for words that would not come. How did he tell the woman who had become an extension of himself that he couldn't see her again?

"The meeting went well for you," he said, resorting to the platitudes he had not bothered with earlier.

Tatum fiddled with the ice in her glass with the tip of one finger. "And you resent that." It was a statement, not a question.

Jonathan thought he had kept his tone neutral, noncommittal, and maybe he had. Maybe she just knew him too well. Because she was right. He did resent the impact she was having on his constituents. But he resented it for a damn good reason.

"I do," he agreed. After all, this was a large part of their problem. This was what he had come here for. To face up to the problem and to end it. He just hadn't expected to feel so helpless, so desolate, nor had he expected to see the tears that sprang to Tatum's eyes before she quickly blinked them away.

He reached out a hand, intending to draw her around the bar and into his arms, to hold her one last time, to cushion the despair.

"Come here, hon."

She leaned toward him just a fraction, and then Jonathan watched as resolution came over Tatum's expression, taking all her warmth away.

"No, Jonathan. That's the last thing we need."

And that was when he finally admitted that there was a lot more than due-notice and public obligations standing between him and Tatum.

He stood up, leaving his iced tea untouched on the counter. "The last thing *you* need, maybe. Don't include me in your house of ice, Tatum. I need an occasional hug now and then, a little comfort from those around me. But you can't let yourself do that, can you? You've got yourself so barricaded you can't even accept a little solace from a friend."

His words seemed to be having no effect on her at all. She was looking at him as if he were a member of a jury or a judge handing down a sentence. Her indifference hurt more than anything that had gone before. Had he misjudged her so completely? Was he the only one who had something other than time invested in this relationship? Sadness gave way to anger.

"What gives you the right to be so selfish? You aren't the only person living on this earth, the only one to have suffered from having been here. You're all shut away, wasting the most precious gift of all, life itself." Now that he had started, he couldn't seem to stop. "Hell, I thought we were friends. Much more than friends, but you didn't even bother to call when you lost one of the most important cases in your career. I had to hear the outcome on the news like some stranger."

"I called." Her words were barely audible, but they stopped his flow of venom instantly. "As soon as I could, after the trial. I found a pay phone."

"I didn't get any message." Why hadn't he heard that she had called? He had left specific instructions with Mandy the night Tatum lost the trial. If Tatum called, Mandy was to find out where she was and tell Tatum that he'd call just as soon as he got back. According to Mandy, Tatum had never called.

And Mandy had assured him she had passed his instructions on to Laura for the short time Mandy had been upstairs helping Cinci get ready for Sam. Laura had not taken a call from Tatum, either. His answering machine at home was working perfectly also. It had collected several messages over the past two days. Just none from Tatum.

"I didn't leave one. When I called the center, one of the children answered the phone. Mandy was apparently upstairs helping Cinci get ready for a new boy, and her fill-in, Laura, was in the restroom. You had just left to go down to the police station. There didn't seem to be much point in leaving a message."

"Damn it, Tatum. I'd have come. I'd have been here just as soon as I could have if you'd only given me the chance."

"I know," she said, her chin in her chest.

"So?" Jonathan prompted. Didn't this just prove his point all over again.

Tatum looked up, tears slipping silently down her cheeks, allowing him to see finally the despair she was hiding so well.

"So what time would that have been?" she asked. "Midnight? What was I supposed to do in the meantime? I was a basket case at five. How can I let myself rely on you, Jonathan, when I know I will never come first?"

Her voice was trembling and she sounded needier than he had ever heard her. And there wasn't a damn thing he could do about it. Because she was right again. How could he ask her to depend on him when he could not guarantee that he would be there?

"And how can I turn my back on people, *children,* who need me, for someone who doesn't?"

Tatum shrugged. Stalemate. They had reached the bitter end.

Jonathan met her gaze with his own, saying goodbye with his heart. "I'm sorry," was all he said, meaning those two words more than he ever had in his life.

She smiled the unhappiest smile he had ever seen, a smile that he knew he would take with him to his grave. "Me, too."

And then there was nothing more to say. Jonathan took one last long look at Tatum, wishing with all of his heart that things could be different, that he were not who or what he was, that she had not been so bruised by life's battles, and then he turned to go. He was going back to his public, to his calling, but he was leaving a part, a very private part of himself behind.

"Jonathan?" Tatum's voice reached him as he opened her front door.

His heart thumped rapidly, hope springing foolishly forth, as if she could have suddenly come up with a solution that would meet the needs of both of them. He turned to face her.

"Yeah?"

She was standing at the end of the hall. She had removed her high heels sometime while they were in the kitchen, and now she stood with her bare feet visible through her hose. Jonathan remembered a time when he had seen those toes peeking up through a tub of bubbles.

"You ever stop to think that maybe you're hiding, too?" Her words brought him abruptly back to the present. "That maybe caring for so many people relieves you of the responsibility of caring too deeply for just one?"

No, he never had thought that. And he wasn't going to now, either. She was not going to pin her emotional cowardice on him, too. He had been caring for people all of his life. But if it made it easier for her to believe otherwise...

He walked out the door and out to his car without looking back.

LUNCH WAS THE ANSWER. Tatum had been to the office. She had as solid a defense as she was going to get to present to her peers at her impeachment trial. She had been to the prison several times. She had spring-cleaned the house and written her presentation for the upcoming local television appearance she and Jonathan had agreed to weeks before when they had shared the radio appearance so successfully. She had swam laps, taken long walks, cooked meals she had no interest in eating and still, just a week after Jonathan had walked out of her life, she felt ready to climb her walls. For so long her work had consumed her life, and now she had virtually no work. After all, what point was there in having her involved in cases she might not be around to fight?

It was Friday, Mandy's day off. She would call and see if the teenager could meet her for lunch.

Two hours later Tatum sat alone in a plush booth at one of the city's current hot lunch spots, once again tense enough to climb walls. She wiped her palms slowly up and down the seam of her linen slacks in an effort to find some measure of calm. Mandy had cheerfully agreed to meet Tatum at the Hungry Hunter for lunch, but she was over half an hour late. Mandy was too darn reliable to be negligently late. Had she been in an accident? Or was something wrong at the center?

Giving her passing waitress a worried smile, Tatum slid from the booth and headed for the pay phone out in the lobby. She dialed with shaking fingers. If anything had happened to Mandy...

"Children's Crisis Center. This is Cinci." Tatum felt like her heart dropped into her stomach when she heard the other woman's voice. She had been hoping that Mandy would answer, that the girl had been un-

avoidably detained—or that Jonathan would, and
quiet her fears.

"Hi, Cinci, it's Tatum. Is Mandy there?" She tried
to keep the concern out of her voice.

"No... Isn't she with you?" Cinci sounded confused.

Tatum's heart was beating a tattoo against the inside of her rib cage. Something was not right. She was
sure of it. "She's almost forty-five minutes late,
Cinci. I'm getting worried."

"Now don't fret, honey. I'm sure there's a perfectly logical explanation. She went on home to the
Gaineys' to get freshened up just over an hour ago.
She probably just misunderstood what time to meet
you. I'm sure she'll be right along."

Tatum tried to convince herself that Cinci was
right, that Mandy was fine and would be walking in
the door any moment with a harried expression and
a hurried explanation, but she didn't believe it. She
called the Gaineys' house just in case Mandy was still
there, but after listening to the line ring more than
twenty times, she finally gave up. She returned to the
table, telling herself that Mandy would be walking in
any second, that she was worrying over nothing. Fifteen minutes later she flagged the waitress, added a
generous tip to the bill for her cola and once more
headed toward the lobby.

She called Cinci again to get directions to the
Gaineys' and with a quick promise to call the center
as soon as she knew anything more, Tatum headed
out to her car. Her stomach felt like lead, and there

were knots in the muscles along the back of her neck. She hoped she was experiencing nothing more than an embarrassing anxiety attack, but she was just not convinced. Something just didn't sit right.

The Gaineys' home was a medium-sized, nondescript stucco building set in the midst of a hundred more just like it. With all the children in school, the neighborhood was quiet, peaceful looking, though its eclectic mixture of desert landscaping and green grass, cacti and fruit trees kept it from appearing sleepy.

Tatum breathed a sigh of relief as she finally arrived, having made it all the way from the restaurant with no sign of any traffic fatalities. But she broke out into a cold sweat as soon as she saw the unfamiliar car parked behind Mandy's in the Gaineys' driveway.

She pulled up across the street and thought briefly of going for help before she went inside, but the thought of driving away and leaving Mandy in possible danger froze her on the spot. If Mandy was indeed in trouble, Tatum would have surprise on her side. And chances were, the car belonged to the plumber or a friend of the Gaineys who had stopped by, unaware that the family was out of town. Either scenario would explain Mandy's tardiness and be cause for undue embarrassment if Tatum arrived on the scene complete with backups.

No one answered Tatum's knock on the front door, but she couldn't hear any signs of wrongdoing inside, either. Thinking that maybe Mandy was out back with her visitor, Tatum walked around the side of the house. She did not see anybody outside, but she noticed that the sliding glass door in the back of the house was off the track. Maybe Mandy had tried to get out back, probably to the clothesline stretched between two fruit trees in the backyard, and had had problems with the door.

Tatum stepped into the kitchen from the opened glass door. A strange, sharp sound came from the next room, immediately followed by a short, quiet howl.

Thankful for the soft-soled canvas shoes she had donned with her slacks and pullover that morning, Tatum crossed the kitchen floor, heading toward the sound. She had almost reached the door when she heard the voice. It was a man's voice—an angry man's voice.

"That's what you get for rattin' on your old man, girl. I told ya I'd make ya pay good and hard if you ever ran away at the mouth and by God I meant it. A girl's gotta learn her place."

Tatum shivered, her blood running like iced water through her veins. *Your old man?* Could Mandy's father be in the next room? But the man was in prison, wasn't he? *Wasn't he?* Arizona did not have any provisions for notifying victims of a criminal's status. The man could have been released from jail without anybody knowing.

"I didn't just give you life, girl. I raised ya, too. I kept ya when your sluttin' mama run off. I kept your back warm and your cheatin' belly full, and what thanks do I git? Three years locked in a rat hole, that's what."

Tatum was sick with terror as the scene in the next room played itself out in her mind. She moved over to the wall, inching along it toward the doorway. Another crack resounded through the silent house. There was no mistaking it this time. It was flesh hitting flesh. She did not have time to go for help. The man was hurting his daughter—again.

Bile rose in her throat as she reached the door and peered carefully through the opening, but she could not see the teenager from her vantage point. A large, dangerous-looking man was blocking her view, but at least his back was to the door. If she could just figure out a way to warn Mandy to be ready, Tatum could jump the man from behind, counting on the element of surprise to make up for her lesser body weight, and give Mandy enough time to run for help.

"Tell me, girl. Tell Daddy you're sorry. Beg me to take care of you jes' like you always done. Tell me or I'll hurt ya some more." He nodded his head with each word, punctuating his threat, while his long greasy hair bobbed in and out of the collar of his faded blue shirt.

There was no reply from Mandy. Tatum had never been so scared in her life—not even when they had hauled Pop away with his hands cuffed behind his back. Had Schroeder already beat Mandy senseless? Was he threatening an unconscious child? Had he...

Schroeder turned then, just a fraction of an inch, but it was enough for Tatum to see the shiny little pistol he held in his hand. It was aimed in front of him where, Tatum supposed, Mandy was cowering in fear. Surely the man would not shoot his own daughter... would he?

Tatum knew she had to make her move and hope that Mandy was still capable of getting away. She could not afford to wait to warn the girl.

Refusing to consider that she might already be too late, she moved quickly but soundlessly into the doorway, on her way to charge the wide shoulders halfway across the room.

"No!" The sharp cry made Tatum stop in her tracks. It had to be from Mandy, but it was strong and angry and lacked any of the tenderness Tatum had come to associate with the girl.

Just as the sound echoed around the room, the gun in Schroeder's hand came sailing across the floor to land about five feet from Tatum. She barely had time to realize that Mandy's foot had sent the weapon her way before she was moving, too. Propelled by sheer instinct, Tatum picked up the gun, cocked it and aimed it at the big man standing between her and her friend.

He raised his hand as if to hit Mandy again.

"No!" This time it was Tatum's voice calling the command. "You touch her again, and I'll shoot this thing," she said, surprised to find that she would not hesitate to follow through on her threat. She would do whatever was necessary to protect the young girl on the other side of the room.

Schroeder whirled around as he heard her voice, finally realizing he and his daughter were no longer alone, and Tatum had her first glance at Mandy. The teenager had a cut on her lip, and her left eye was almost swollen shut.

Tatum almost dropped the gun in her hand as she cried out against the violation to her young friend, but she stopped herself just in time. She focused on the man in front of her instead. She would not allow her emotions to give this detestable excuse for a father an opportunity to overpower her. She would see to Mandy's safety first, and then she could do her best to comfort her.

"Tatum!" Mandy's good eye glowed with relief as the girl realized she was no longer alone with the maniac whose only good deed had been to give her the seed of life.

"Call the police, Mandy, and then call Jonathan," Tatum said, keeping both hands on the gun she was holding up in front of her. She did not dare look at the girl again. She could not take her eyes off Schroeder for the second it would take for one more glance, nor could she trust her trigger finger to the rage Mandy's ravaged face wrought within her.

"Don't do it, girl. You'll be sorry all over again," the man dared to threaten.

He may have had power over Mandy at one time, power based solely on his physical domination of the girl, but he held it no longer. Mandy didn't even hesitate as she crossed the room and picked up the phone.

CHAPTER THIRTEEN

"JONATHAN'S COMING." Mandy hung up the phone and turned to report what Tatum had already deduced from the part of the conversation she had overheard. The teenager's voice was not quite as strong as it had been moments before.

Tatum was not surprised that the girl had chosen to call Jonathan first. It was thanks to his tutelage that Mandy had had the courage to fight back against her abusive father.

Tatum didn't take her eyes off her captive. "What about the police?"

"He's calling them."

Schroeder glanced from one woman to the other, his face marred with years of hard living and hatred. He looked around the room, stopping to study the bay window to his left.

"Move, and I'll shoot," Tatum said, her words filled with deadly intent. This man wasn't going to get away from her. He wasn't going to go back out into the world where he would be free to hurt Mandy again. The teenager was not going to have to live her entire life looking over her shoulder, afraid to ever be alone, always wondering when the man who had fathered her was going to find her again.

Tatum froze inside when she realized where her thoughts had just taken her. Mandy needed due-notice. Had the law been in effect, this afternoon might never have happened. Without the law, it could happen again—to Mandy and to all the women and children just like her, victims of domestic abuse. It was what Jonathan had been trying to tell her all along. Without due-notice Mandy and thousands of other children were going to be running scared for the rest of their lives. *Just like the victims Tatum was trying to protect by seeing the bill fail.*

Schroeder spit on the steel gray carpet. "Pretty tough for a lady, ain't ya?"

Tatum had never felt less tough in her life, but she was not going to let him know that he was making her insides quake. "Maybe, maybe not, but I'm the one with the gun so I guess that answers it, doesn't it?" she said in her best courtroom voice. She could not let him intimidate her.

Schroeder gave her one last disgusted snort and then turned on his daughter. "You'll pay for this, girl. They can't keep me in there forever. An' next time I git out, I'll make sure it's just you an' me."

Mandy left the room.

Tatum was alone with Schroeder for no more than sixty seconds, but it was enough to tax what strength she had left.

"We'll take it from here, ma'am."

Tatum had never been so glad to hear another voice in her life, but she could not take her eyes off her charge long enough to see whom it belonged to. She held the gun in front of her with both hands, shaking.

"It's okay, ma'am, we've got him." She heard the words just as the two armed policemen came into her line of vision. With his gun firmly aimed, one approached Schroeder, ordering him down to the floor, while the other gently unarmed Tatum.

She watched just long enough to see Schroeder's bloodstained hands being cuffed, and then she turned and fled. She was afraid she was going to be sick all over that gunmetal gray carpet.

Taking big gulps of air, she searched the house for Mandy, sure that the girl would want to know that her father was safely in custody, but the girl was nowhere in the house. Tatum ran out through the broken back door, afraid for Mandy, afraid that in trying to get as far from her father as possible, the girl would do something foolish. Mandy should not be alone. No one could be expected to deal rationally with the aftermath of the past hour's horrors. The young woman needed reassurance—and a doctor.

Tatum's eyes were still adjusting to the sunlight as she rounded the corner of the house, and she almost ran straight into the back of Jonathan's strong, comforting shoulders. Mandy's trembling body was locked in his embrace, and the teenager was sobbing almost incoherently.

"They've got him," Tatum said softly, afraid to admit how badly she had needed to see Jonathan, how much she had depended on the knowledge of his coming during those horrible minutes when she had pointed a gun at another human being with full intent to shoot if the need arose. But she couldn't deny the calm that swept away her panic as their eyes met or the sudden need to put distance between them.

Jonathan looked up from the hysterical, bleeding young woman in his arms as Tatum's voice shot through him. He couldn't stem the longing he felt when he first saw her, nor could he stop the flow of gratitude that swept through him as he acknowledged that if it had not been for her brave actions, Mandy might well be dead.

He continued to murmur comforting assurances to Mandy as his eyes spoke to Tatum. Thanking her. He wanted to pull her into his arms, too, to assure himself that she was fine, to protect her, but he couldn't release his hold on Mandy. The girl would fall on her face on the hard concrete.

"Call me if she needs anything," Tatum said, looking at Mandy. And then, turning away, she walked swiftly down the driveway to her car parked across the street.

Jonathan's eyes looked resigned as he watched Tatum turn her car around and drive off down the street as if a herd of hunting dogs were chasing her down. The lady was strong enough to stay afloat in the middle of a raging ocean. She did not need anyone. But it wasn't that knowledge that hurt so bad—it was the brief glimpse he had seen of her hunger to be held, the knowledge that she had *wanted* him to comfort her and his arms had already been full.

But he was Jonathan Wright, *Senator* Jonathan Wright, founder and director of the Phoenix Children's Crisis Center, son of a Nobel Prize winner. He had his obligations, and he would fulfill them even if his heart ached for the rest of his life.

He squeezed the young woman nestled against his chest. "Come on, baby. Let's get you to the clinic and then home to Cinci."

FIGHTING THE AGONIZING loneliness that was threatening to consume her, Tatum spent every spare moment of the next two days poring over law books, articles and pages of legislation, trying to read every word that had ever been written about due-notice. She studied precedents and percentages, various states' before-and-after-due-notice figures, parole statistics and victims' personal accounts. Burying personal thoughts of Jonathan way down deep inside, she wrestled with her conscience, her emotions and her logic, but still could find no workable solution to the due-notice issue. It still remained that more people would benefit from the failure of the bill than the passage of it. But that did not stop both sides of the issue from raging inside of Tatum's heart.

During her Sunday-morning visit to her father, she listened to him struggle for breath until she was exhausted from the effort. She filled her lungs to capacity again and again, as if she could somehow store air for him, as if her oxygen could become his. She held his hand, smoothed her fingers over his thinning, blue-veined skin and told him all about the trial she had lost, the job she may be losing, due-notice and Mandy. She spoke of the past and the future, of memories and fears. She spoke of everything in her heart, except for Jonathan.

And when she ran out of words, she leaned over, kissed him and held her cheek pressed gently against his for several long seconds. Pop did not wake up once the entire morning.

She stopped by the center on the way home. Cinci greeted her at the door with a hug.

"Thank you. Thank God for you, Tatum McGillus," she said, the words muffled against Tatum's hair.

Tatum returned Cinci's hug, more comforted than the other women would ever have imagined by the physical contact, but she had to pull back long before she had received the sustenance she needed. She could only take so much without breaking down completely.

"How is she?" Tatum asked, still holding Cinci's hand.

Cinci nodded and smiled weakly. "Better. She's already asking how soon she can come back to work. She's been asking for you."

Cinci led Tatum down the hall to one of the smaller multi-purpose rooms. Mandy was sitting in an armchair in the far corner of the room, wrapped from her ears to her toes in a big furry blanket. It looked to Tatum as if she had her knees pulled up protectively to her chest, her arms wrapped around them, with the blanket tucked tightly around the ball she made. She had a book on her lap, but judging from her vacant stare, she didn't appear to be reading.

"Hi, hon," Tatum said softly, leaving Cinci at the door of the room as she approached Mandy.

Mandy's head jerked up, but she smiled when she saw Tatum, as much as her swollen lip would allow.

"Tatum! I've been thinking about you," Mandy said with a lisp. "I owe my life to you."

Tatum sat on the floor at Mandy's feet, not sure whether she should touch the young woman or not. Other than the time she had accompanied Pop to bring a fourteen-year-old Mandy to the center, Tatum had never dealt one-on-one with a victim of domestic abuse. She had no idea what Mandy needed or didn't need.

"You don't owe me anything," she said, smiling up at her young friend. "Except maybe a hug, if you're up to it."

Tatum swallowed thickly when she saw the tears fill Mandy's eyes, but she knew she had done the right thing as she watched the girl unravel herself from her cocoon and hold out her arms to Tatum. Tatum pulled Mandy out of the chair and down onto the floor and into her arms. She held her friend carefully, mindful of Mandy's bruised body, and listened while Mandy cried out her fear, her embarrassment, her loss of dignity. And sometime during those moments, Tatum began to mix her own tears with Mandy's. And when Mandy finally lifted her head from Tatum's shoulder, she was smiling again, really smiling, even through the bruises. "What a pair we make, huh?" she said.

"I think we do okay," Tatum replied. "We sure won this round."

Tatum was surprised as a frown crossed Mandy's face.

"But we can't win, Tatum. You and Detective McGillus and me. People like you shouldn't have to hear about jail releases, but I *gotta* hear, Tatum. I need due-notice. I know that now. Jonathan was right all along."

Tatum nodded, not knowing what to say. She had no words of wisdom. She had no answers. But she understood. Mandy was right.

Mandy looked across at Tatum, meeting Tatum's gaze with her own. "Are you disappointed in me for backing out on you—on our fight?" Mandy asked.

"Absolutely not!" Tatum said. That was one thing she was sure of. Mandy had to fight for due-notice. If it passed in Arizona, due-notice could save Mandy's life some day, just as Florida's due-notice was taking Pop's.

Tatum knew what Mandy had to do about due-notice. She just didn't know what *she* was going to do about anything.

She was still struggling with the dilemma Sunday evening, no closer to deciding what kind of stand she was going to take when she appeared on television the next day, when the phone rang. Afraid that it might be Danny with bad news about Pop, she rushed into her home office to answer it.

"Hello?" Her voice was breathy, barely above a whisper. Her heart was drumming a rapid beat beneath her breast.

"Ms. McGillus?" Tatum swallowed her disappointment, instantly alert.

"Who is this?" she asked. The voice sounded familiar, but she couldn't place it.

"It's Bobby Rhodes, ma'am. I'm sorry to bother you, but I keep thinking about that smell."

Tatum sank down into the chair behind her desk. "What smell, Bobby?" she asked. She was aware that she should resent the intrusion, that she should resent any contact at all from the young man who may have cost her her career, but she had liked Bobby from the beginning. She was curious about his call.

"The one that wasn't gunpowder. You know, like my cousin's perfume?"

Tatum sat up straighter. "Do you know what it was?" she asked.

"Yes, ma'am. Lily was over with her new baby today, and as soon as she walked in the door, I smelled it again—you know, the smell that was unfamiliar the night of the murder. I asked her what it was. She said it was a cologne made naturally from herbs by some old lady here on the west side. There's a shop down by Miguel's that sells it."

Tatum's heart began to pound as healthy, invigorating adrenaline started flowing through her veins. "So someone else *was* in your home that night, after you left for Miguel's—presumably, a woman."

"That's what I've been thinking about all afternoon, ma'am. I just don't know where to go from here."

"Have Lily take you to that shop, Bobby. Find out who's purchased that cologne recently. See if you can meet with the woman who makes it. She may sell some of it herself. Go to Roy's work, ask around. See if anyone remembers seeing him with another woman. And then call me back here at home. As district attorney, I can't pursue this, but there are no laws against a private citizen asking questions. If someone else was in your home that night, if someone else killed Roy, we need to find out who it was before asking the police to open the case again...."

Tatum still was not sure whether Bobby was innocent or whether she had just lost her ability to "feel" the difference between guilty and not guilty, but hope was reborn in her heart as she headed back to the kitchen.

JONATHAN DRESSED slowly for his television appearance Monday morning, wondering how the world had ever gotten so crazy. Forgetting Tatum was proving even harder than he had expected, and was made still harder by the fact that he had to face her on opposite sides of an issue that meant everything to both of them.

Tying his maroon paisley tie with the help of the bathroom mirror, he shook his head at the irony of it all. He was in love with a woman who did not need him, and he was committed to people who did. He was fighting a battle to protect those he was committed to, but in winning, he had to defeat the woman he loved.

And there was no way he could back down on the due-notice issue. Especially now. Mandy's near tragedy had not only filled him with rage; it had also filled him with panic. If he never did another thing, he had to provide his kids with the promise of some measure of security in their battered lives. It was the only way they were ever going to recover from the cruel blows life had dealt them. It was the only way they would ever be able to conquer the instinctive fear that had been cruelly instilled in them at such a young age. His love for Tatum was nowhere near a good enough reason to desert those children.

Jonathan took one last cursory glance at himself as he buttoned his white cuffs. Bolstered by his good intentions, he slipped on his navy suit coat and left to defeat the woman who had become as much a part of him as his own arms and legs. He could live without her if he had to, but her loss had brought irrevocable changes to his life. He had joined the ranks of the walking wounded.

TATUM ARRIVED at the television station purposely late, leaving herself only enough time for makeup touch-ups and last-minute instructions before she was due to go on the air. She didn't want time alone with Jonathan before the live talk show began, since she feared that her limited composure would crack under the strain of small talk.

"You have four minutes until you're on, Ms. McGillus. If you'd like to wait in the room to the right of the set with Senator Wright, we'll signal when we're ready," the young assistant assured Tatum as she led her down the hall.

Tatum's stomach clenched. "Four minutes?" Her watch must be fast. Tatum thought quickly. "Is there a ladies' room close by? I'd have just enough time..." She let her words trail off.

"Certainly. It's right through those doors," the young woman replied, pointing to her left. "Just be sure you're out here in exactly three and a half minutes."

Tatum spent the next three minutes pacing the ladies' room. She had made some major decisions over the past forty-eight hours, but she still wasn't completely comfortable with them. She only knew that no matter how unhappy she might be at some time in the future, she could no longer go on soaking pillow-cases with useless tears.

The assistant met Tatum just as she emerged from the ladies' room. "It's time. They're on commercial break for sixty seconds. Senator Wright is already in place on the set," she said, leading Tatum around the corner.

Tatum had never been on television in her life, and was surprised and a little disappointed when she first saw the tiny plywood platform that held three chairs, a coffee table, an end table and little else, set in the midst of a shadowed, cluttered room. She stepped up onto the platform, joining the host, Mike Tarryton, and Jonathan. Both men stood up at her approach.

Bright lights shone down on Jonathan's hair, making its brown strands shine like burnished gold. Tatum clutched her hands together and forced herself to look away as she took her seat. She felt his eyes on her, though, and had to consciously restrain herself from glancing up to meet his gaze. She was thankful when Mike sat down between them.

"Four, three, two, one ..."

"Good morning, and welcome to 'Arizona Avenues,' the show where we discover Arizona, and Arizonians, together...."

Tatum listened to Mike introduce her and Jonathan, smiled in the right places and realized that as long as she concentrated on the matter at hand, as long as she didn't glance to the left where Jonathan was seated, she was going to make it through the next twenty minutes. She was excited about the solution she had found to bring together both sides of the due-notice issue, and was eager to impart her findings not only to the public, but to Jonathan, as well. She only hoped that he would approve of her compromise.

"We'll hear from you first, Ms. McGillus. Then, after Senator Wright has a chance to speak, we'll open the phone lines."

Tatum felt a little nervous as she faced the dark-ened roomful of cords, lighting paraphernalia, stray pieces of filming sets and jean-clad shapes moving around with bulky cameras on their shoulders. What if Jonathan didn't agree with her proposition? How could she ever choose between saving people like herself, whose lives would be ruined by due-notice, and children like Mandy, whose only hope was the passage of the bill?

Tatum thanked Mike for having her on the show and then, with her hands clasped calmly in her lap, she faced the camera directly in front of her and gave the speech she had prepared the night before.

"I agreed to be a guest on 'Arizona Avenues' with the sole purpose of convincing Arizona citizens that Senator Wright's proposed due-notice law would rob them of their freedom to live normal lives. I have evidence that in many cases, that is exactly what happens when a crime victim is informed that the perpetrator of said crime is once again free on the streets. The victim loses his freedom. He lives in fear. Or if he is a family member of a deceased victim, he lives with a bitterness so encompassing that it clouds every thought he has, every thing he does. And for what good? What good comes to any of these people from the knowledge being forced upon them?''

Out of her peripheral vision, Tatum saw Jonathan bow his head. She heard his troubled sigh.

''But recently I had cause to witness firsthand the harm that can come to certain individuals who do not yet have the protection of due-notice.''

Tatum paused. Her heart began a rapid thud as Jonathan sat up straighter. She could feel his piercing brown gaze locked firmly on her face. She glanced at Mike, saw the question stamped across his startled features and continued before she lost her chance to be heard.

''There are those individuals, victims of domestic crimes mainly, who desperately need the protection of knowing when an abusive family member is being released from captivity. The statistics of repeated abuse from such criminals are alarming. And as things stand currently, the related victims are little more than sitting ducks, waiting to be found. Last Friday one such victim, a seventeen-year-old friend of mine, was found.''

''Excuse me, Ms. McGillus. Are you saying that you now support the due-notice issue?'' Mike asked, sounding almost disappointed. Tatum wasn't sure if it was because he saw the fireworks dwindling out of a show that was supposed to have been controversial enough to guarantee him good ratings, or if it was because he had sympathized with her side of the issue.

Tatum forced herself to look at Jonathan. After all, he was the senator who was writing the bill. She had to have his approval to change it. He met her gaze thoughtfully, waiting for her to speak, giving her the courage to continue.

"Not as it stands, I don't," she answered the host. As the look in Jonathan's eyes turned stony, she quickly continued, her throat constricted. "But when I looked at my young friend and saw patches of swollen skin still wet with blood on her pretty face, it suddenly hit me that if the due-notice proposal were defeated, I would be partially to blame for such atrocities. I'm ashamed to admit that it took a near tragedy to someone very dear to me to enable me to see the issue from a different angle for the first time. I've spent the last couple of days poring over legal briefs and recorded laws from all the other states that have due-notice laws on their books, and have finally determined that if we can rewrite the bill, if we can combine it with an addendum that I have taken from similar laws in other states and an added clause of my own, I think we could have a law that, while highly unusual, would give the best overall protection."

She was speaking only to Jonathan now, hoping he would take her olive branch, knowing that if he did not, they would both lose.

"What exactly do these addenda entail?" Jonathan asked before Mike had the chance. At least he was still listening to her. Her heart continued to beat rapidly.

"That due-notice be given only to victims who request it," she began, opening with the hardest sell.

"But..." Jonathan started to interrupt, his features showing his frustration.

"And that *all* victims of domestic abuse be notified automatically, unless they specifically request not to be," she finished. As far as she could see, this was the only answer. She could only hope that Jonathan saw it that way, too.

He was silent for a full minute, studying her, obviously weighing her words with great care. Mike sat silently between them, glancing from one to the next, seeming to realize that his best move was to simply let the scene play itself out.

Tatum's gaze never wavered from Jonathan's, whose features softened imperceptibly. For an instant she felt him looking at her as if she might be a miracle worker, and for that single moment in time, she felt like one. The ice around her heart was not quite so cold, her loneliness not quite so acute.

Jonathan was still frowning, but it was more a frown of concentration than displeasure. "The extra paperwork will be costly for the state," he said, voicing what was also her biggest concern.

Tatum nodded. She couldn't argue with him there; she just hoped the extra tug on the state's budget would not be reason enough to stop him.

"People have a tendency to vote more conservatively when money is involved, which means that these addenda might lose some due-notice supporters," he said, more to himself than to Mike or Tatum.

"But not nearly as many as if I continue my campaign against you," Tatum said, playing her ace.

Jonathan looked at her directly as she issued her challenge, studying her with his intent brown gaze, and then, after a very long minute, he nodded.

"I'll see that the changes are made," he said, making official what her heart already knew. As far as due-notice was concerned, they had both won.

"And there you have it, folks, Arizona laws in the making. All it takes is a couple of concerned citizens like you and me, and we can make our world a better place...."

Jonathan felt a huge weight lift from his chest as he listened to Mike Tarryton lead them into a commercial break. He smiled at Tatum, silently thanking her for finding the solution that had been eluding him, for being willing to meet him halfway, to announce publicly to all of her supporters that their Senator's bill had merit after all.

But that was Tatum's way, he thought with a twinge of sadness. She could do anything, handle anything, solve anything, and she didn't need his or anyone else's help to do so. He thought of the children waiting back at the center, of Mandy, who had had a change of heart about the bill now that she saw firsthand what Jonathan had been fighting against. He was suddenly very eager to return to the place where he knew he was needed, where he never doubted that he belonged.

TATUM HURRIED off the set as soon as the commercial break was called, but she waited in the wings for Jonathan to follow her. Whatever other problems still lay between them, they had overcome a huge hurdle that morning. The event deserved a little celebration, if nothing else.

She only hoped she could talk Jonathan into having lunch with her. Then maybe she could talk to him about some of the other things she had been thinking about, as well. Things like maybe he'd been right when he had called her selfish. Maybe she *was* so busy protecting herself against being hurt that she had begun to exist rather than live.

"Hi, I thought you'd left," Jonathan said as he came around the corner where she was waiting.

"I thought maybe we could have lunch," Tatum replied, hardly daring to hope that the next hour would go as smoothly as the previous one had.

"I'd like to, but I promised a couple of the kids a game of table tennis this afternoon," he said with an apologetic look, as if he knew his excuse sounded lame.

"Couldn't you put it off for an hour?" Tatum pressed, refusing to be daunted by his evasive tactics.

After all, he did not yet know just what she had to say over lunch.

Jonathan shook his head. "I've got to help Cook figure out how to work the new dishwasher this afternoon, and I promised Cinci an evening off. She has some shopping to catch up on. Maybe some other time," he said, putting her off with a suggestion they both knew he did not really mean.

"Yeah, some other time," Tatum echoed as she watched him walk away. She had just been saved from making the biggest mistake of her life. So why didn't she feel better about that? If Jonathan had really cared for her, if he was hurting at all, if he missed her even half as much as she missed him, surely he would have made the time to spend a measly hour with her. Instead, he'd seemed almost anxious to get back to the center, to the people who *needed* him. He was still caring for the people rather than the person. He was still putting his public obligations first. He was still hiding. How could she have allowed herself to love him, knowing he was not capable of loving her back? And how was she ever going to stop?

TATUM WAS STILL ASKING herself that question two nights later as she lay wide-awake in her big lonely bed. Would she ever stop longing for Jonathan? His presence haunted the room, taunting her with warm memories. The bedroom was the one place where she had always come first in Jonathan's life. If only they could have locked themselves in and never come out.

Tatum's thoughts drifted as her exhausted psyche imagined a lifetime lived solely in that one room. There was a bathroom attached. And they could send out for food, but how would they pay for it after the first year or so when all their savings ran out?

The phone rang, startling her back to full consciousness. Who could be calling this late? Did she dare hope that it was Jonathan? Could he feel how she longed for him?

She fumbled for the bedside phone. "Hello?" She hoped her voice didn't sound as lonely as she felt.

"Ms. McGillus?"

Tatum recognized the voice this time. She sat up in bed.

"Yes, Bobby. Have you found anything yet?"

"I know who killed Roy, ma'am."

Tatum smiled, falling back against her pillows, not the least bit surprised when she heard Bobby's words. She wasn't surprised that he had moved so quickly or that he had found his answers. It was just what Jonathan would have done, or Pop, or Cale.... Blessed relief washed over her, leaving her lightheaded. She had not been wrong about the young man after all.

"Who?" The single word was more for curiosity's sake than anything else. She didn't need the facts to know that Bobby had found his truth.

"He had a lover, ma'am. I did like you said and went down to Roy's work. He'd been carrying on with one of his co-workers for months. With a little friendly persuasion, it wasn't hard to link her to the cologne. She bought some the day of the murder. Getting her to admit to killing Roy was a little harder, but I was not leaving her without finding out what happened that night.''

Tatum's professional adrenaline began to flow. The feeling that she was hearing the truth was too strong to ignore. "What did happen, Bobby?" she asked.

"She says she thought she was pregnant and came to the house demanding that Roy leave Jenny like he'd been promising to do for months. When Roy refused, she went a little crazy, started crying and hitting him. He backed into the side table, spilling the drawer that held my gun. She grabbed for it, but she says she didn't mean to kill him, that she only wanted to threaten him to get him to take her seriously. But Roy wrestled her for it, and it went off during their struggle. I think she's telling the truth, but that is for you folks to determine. She found out a couple of days later that she wasn't pregnant after all.''

"Who is she, Bobby?" Tatum asked, sure that the young man wasn't going to tell her. That, after all, was the code of the streets. It was probably why Bobby had been able to find his answers so quickly. It was certainly the only reason the woman would have dared to confess to him. It was the reason Bobby had had a police record to begin with.

"Her name is Patty LaTina. She's working a second job, nights at Arthur's Food Mart. She's there now, I suppose.''

Tatum's face broke into an all-out grin. She hadn't felt this good in a long, long time.

"Why, Bobby?" she asked. "Why are you telling me this?"

"You gave me a fair trial ma'am. The law worked for me. I would like to see it work for Jenny, too."

CHAPTER FOURTEEN

JONATHAN READ about it in the paper. District Attorney Tatum McGillus had assisted in the arrest of one Patty LaTina for the murder of Roy Ingram. After a brief vacation Ms. McGillus was back to work full-time and would be trying the case herself.

He read the article again. They were making Tatum out to be a hero. Not for finding Patty—apparently Bobby Rhodes had had the bigger hand in that, but people were making a big deal out of the fact that the district attorney was out to see that justice was done, not how many cases she could win or lose. No mention was even made of Tatum's connection to ex-detective Jack McGillus.

Jonathan reached for the phone, intending to call her to congratulate her, to tell her how proud he was of her, but his hand fell limply on top of a pile of folders on the right corner of his desk. He could not call Tatum. She was no longer a part of his life.

It had been eight days since he had seen her, eight days since she had saved the due-notice issue for both of them, and he had felt her loss every minute of those days. It didn't make sense to him—he simply couldn't get on with his life. How could anyone have become such an integral part of him in just three short months? And how long was it going to take before he was himself again?

MANDY CALLED Tatum to congratulate her on the surprising development of the Bobby Rhodes murder trial. Though she had been hoping Jonathan would be the one to call, Tatum was delighted to hear from Mandy, and relieved to find that her young friend's voice was almost back to normal.

"I guess you're real busy again, huh?" Mandy asked.

"I'm not busy Friday night, how about you?"

"Nope." Tatum could hear the smile in the young woman's voice.

"Wanna have dinner and spend the night?" Tatum asked, waiting more anxiously than she should have been for the girl's reply. She just really needed something to look forward to.

"Sure!"

It had been decades since Tatum had had a girlfriend over for the night, but the more she thought about it, the more fun it sounded.

"Should we do Italian this time?" she asked, wondering when she would find the time to shop for semolina. "I don't usually shop until Saturday morning, but I could stop on my way home from work."

"You don't have to do that, Tatum. I make a great lasagna. How about if I come early and do the cooking and we can eat whenever you get home?"

Tatum's grin broadened. How could she ever have contemplated living her life without friends?

"You sure you don't mind?" she asked, not wanting to abuse Mandy's generosity.

"I'm sure. I'm off at noon on Friday, and hanging around here isn't my idea of fun right now. Jonathan's being a bear...."

"HOW OLD DO YOU HAVE to be to adopt a child?"

Tatum almost choked when Mandy threw out the question. The two women were sitting on Tatum's couch, having settled there after feasting on Mandy's lasagna, salad, strawberries and ice cream.

"Each case is different, hon, but you do at least have to be a legal adult," Tatum answered, worried about where Mandy's question might be leading.

Mandy raised one ankle to her knee and fiddled with a string on the hem of her jeans. "I'm worried about Abby."

Tatum had not heard Mandy mention the little girl since the night Abby had left. "Have you heard from her?" she asked. Concern for little Abby sprang up within Tatum, and concern for Mandy, as well. The teenager was barely over her own tragic ordeal, the bruises were only just now fading away, and already Mandy was thinking about someone else's troubles.

"Sylvia Reynolds was in a couple of days ago. She says Abby's already been through two foster homes. She's gonna get hard real quick if it keeps up." Tatum heard the words Mandy was not saying as clearly as the ones she was. Little Abby was being stripped of her childhood, too.

"You don't have any means of supporting a toddler, hon," Tatum said, wishing she could relieve some of the burden Mandy had taken upon her young shoulders, wishing, too, that she had the power to snatch Abby away from the cold world that had her in its grasp.

"No..." Mandy's fingers were suddenly still against her ankle, her eyes earnest and pleading as they searched Tatum's face. "But you could."

The words dropped into the silent room. Tatum's first instinct was to recoil, to reject any possibility that she could be a mother to Abby, to any child, that she could once again be a part of a loving family. But even as she fought against it, the idea began to take form, to weave itself into possibilities, into hope.

"You'd make a wonderful mother." Mandy's words were spoken softly, floating into Tatum's consciousness to mingle with the dreams she'd suppressed for so long.

"Adoption is a huge commitment, Mandy—a lifetime commitment. It takes a lot of thought, of consideration. Children are not Christmas trees. You don't just decide to get one, go pick it out and bring it home, and you can't throw it out when the sea-son's over, either. What you're suggesting would alter my entire life. A child, any child, would require years and years of responsibility."

Tatum's words were intended for her own foolish heart, as well as Mandy's. How could she even be considering the possibility of adopting Abby? The idea was ludicrous.

"But wouldn't it be great?" Mandy asked, a half impish, half wistful grin on her face.

Tatum could not allow the silly fantasy to continue. She could not allow herself to think about the upside of being a mother. She had reality to deal with.

"I'd be pushing any possibility that I may someday marry even further away than it is right now," she said to Mandy. "I can't expect some guy to take on another person's child."

"If he were the right guy, he wouldn't mind," Mandy persisted, undeterred by Tatum's reasoning. After a pause she added, "Jonathan would do it, if you'd let him."

So that's what she's getting at, Tatum thought ruefully. This was not just about adoption—it was about dreams coming true, about fairy tales coming to life.

Tatum got up, poured herself a glass of wine and returned to her place on the couch.

"It's not a matter of me letting him, hon," she said, knowing that she and Jonathan owed Mandy some kind of explanation. They had done her a great disservice in failing to see that she was hurting for both of them. If only Tatum could help Mandy understand that sometimes love was not enough. If only she believed that herself.

"I know he cares about you, Tatum. I've never seen Jonathan like this before. He's grouchy all the time. Cinci says it's 'cause he misses you."

Tatum took a sip of her wine. "I miss him, too. More than I would ever have thought possible. Enough that I finally realized that some of Jonathan would be better than none of Jonathan, that coming second in his life was better than not coming at all. But I don't think Jonathan is ready to hear that. I think part of the reason he's so good at what he does is that caring for bunches is a lot safer than caring for one. And I also think he's afraid that if he does commit himself to me, or to any other single person, the people who are already counting on him will suffer."

Mandy frowned. "So you're saying that all of this is Jonathan's fault?" she asked.

"It's no one's fault. I was wrong, too, you know. Jonathan once accused me of being selfish, of being so bent on protecting myself from pain that I was shutting myself off from all that life had to offer—"

"You don't do that!" Mandy said, breaking into Tatum's explanation.

Tatum set her glass down. "I did. He was right, Mandy. But after watching you, after seeing how no matter how many times you're knocked down you keep getting back up, keep reaching out, I wasn't very proud of myself. I knew then that I didn't have the right to hide anymore.''

Mandy was fiddling with her string again. "So where do you go from here?''

Tatum flicked a piece of Mandy's hair affectionately. "To bed. And then, maybe tomorrow, to a movie with you?''

Mandy studied Tatum's expression for a long moment, and Tatum braced herself for more of the teenager's persuasion. But Mandy just shrugged.

"Sure. I'm off at three. What do you want to see?'' Mandy asked.

Tatum breathed a sigh of relief at Mandy's willingness to let the topic drop. She only hoped she would be better prepared if or when it came up again.

"Tatum?'' Mandy asked a few minutes later as the women were crawling into bed.

"Yeah?''

"Will you at least think about Abby?''

Tatum had a feeling she didn't have much say in the matter. The obstacles might prove to be too great to overcome, but hope had been born. The thought of mothering little Abby was just too tempting to ignore.

JONATHAN THREW his reading glasses down on his desk, having read the same memorandum six times without knowing what it said. He had heard Mandy come in a few hours earlier, and he had spent most of that time trying to come up with a way to ask about

Tatum without appearing to be doing that. The last thing he wanted to do, he thought as he clambered down the stairs, was to put Mandy in the middle of something that didn't concern her.

Mandy was talking on the phone when Jonathan reached the lobby, and he leaned against the wall of the entryway, waiting for her to finish. It was good to see Mandy back, sitting in her usual place behind the receptionist's desk, looking as if nothing bad had ever happened to her. Her bruises had faded, as had the haunted look in her eyes. He knew Tatum had a lot to do with that. She had been spending a lot of time with the teenager.

"Oh, God, no."

Jonathan straightened, instantly alert as Mandy's words reached him. The young woman's face had gone white.

"We'll find her. Yes, sir. She'll be there." Tears pooled in Mandy's eyes as she hung up the phone and saw Jonathan standing there.

Jonathan approached her slowly. "What is it, hon? What's happened?" he asked, trying to keep his voice calm.

Mandy looked up at him, her despair clearly evident. "It's Tatum's pop.... Detective McGillus had another heart attack about half an hour ago. They can't reach Tatum at home, and she's not answering at her office. They left a message on her machine. We can't let her hear about this over the phone, Jonathan. We have to find her. They don't think Detective McGillus is going to make it...."

Jonathan pulled the teenager out of her chair and into his arms as her tears overflowed and spilled down her cheeks. She clung to him briefly and then pulled back. "She said she was going grocery shopping," she said, looking at him with pleading eyes.

Jonathan understood. But she needn't have worried. Nothing was going to keep him from finding Tatum. "You want to come along?"

Mandy sat back down. "She'd probably rather just have you," she said, as if trying to tell him something. He wondered if the two women had spent time talking about him, then reminded himself that now was not the time to pursue such thoughts.

"She goes to that new Safeway...." Mandy's words followed him out into the early November sunshine.

JONATHAN FOUND Tatum in the Safeway parking lot. She was loading plastic bags full of groceries into her trunk. He watched her for a few seconds, unable to hurt her, to bring her more pain. Finally, realizing that time was of the essence, he got out of his Bronco.

Tatum glanced up as he reached her side and did not immediately shrug him off when he slipped an arm around her waist.

"Jonathan!" For a split second Tatum's face registered the joy he heard in her greeting, and then she stiffened beside him.

"What is it? What's happened?" she asked. Something in his expression must have given him away.

Jonathan felt déjà vu sweep over him as he once again found himself telling her the bad news. "It's your father, Tatum. He's had a second attack. His time is limited," he said, knowing that she would want to hear it all.

He expected her to pull away from him, to turn into the automaton she had before, but instead she collapsed against his chest.

"Oh, Jonathan."

There was nothing he could do except hold her against him with all of his strength. Tatum needed him. After months of his wishing it so, after finally giving up hope that it would ever be, she was here, in his arms, needing him. He felt an instant of panic like he had never known before.

Shamed by the unexpected emotion, he pulled her more firmly against himself. "We need to go to him, honey. We should hurry," he whispered just above her ear.

Tatum nodded, but she continued to cling to him. He felt her shudder, heard her sniffle, and then she drew back.

"I'm ready," she said.

She stood before him, teary eyed but in control, waiting for him to lead the way. She never suggested going by herself.

Once again Jonathan made the forty-five-minute trip to the prison. But this time it was not a silent drive. Tatum talked the entire way. She talked about how Jack McGillus had made a home for her and Cale after their mother had left him, how he had never once made them feel unloved, how he had been the best mother a girl could ever want, as well as a pretty terrific father. She told him about her father's fumbling attempts to help her through puberty, about her first date that he'd insisted on chaperoning, about the nights she had worried about him, afraid he was not going to make it back from the streets.

She told Jonathan more in those forty-five minutes than she had in all the weeks he had known her. And while he fell more surely in love with her with every word she spoke, he also felt his earlier moment of panic settle into outright fear. Which made no sense to him at all. People had been turning to him his entire life. His whole existence was based on taking care of others, and it had never scared him before. So why should Tatum be any different?

Danny Torunta was waiting for them at the prison gates. Telling the guard to see to Jonathan's Bronco, he ushered Tatum and Jonathan onto a golf cart and sped them across the grounds toward the infirmary.

"Is he...?" she began as they walked down the hall toward Jack's room.

"You've got time," Danny replied. He just didn't say how much.

Jim Marsh was just coming from Jack's hospital room as they approached. He nodded at all three of them, but without his usual toothy grin. Tatum picked up her pace and hurried through the door of her father's room.

Jack McGillus was awake, his pain-filled eyes trained on the door as they walked in. Relief was evident in the relaxing of his wrinkled features as soon as he recognized Tatum. Running to the bed, Tatum didn't even try to hide her tears. They streamed freely down her cheeks as she sat on the side of his bed, weaved herself in between the equipment and tubes hooked up to her father and gently laid her head against the chest that was laboring so hard just to draw the next breath.

"I love you, Pop." Jonathan barely heard the whispered words, but it was obvious from the peace that settled on the older man's features that Jack had heard them loud and clear.

Jack did not speak. Jonathan wondered if maybe he couldn't, if maybe the man was too weak, too breathless to make sounds, but neither Tatum nor her father seemed to need the words. They spoke with their hearts, with eyes that clung as Tatum lifted her head to kiss her father's cheek, with a weakly moving hand that slid slowly across the bed sheet to rest against Tatum's thigh.

Jonathan slipped over to the far corner of the room. He tried to empathize with Tatum, to put himself in her shoes, and was stunned when he could not. As the minutes ticked by, and he continued to witness the silent communication, Jonathan was ashamed to find himself feeling envious—of Jack McGillus, for having such a large piece of Tatum's heart, but even more of Tatum, for having the unconditional love of another human being. It was something he'd never known.

The more he watched, the more Jonathan was able to tune in to the messages passing between them. Jack was being told that he was the best father to have ever walked on God's earth. And Tatum was receiving the assurance that she would never be truly alone. Jack would continue to always be there for her, just as he had his entire life, even if only in spirit.

And as the minutes turned into an hour, and Tatum continued to sit on the side of her father's bed, watching him slip in and out of consciousness, Jonathan finally had to admit that she had been right about him all along. He had learned, probably from his crib, to guard himself against loving too deeply. His parents, while not physically neglectful of him, were so committed to their causes that they had not always had time for his emotional needs. And as he grew a little older, and he began to make friends, it was always with the knowledge that he had better not get too close, because he would be moving on to another tribe, another uneducated jungle, another war-massacred country. He had learned that it was easier to care for the people he was helping as a whole, rather than as individual human beings whom he might miss too much if he got to know them too well.

In adulthood he had continued to live his life that way. The pattern was so clear to him now, that he had uncovered it. The politics, the center... He'd cared for a lot of people, but very few persons. Was it too late to break out of the pattern?

Jonathan found himself watching Jack as the older man again regained consciousness, looking for signs of turmoil but seeing only peace—the kind of peace he had seen once on the face of a one-hundred-year-old voodoo doctor who had refused treatment to cure the malaria that was killing him. Not only had the old doctor done his best with the calling he had been given, but he had experienced life to the fullest extent and was content to pass on to the next phase of his existence.

Suddenly Jonathan knew, with absolute certainty, that if he continued as he was, he would never find that peace—not if he lived the rest of his life running from the kind of committed love that Tatum and Jack shared. He might reach the point of death feeling that he had answered his calling, but he would never have known what it felt like to live life to its fullest extent. There was a whole other realm of giving and receiving that he had yet to experience.

Jonathan felt a resurgence of the fear that had been gnawing at him since Tatum had turned to him at the supermarket. He was smart enough to realize that a lifetime's worth of walls were not going to crumble without some discomfort, but the alternative, to die without ever having fully loved, would be tantamount to not having lived at all.

When Jack slipped into unconsciousness again, Jonathan moved up to stand behind Tatum. She rested her back against his torso, and as he supported her weight, he knew he was committing himself to be there for her, to put her first whenever she needed him. He put his hands on her shoulders, offering what comfort he could with a love that was hers for eternity.

He was still standing there when Jack struggled one last time for air and slid peacefully away.

TATUM WANTED the funeral to be a quiet ceremony limited to family and a few close friends. But as word of Jack's death got out, she was deluged with condolences from hundreds of people whose lives the ex-detective had touched through the years. She was just hanging up the phone from an old man whose corner market had been robbed twenty years before and who had not lost his life's savings because Detective McGillus had arrived on the scene in the nick of time, when the doorbell rang. Jonathan was back. It had taken him less than hour to make his stops and get back to her.

Her lashes were still moist from the phone call when she opened the door to him.

Jonathan took one look at her tears and pulled her into his arms. "I'm so sorry, honey. I shouldn't have left you alone, not even for a minute," he murmured against her ear.

"It's okay, Jonathan. It's just that so many people still believe that Pop was a good man. I wish he could know it, that's all." Tatum burrowed her head into the security of his chest. She was not going to worry about the fact that leaning on Jonathan was only going to hurt her later. Right now he was here, and she needed him too badly to care about what lay ahead.

"He does know it," Jonathan said, running his hands up and down her back. "He knew it before, too," he added.

Tatum believed him, more because she knew she would never know for sure if he was wrong than because she was sure he was right, but the belief brought some measure of comfort anyway.

JONATHAN STAYED firmly by her side over the next two days, fielding phone calls, ushering in visitors, helping Mandy serve the meals that people brought over. And Tatum loved him for all that he was doing. She never would have held up so well through it all without him. He was there, holding her when the night got too dark or just touching her across the room with a loving look when someone told a story about another one of Detective McGillus's acts of courage.

She knew it could not last. She knew that Jonathan was only there because she had been lucky enough to not have the center, or anyone else out there, need him. And she prayed that she could at least have him until after the funeral.

It was going to be much larger than Tatum had at first planned, but Pop deserved the grand exit his mourners wished to give him. Just the thought of the number of people who cared was a huge comfort to Tatum. Even the police department sent flowers.

The call came the morning of the funeral. She was in the kitchen with Jonathan, pretending to eat the breakfast he had prepared, and she knew the instant he answered the phone that there was a problem somewhere that needed his attention. She felt the old familiar wall close around her heart, freezing anything good inside her as it also froze out the bad.

"How old?"

She heard Jonathan's words with dread, knowing that he was going to leave her—that she was going to have to say goodbye to Pop on her own. Knowing too, that another child was suffering.

"How bad is she?"

He was not even looking at her, as if she had already been wiped from his mind. It was not that Tatum begrudged the child the care she needed; she just didn't believe that Jonathan was the only one who could help. She had been around the center. She knew that there were others who were qualified to take charge and who cared as much as he did.

"So she won't need to go to the hospital? Good, then you can take her to the center immediately. I'll have someone waiting for you when you get there."

Had she just heard that? Jonathan was not going to go collect that child personally? She listened, stunned, as he put in a call to the center.

"Cinci? We've got one coming in. Seven years old. They found her sleeping under some newspapers in a trash bin. Mandy'll help if you need her."

There was a brief pause.

"She's okay. The funeral's in less than an hour."

Another pause. Tatum knew that Jonathan had just made a choice, and she had not come second.

"We'll be by this afternoon if Tatum's up to it."

She would be up to it. She would make herself be up to it. The little one was bound to need as much re-assurance as it could get.

"I'll tell her.... Call if there's a problem.... Talk to you later."

Tatum knew there were tears in her eyes again as Jonathan turned from the phone, but for the first time in longer than she could remember, they were happy tears.

IT TORE Tatum's heart to say goodbye to her father that day, but when she and Jonathan pulled away from the crowded cemetery, she knew she was not re-ally leaving Pop behind. She would carry him in her heart for as long as she lived.

Danny Torunta was one of the first people who came back to the house after the funeral. He re-minded Tatum that he had always been considered family when her father was alive, and he wanted her to continue to think of him as such. If she ever needed anything, she was to call.

He also had another piece of news.

"Did you hear about Jim Marsh?" he asked Tatum as they sat together on the living-room couch, accepting the condolences of those who stopped by.

"The custodian at the prison?" She felt sad for the man, still stuck away behind bars without a friend now that Pop was gone. She would just have to make a point to visit him on Sundays now instead of Pop. It was the least she could do. And Pop would approve.

Danny nodded. "Seems he was in prison for nine years for a robbery he didn't commit, just like he said. They caught the guy who did it on another charge, and Marsh is due to be released this next week."

Tatum's grin spread clear across her face. She was glad to hear that at least one good man was going to leave that hole alive.

"What'll he do? Does he have family around here?"

Danny shrugged. "Not that I know of. It'll be rough for him for a while, adjusting, accounting for the past ten years of his life everywhere he goes, but he'll make it. He's a survivor. Just like someone else I know," he added, patting Tatum's hand where it lay on her lap.

Tatum smiled and talked to Danny for another few minutes before they were once again interrupted by another new arrival. Danny left shortly after that with another reminder that she was not alone.

TWO DAYS LATER Tatum was almost wishing for a little time to herself. Her house was still being besieged with cards and visits, and when she was not at home, she was at the center, spending time with Jonathan and Mandy and little Theresa Coughlin, the seven-year-old who had been brought in the day of Pop's funeral. She and Jonathan had not shared anything more private than a car ride in days.

He drove her home Thursday evening, after they had had dinner at the center, and she was a little nervous as she invited him in to her empty house. He looked so good to her, dressed casually in the blue jeans and polo shirt he had put on after coming home from a luncheon he had attended that afternoon. And yet nothing had been formally resolved between them yet. She knew what she wanted with all of her heart; she just wasn't positive it was what Jonathan wanted. But she had a feeling, now that they were finally alone, that she was about to find out.

"Did I ever tell you I like you in blue?" he asked as he followed her into the house.

Tatum turned and locked the front door, letting him know, just in case he was not sure, that she wanted him to stay. "No, you never have," she said, thinking that her blue slacks and cotton blouse were rather plain.

He slipped his arms around her. "It makes you look so cool and collected, when I know what's really underneath," he murmured, lowering his lips to hers.

It was the first kiss they had shared since long before Pop died, and Tatum clung to him like a drowning person to a raft. She felt desire pool in her belly, but overshadowing that was the warmth encasing her heart.

"Marry me." The words were spoken against her lips.

Tatum's heart stopped, and then started back up again in double time, as if making up for the beat it had lost. "What did you say?" she asked, not because she hadn't heard, but because she so badly needed to hear the words again. She hoped some day he would tell her how the change in him had come about.

Jonathan lifted his lips from hers, even as he pulled her body more firmly into his. "I said 'marry me.' But what I meant was that I love you more than life itself. Will you please marry me?"

Tatum didn't need to be asked a third time. "Yes, oh, yes!" she said, knowing that for the rest of her life she was never going to have to build walls again. If life ever saw her alone again, she would only have to look as far as her heart to find those whose love would always give her the strength to carry on. Her well was full.

EPILOGUE

"I'M HOME!"

Tatum smiled as the cheery feminine tones rang from the kitchen.

"In here, honey!" she called, sitting back from Pop's old desk as she waited for Mandy to come find her.

"I thought you were taking the day off to get ready for your twice-postponed honeymoon," the teenager said with a grin as she entered Tatum's office.

"I was, but I got a call on another child-abuse case, ten-year-old twins, and I wanted to get the essentials done before I go." Tatum, having resigned her position as district attorney, was already gaining quite a reputation as the state-appointed lawyer for cases of child abuse.

"Did Jonathan take the kids to the center?" Mandy asked, concern marring her pretty brow.

Tatum shook her head. "They're with an aunt who would like to keep them if she can." It gave her hope to see that not all abused children were abandoned children, as well. "So how was school?" she asked, hoping to bring a smile back to Mandy's face.

Mandy had started college in January and was soaking up the experience like the desert would a rainstorm. And she hadn't been able to resist Tatum and Jonathan's offer to have her live with them rather than in a dormitory.

"Great. Got an A-minus on that composition," she said, crunching on the apple she had brought in with her.

"I'm proud of you, sweetie," Tatum told the girl, referring to far more than a freshman composition assignment.

Mandy blushed a pretty crimson. "So, you all ready to take Mexico City by storm?" she asked to cover her embarrassment.

"Just about. And this time I think we're really going to get to go. Jonathan just went over to give last-minute instructions to Jim and Cinci before we go. As if they don't already know how to handle any crisis that might come up."

She and Mandy shared a smile at Jonathan's overprotective ways. It was one of the things they both loved so much about him.

"I still can't believe that Cinci eloped!" Mandy said, plopping down in the chair in front of Tatum's desk.

"I guess she figured that if she didn't grab Jim up before he'd been out of prison long enough to get around, she'd lose him to the first young thing who figured out what a great catch he is."

Mandy chuckled. "Well, at least he loves kids, or we'd be in real trouble."

Tatum laughed with Mandy. "And he's good at fixing things, too."

"It's about time somebody around here realized my worth."

Both women glanced up as Jonathan walked into the room. Tatum was around her desk and in his arms in one lithe movement, unconcerned that Mandy's broad grin was following her all the way.

"I can see I'm needed elsewhere," Mandy said, heading toward the doorway.

"Did you get your paper back yet?" Jonathan asked before Mandy made it to the door.

"A-minus," she said, giving him a saucy grin.

Jonathan looked at Tatum. "A-minus? She writes an exposition on the importance of due-notice, a paper which both of her highly qualified guardians critiqued and approved, and she only gets an A-minus? What's the matter with that teacher?"

"Guess she's just not as smart as we are. Now, are you going to tell her, or am I?" Tatum asked, her words a mixture of excitement and exasperation.

Mandy turned back from the doorway, alarm lining her forehead.

"Tell me what?" she asked.

Jonathan and Tatum walked over to include the young woman in their embrace.

"There'll be some redecorating going on while we're in Mexico City—some pink paint and frilly things are going to be added to Cale's old room. And the day after we get back, you'll be the proud sister of a very anxious little girl.''

Mandy pulled back, hope mingling with doubt on her features. "A little girl?"

Her gaze settled on Tatum's, read the message there, but still the young woman did not quite believe.

"You don't mean Abby do you?" she asked as if afraid to even voice the possibility for fear that it might slip away.

Tatum and Jonathan both grinned, stumbling over their tongues in their eagerness to explain, but Mandy didn't wait for their jumbled words.

"We're getting Abby? It's all final and everything? She's really ours—permanently?"

Tatum and Jonathan nodded in unison and then nearly landed in a heap on the floor as Mandy pounced on them. She clutched them so tightly Tatum could hardly breathe, and shortness of breath had never felt so good. Mandy was laughing and crying all at once, but even through her sobs, Tatum had no trouble making out Mandy's next words.

"You see, fairy tales really can come true...."

HARLEQUIN SUPERROMANCE ®

TIRED OF WINTER?

ESCAPE THE WINTER BLUES THIS SPRING WITH HARLEQUIN SUPERROMANCE and MARRIOTT'S CAMELBACK INN, RESORT, GOLF CLUB AND SPA!

March is **Spring Break** month and Superromance wants to give you a price break! Look for 30¢-off coupons in the back pages of all Harlequin Superromance novels, good for the purchase of your next Superromance title.

April Showers brings a shower of new authors! Harlequin Superromance is highlighting four simply sensational new authors. Four provocative, passionate, romantic stories guaranteed to put Spring into your heart!

May is the month for flowers, and with flowers comes **ROMANCE**! Join us in May as four of our most popular authors bring you four of their most romantic Superromance novels. Tracy Hughes, Janice Kaiser, Lynn Erickson and Bobby Hutchinson will make this Spring special.

And to really escape the winter blues, enter our Superromantic Weekend Sweepstakes. You could win an exciting weekend at **the Marriott's Camelback Inn, Resort, Golf Club and Spa in Scottsdale, Arizona.** Look for further details in Harlequin Superromance novels beginning in March.

HARLEQUIN SUPERROMANCE— NOT THE SAME OLD STORY!

HSREL1

My Valentine 1994

Celebrate the most romantic day of the year with
MY VALENTINE 1994
a collection of original stories, written by
four of Harlequin's most popular authors...

MARGOT DALTON
MURIEL JENSEN
MARISA CARROLL
KAREN YOUNG

Available in February, wherever
Harlequin Books are sold.

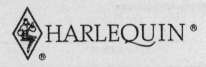

HARLEQUIN ®

VAL94

Where do you find hot Texas nights, smooth Texas charm and dangerously sexy cowboys?

Crystal Creek reverberates with the exciting rhythm of Texas. Each story features the rugged individuals who live and love in the Lone Star State.

"...Crystal Creek wonderfully evokes the hot days and steamy nights of a small Texas community."   —*Romantic Times*

"...a series that should hook any romance reader. Outstanding."
                                                    —*Rendezvous*

"Altogether, it couldn't be better."

                                                    —*Rendezvous*

Don't miss the next book in this exciting series.
MUSTANG HEART by **MARGOT DALTON**

Available in March wherever Harlequin books are sold.

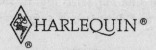

HARLEQUIN®

COMING SOON TO
A STORE NEAR YOU...

THE MAIN ATTRACTION

By *New York Times* Bestselling Author

This March, look for THE MAIN ATTRACTION by popular author Jayne Ann Krentz.

Ten years ago, Filomena Cromwell had left her small town in shame. Now she is back determined to get her sweet, sweet revenge....

Soon she has her ex-fiancé, who cheated on her with another woman, chasing her all over town. And he isn't the only one. Filomena lets Trent Ravinder catch her.

Can she control the fireworks she's set into motion?

BOB8

When the only time you have for yourself is...

Spring into spring—by giving yourself a March Break! Take a few *stolen moments* and treat yourself to a Great Escape. Relax with one of our brand-new stories (or with all six!).

Each STOLEN MOMENTS title in our Great Escapes collection is a complete and never-before-published *short* novel. These contemporary romances are 96 pages long—the perfect length for the busy woman of the nineties!

Look for Great Escapes in our Stolen Moments display this March!

SIZZLE by Jennifer Crusie
ANNIVERSARY WALTZ
by Anne Marie Duquette
MAGGIE AND HER COLONEL
by Merline Lovelace
PRAIRIE SUMMER by Alina Roberts
THE SUGAR CUP by Annie Sims
LOVE ME NOT by Barbara Stewart

Wherever Harlequin and Silhouette books are sold.

HARLEQUIN®

Don't miss these Harlequin favorites by some of our most distin-
guished authors!
And now, you can receive a discount by ordering two or more titles!

HT#25409	THE NIGHT IN SHINING ARMOR by JoAnn Ross	$2.99	☐
HT#25471	LOVESTORM by JoAnn Ross	$2.99	☐
HP#11463	THE WEDDING by Emma Darcy	$2.89	☐
HP#11592	THE LAST GRAND PASSION by Emma Darcy	$2.99	☐
HR#03188	DOUBLY DELICIOUS by Emma Goldrick	$2.89	☐
HR#03248	SAFE IN MY HEART by Leigh Michaels	$2.89	☐
HS#70464	CHILDREN OF THE HEART by Sally Garrett	$3.25	☐
HS#70524	STRING OF MIRACLES by Sally Garrett	$3.39	☐
HS#70500	THE SILENCE OF MIDNIGHT by Karen Young	$3.39	☐
HI#22178	SCHOOL FOR SPIES by Vickie York	$2.79	☐
HI#22212	DANGEROUS VINTAGE by Laura Pender	$2.89	☐
HI#22219	TORCH JOB by Patricia Rosemoor	$2.89	☐
HAR#16459	MACKENZIE'S BABY by Anne McAllister	$3.39	☐
HAR#16466	A COWBOY FOR CHRISTMAS by Anne McAllister	$3.39	☐
HAR#16462	THE PIRATE AND HIS LADY by Margaret St. George	$3.39	☐
HAR#16477	THE LAST REAL MAN by Rebecca Flanders	$3.39	☐
HH#28704	A CORNER OF HEAVEN by Theresa Michaels	$3.99	☐
HH#28707	LIGHT ON THE MOUNTAIN by Maura Seger	$3.99	☐

Harlequin Promotional Titles

#83247	YESTERDAY COMES TOMORROW by Rebecca Flanders	$4.99	☐
#83257	MY VALENTINE 1993	$4.99	☐

    (short-story collection featuring Anne Stuart, Judith Arnold,
    Anne McAllister, Linda Randall Wisdom)
(limited quantities available on certain titles)

	AMOUNT	$
DEDUCT:	10% DISCOUNT FOR 2+ BOOKS	$
ADD:	POSTAGE & HANDLING	$
	($1.00 for one book, 50¢ for each additional)	
	APPLICABLE TAXES*	$ _____
	TOTAL PAYABLE	$ _____
	(check or money order—please do not send cash)	

To order, complete this form and send it, along with a check or money order for the
total above, payable to Harlequin Books, to: **In the U.S.:** 3010 Walden Avenue,
P.O. Box 9047, Buffalo, NY 14269-9047; **In Canada:** P.O. Box 613, Fort Erie, Ontario,
L2A 5X3.

Name: _____

Address: _____ City: _____

State/Prov.: _____ Zip/Postal Code: _____

*New York residents remit applicable sales taxes.
 Canadian residents remit applicable GST and provincial taxes.

HBACK-JM